THE DROWNING WOMAN

Also by Robyn Harding

The Perfect Family

The Swap

The Arrangement

Her Pretty Face

The Party

THE DROWNING WOMAN

ROBYN HARDING

NEW YORK BOSTON

This book is a work of fiction. Names, characters, places, and incidents are the product of the author's imagination or are used fictitiously. Any resemblance to actual events, locales, or persons, living or dead, is coincidental.

Grand Central Publishing
Hachette Book Group
1290 Avenue of the Americas, New York, NY 10104
grandcentralpublishing.com
twitter.com/grandcentralpub

First Edition: June 2023

Grand Central Publishing is a division of Hachette Book Group, Inc. The Grand Central Publishing name and logo is a trademark of Hachette Book Group, Inc.

Library of Congress Cataloging-in-Publication Data

Names: Harding, Robyn, author.
Title: The drowning woman / Robyn Harding.
Description: First edition. | New York : Grand Central Publishing, 2023.
Identifiers: LCCN 2022053119 | ISBN 9781538726761 (hardcover) | ISBN 9781538726785 (ebook)
Subjects: LCGFT: Thrillers (Fiction) | Novels.
Classification: LCC PR9199.4.H366 D76 2023 | DDC 813/.6--dc23/eng/20221110
LC record available at https://lccn.loc.gov/2022053119

ISBNs: 9781538726761 (hardcover), 9781538726785 (ebook), 9781538756966 (Canadian trade pbk.)

Printed in Canada

MRQ-T

10 9 8 7 6 5 4 3 2 1

For my agent, Joe Veltre
Ride or die since 2003

THE DROWNING WOMAN

Part One

LEE

1

IN SOCIOLOGICAL TERMS, THEY CALL it the *fundamental attribution error.* Basically, it means that when people see someone in a bad situation, they tend to believe that individual brought it on themselves. Of course, there are always external, situational forces at play, but it's human nature to think it could never happen to you. You'd fight back differently if attacked; crawl your way out of the burning building; wouldn't fall for that online scam. And, of course, you'd never end up sleeping on the streets. Those people have drug problems, mental health issues, no work ethic.

What did I think of the homeless before I became one of them? Not much, is the short answer. Each year, I donated to a local shelter that served Thanksgiving dinners. I occasionally tossed coins into hats or empty coffee cups, but I didn't meet their eyes, I didn't ask their names. Sometimes I'd even cross the street to avoid them. I was not without compassion for the displaced, but they were just so separate, so other. There was no way I'd ever become one of them.

I pull the sleeping bag up to my chin and stretch my legs out under the steering column. The back seat would be more comfortable, but I'm too on edge to sleep there. Instead, I doze in the reclined driver's seat, with the doors locked and the keys in the ignition. If anyone comes—the police, thieves, or worse—I can be on my way in a second. My Toyota sedan is just one in a row of bedrooms on wheels, parked on this quiet street, under a dank underpass. Our vehicles form an unsightly border along the edge of a big box hardware store's parking lot. Will I ever relax enough to sleep soundly, horizontally? Hopefully I won't be here long enough to find out.

In these quiet moments, it still baffles me that I ended up like this. I'm bright, educated; I owned a successful business. I'm not hooked on any substances…although I drink more now. In the console beside me sits a bottle of whisky. It's for warmth, to dull the edges and settle my nerves enough to allow me to doze off. Picking it up, I take a sip and for a moment, I feel nothing but this…the warmth traveling down my throat, burning in my belly. It's tempting to take another drink. And another. But I can't overdo it. I need to keep my wits about me, and I mustn't develop a dependency. I replace the cap and set it back in the console.

The light goes out in the motor home in front of me. It's a kerosene lantern; the occupants can't afford to drain their battery using the vehicle lights. Margaux and Doug are in their sixties. Margaux has health issues—cancer, though I'm not sure what kind. Doug worked at a hotel but was laid off, another victim of the pandemic, the economy, life in general. They have a large dog, Luna, a pit bull cross that makes it hard to rent a room. I try to park behind them when I can. Their run-down Winnebago never moves, sporting an intricate addition of tarps that keeps out the rain and creates an awning they can sit under. We're not friends, exactly, but we chat sometimes, and their proximity—and Luna's—makes me feel safer, less alone. They look out for me, too. It was Doug who gave me the knife.

I finger the wooden handle pressing against my right hip. The blade is between the seat and the console, a sort of holster. If I need to, I can pull it out in a second, brandish it at my attacker. "Women aren't safe here." Doug stated the obvious. "Be prepared to use this." I had assured him I was, but could I really stab someone? Pierce their flesh with this sharp blade? Plunge it into their chest or neck or belly? I'm capable of lots of things I never thought possible before. Desperate people will commit desperate acts. When my restaurant was failing, my life's dream crumbling before my eyes, I lied, I cheated, and I manipulated. I destroyed people, hurt the ones I loved. So, could I stab someone to save my own life? Of course.

It is late…and a false sense of peace descends. In the distance, someone is shouting angrily—at someone or no one—but eventually, it peters out. A bottle clinks against another, but it is soft and infrequent. The hum of sporadic traffic on the overpass lulls me. Somehow I don't hear them approaching—either I have drifted off, or they are being stealthy…probably a combination of the two. Suddenly, they're here, on either side of my car, gray, sunken faces peering into my darkened home. Fear twists in my belly. My hand moves to the knife at my side.

"Hey, honey," one man says, and I see missing teeth through the fog of his breath on my window. I meet his eyes for a second and see the blackness, the blankness. He's an addict; I know the look by now. His humanity has been usurped by his need for drugs. Judging by the sores on his face, he's hooked on meth. The chemical can turn humans into wild animals: angry, aggressive, unpredictable.

The man on the other side of the vehicle has his face to the passenger-side glass. His eyes dart around the car and its contents, sizing up anything valuable. In the weeks I've been sleeping here, I've had to speed away once before. I heard them that time; they broke a window in a van farther up the line. That night, I started my car and pulled away before they got to me. Since then, I've practiced this scenario in my mind: pull the lever to return the seat to its upright position, turn the key, stomp on the gas.

"Open up, pretty lady," the toothless man says, and a frisson of disgust shudders through my body. Does he want more than my belongings? I grab the knife and hold it to the window. The blade taps on the glass: a threat. But he doesn't back away, and he doesn't look concerned. In fact, his rotten mouth smiles at me.

My hands feel sweaty and slippery as I fumble to right my seat. I'm not drunk but the whisky has made me slow and dull. And I'm terrified. My seat pops forward and I drop the knife, reach for the key. *It's okay, Lee,* I assure myself as I turn the ignition. *You're safe. You're out of here.*

And then the passenger window shatters. I scream as a hand dives into the car, feeling blindly for something, anything to grab. It's not me he's after, at least, but my backpack is right there on the seat, my purse is on the floor. Before I can put the car into gear, the backpack disappears through the broken window. That, I can live without. It's got clothes, toiletries, things I can just afford to replace. I slam the gear shift into drive as the arm dives back inside, reaching for my purse.

No, no, no, not that. While I'm smart enough not to keep all my cash in it, my phone and my ID are in that stylish Coach bag, a remnant of my old life. As the car shoots forward, I lunge for the purse on the floorboard, trying to drag it into my lap. But the arm is still inside, and it grabs my wrist. Dirty fingernails pierce my skin and I gasp with the pain. I lean on the horn, hoping someone—Margaux and Doug—will wake up. If they open the door and release Luna, these men will run. I'll be able to get away. But the motor home stays dark.

I gun the engine, but the hand is still inside the car. He's got my purse in his grasp and he won't let go. Gathering speed, I swerve on the empty road, trying to dislodge him, but he holds on. And he's fast, sprinting along at pace, and he won't let go. He won't fucking let go! Using my right hand with its damaged wrist, I grab for the knife and swipe blindly at his arm. I slice into his skin, but he doesn't flinch. The meth has given him superhuman strength and speed, made him impervious to pain. The purse, with all the documents that make me a person, slips through the window. Gone…

And just like that, I am nobody.

2

THE STING OF CHLORINE ASSAULTS my nostrils and sends a swell of nostalgia through me. The neighborhood pool was a regular and sustained part of my childhood. Growing up, my family had a summer house in the Catskills. It wasn't opulent, but it was comfortable and lakefront. My mother insisted my sister and I take years of swimming lessons so that she didn't have to worry about us drowning while she sipped gin and tonics on the sunporch with her girlfriends. Teresa and I spent hours paddling in the water, floating in our dinghy, or just lying on damp towels on the dock, staring up at the endless blue as the sun fried the water on our skin. We talked about horses, and boys, and what we wanted to be when we grew up. Teresa wanted to be a veterinarian. I wanted to be a movie star, or a rock star, someone shiny and bright.

The lobby is warm and damp and cloying as I approach the woman at the chipped Formica counter. She looks up, her eyes wary. "I lost my pass," I mumble, the familiar sweep of shame making my cheeks hot. She knows I'm lying. She knows I'm not here to swim. I see myself through her eyes: haunted, disheveled, carrying two canvas bags stuffed with clothing, food, a few dishes...the items that I couldn't stuff into my trunk. A plastic bag is taped over the broken window, but my car is no longer secure. *This is not me,* I want to tell the receptionist. *I'm a restauranteur. A businesswoman. An entrepreneur.* She gives me a begrudging nod. "Go ahead. But make it quick."

"Thank you."

A dingy path worn into the linoleum guides me toward the changeroom. It's vacant except for a couple of seniors fitting their bathing caps in the mirror. I wait for them to leave before heading straight to the showers. A large sign on the cinder-block wall reads:

CHANGE ROOMS ARE FOR
POOL CUSTOMERS ONLY

Vagrants, people like me who are here for a hot shower and some free soap, are not permitted. But the staff will look the other way if it's not too busy, if I am quick and quiet. Admission is seven dollars. I could pay but every penny counts. I need to save up the deposit to rent an apartment; I won't survive living in my car for much longer. There are free showers at some of the shelters, but terrifying stories of theft, rape, even murder swirl around them. And going to a shelter will make my homelessness *official*, and it is not. It's a temporary, ephemeral state.

Stripping off my clothes, I step into the tiled stall. I kick at a soggy Band-Aid left on the floor and punch the button to turn on the water. My right index finger throbs with the effort, and the scratches on my wrist sting as the hot stream hits them. I probably need a tetanus shot, but that's not going to happen without insurance. For a moment, I close my eyes, let tears flow down my face. I want to go home. I want to get in my car and drive back across the country to New York. But I can't. I have torched and burned every bridge behind me. My family hates me. I have no friends left. And then there is Damon, who will hurt me. Even kill me.

We met when I was working at a swanky brasserie in the

Meatpacking District. He was a regular, occupying a prime booth near the back, accompanied by burly associates or beautiful women, frequently both. Oysters, steak frites, vodka for the table. It never changed. Damon was polite and generous, so we all ignored the pervasive sense of danger surrounding him. It was not uncommon in that restaurant, in the industry at large. Men in flashy suits, with significant money to spend but no discernible career.

One night, as service wound down, he summoned me from the kitchen. He told me he loved my cooking. I told him about my plans for the Aviary. My vision was clear: I'd serve elevated but accessible food—short ribs with duck-fat potatoes, buttermilk-fried chicken drizzled with spiced honey, chanterelle mushroom risotto. The tables would be six-tops and four-tops, only a handful of two-tops. Every night would feel like a dinner party in my home. I'd recently found a space in the East Village that would be perfect.

"I want in," he'd said, so confident, so casual. "How much do you need?"

I needed a lot. I had only two other interested investors. Damon's money was shady, I knew that, but I took it anyway. Because the Aviary was my life's dream. I was done working for egotistical, demeaning, or downright abusive bosses. And I was confident in my concept, my capabilities, and my connections. The restaurant would thrive, even in the highly competitive New York market. I'd make my payments on time, so the way Damon made his money was none of my concern.

And then the pandemic. People stopped coming. I knew I was going to have to close my doors, even before the mayor forced me to. When restaurants reopened, I tried again, but I was too new; the momentum was lost. I hung on as long as I could, but omicron was the final straw. My servers got sick, followed by my kitchen staff, and then I went down. We tried to operate short-staffed, pivoted to takeout, but it wasn't enough. I had to admit that my business, my dream, had failed.

I worried about my staff, my vendors, my health insurance, and my investors, in that order. Because this was force majeure. They wouldn't expect me to pay. And yet...they did. I tried to apply for a disaster loan, but the website kept crashing. I asked for a line of credit but was turned down due to "inadequate business," which was the reason I needed it in the first place. My lead line cook suggested a GoFundMe page, but everyone in the industry was suffering. How could I ask for money to keep *my* restaurant afloat? Finally, my accountant advised me to declare bankruptcy. It would mean I could walk away from all my debts, leaving a trail of spurned and angry suppliers, staff, and investors.

That's when Damon crushed my finger with a meat mallet.

What had I expected of him? Forgiveness for the money I owed? Understanding at least? Damon was a gangster. Violence was his currency. But still, I was shocked by the cruelty, the ruthlessness. He promised to break a finger a week until I paid. I'd lose my ability to cook. There was no choice but to run.

I kept moving, from city to town, ensuring that I never stayed in one place for too long. Damon had other avenues of income, other businesses that would be making their payments on time. He didn't need my money badly enough to send his thugs chasing me across the country. But still...I pushed onward, until I reached Seattle. The Pacific. The end of the line. One of the farthest geographical points from New York in the country.

With my elbow, I pump the lemon-scented soap into my hand, wash my body, and use it as shampoo. The harsh detergent will dry my skin, make my hair stiff and frizzy, but all my toiletries were in my backpack. I try to wash away the fear, the loss, the utter sense of desolation that threatens to overwhelm me. Because I have no choice but to keep trying, keep moving forward, keep existing.

Stepping from the shower, I dig a towel from my bag. It smells musty, but I pat at the droplets on my skin, hoping the scent won't cling to me. Clean laundry has become a luxury I can afford only once a week. A woman with a toddler on her hip enters and gives me a side-eyed glance. I see her brow furrow as she spots the angry red scratches on my arm, clocks my pile of belongings, puts the pieces together. I need to hurry.

I used to wear makeup—just a little concealer and mascara, a pop of color on my lips and cheeks, but it's all gone now, taken with my purse. I finger-comb my tangle of dark hair, the highlights grown down to my chin, pressing it into some semblance of a style. It's not really working, but at least I'm clean and presentable if not attractive. I've let that go. In some worlds, you trade on good looks; in others, you hide them. Eventually, they abandon you anyway. Just a lot quicker when you're homeless.

Hurriedly, I slip on a pair of jeans and a black T-shirt, my work "uniform." Thankfully, the diner's dress code is extremely casual. The protective mother is still watching me as she steps out of her clothes, eyes alert and wary. Does she think I'm crazy? Dangerous? That I might steal from her? *I'm not interested in your bag of diapers and animal crackers,* I want to snap, but I don't. I drop the moist towel onto one of my canvas bags and hurry past two more moms and babies coming in for swim class.

The crisp air outside the pool hits me like a slap, sharpens my senses. I'm beginning to feel weak and light-headed. I need food and caffeine. There is a coffee shop a few blocks from the pool that sells discounted day-old muffins, spotted bananas, and mealy apples kept in a basket by the till. I'll order a drip coffee loaded with cream and sugar for breakfast and a stale pastry for lunch. I eat supper at the diner, a definite perk of my otherwise unfulfilling employment.

Sliding into the driver's seat of my car, I feel the knife press into my hip. I shoved it farther down beside the console, but an inch of the handle is still exposed. I pull it out and look at the blood dried on the blade. A shudder runs through me as last night's attack returns to me. I stabbed a man, cut his skin, and yet, he didn't care, he didn't stop. I couldn't protect myself or my belongings.

I know what I have to do. This car is my home, and it must be secure. My survival depends on it.

3

IT'S NOT HARD TO IDENTIFY the type of establishment that will hire illegal staff: people without work permits, or bank accounts, or a home address. People who have criminal records, who come without résumés or references. I have found these types of places across the country, and I found Uncle Jack's. Set in a rough neighborhood just south of Seattle, the peeling paint and faded sign signal a certain willingness to bend the rules. I'd first entered two weeks ago, taken a seat at the scratched orange counter, and nursed a cup of coffee. When "Uncle Jack," whose name is really Randy, left the kitchen for a smoke break, I'd hit him up for a job. Randy has a rap sheet, apparently. I've heard everything from assault to cocaine possession to murder. Whatever he's done, he knows that sometimes people need a second chance.

My usual shift is 4:00 p.m. to midnight, six days a week. It's a lot but it suits me fine. I'd rather waitress than sit in my car, fruitlessly trying to sleep. The café serves an all-day breakfast, burgers, nachos, beer, and wine. Each item is a heart attack on a plate, but there is something comforting about Uncle Jack's greasy fare and generous portions. My restaurant prided itself on quality ingredients, comfort food kicked up a notch. The brasserie

I'd worked at served upscale plates that bordered on pretentious: bone marrow croquettes, cured scallops, Wagyu carpaccio...I'm qualified to work somewhere more high-end, but then, there would be questions.

Uncle Jack's clientele is practically the same every night. There are dealers and prostitutes, club kids and gangbangers. It's the kind of place where people look the other way, eat their cheap food, and conduct their business. The old me wouldn't have set foot in an establishment like this, would have been terrified by Lewis, the guy with the gold front tooth and the slash of a scar across his jaw. He sits at the end of the bar, drinking Sprite and waiting for customers to buy cocaine from him. Or Talia, who comes in between tricks, using the bathroom for up to half an hour at a time. Maybe she's shooting up? Maybe she's just washing? No one asks and no one cares. They're just people...I see that now. They're just doing what they have to.

My boss, Randy, wanders through the long, narrow space, checking on his customers. He's short and stocky in his jeans and pale green T-shirt, and he's sweaty...so sweaty. It's warm in here but it doesn't account for the dark circles under his arms, the droplets on his forehead. I've never seen him use drugs, but it can be a side effect. He's about fifty, I'd guess, but a hard fifty, his skin thick and gray and lined. His eyes are a cold, hard blue.

I refill Lewis's Sprite. At the end of my shift, he'll slip me ten bucks for serving him and looking the other way. It will be the most generous tip I'll receive by far. Uncle Jack's patrons don't have a lot of extra money. A buck or two is standard, but a handful of coins is not uncommon. My eyes track Randy's movements, and when he steps behind the counter, I make my move.

"Hey, Randy. I was wondering...I, uh, need a favor."

He says nothing and shows no curiosity as he slowly pulls a glass of beer from the tap. I clear my throat and press on. "My car was broken into last night. The passenger window was smashed." I leave out the minor detail that I was inside it at the time. "I took it to two different mechanics today and they both said it'll cost over four hundred bucks to fix."

Randy's eyes meet mine over the beer glass. They're blank, impossible to read.

"I was wondering if I could get an advance on my paycheck."

"Check" is not a literal term. Randy pays me cash, under the table. While illegal, it's more profitable for him and essential for me. I don't even have a bank account anymore. If I did, my wages would be garnished to pay back my loans.

"I don't do advances," Randy says, taking a sip of the foamy beer.

"I don't need the whole thing," I continue. "Just a hundred bucks. And it's only for a few days."

"Nope." He sets the glass down on the counter. "It's my policy."

"Please," I say. "I really need this."

Those blank eyes take me in, assessing me. My looks have deteriorated in the weeks since Randy hired me, stress and poverty taking their toll. I'm only thirty-four, but I feel—and look—older. If I still had my makeup, I could mask the fatigue and tension, but it's on full display. I pulled my hair back with an elastic band, but frizzy tendrils have escaped in the humidity from the kitchen. Does my boss think I'm using? That I need the money for drugs?

"My car is parked in the back lot," I add quickly. "You can see the broken window for yourself. The guy stole my purse and my phone."

"If I do it for you, I have to do it for everyone," he says with an indifferent shrug. "Sorry."

A feeling of panic flutters in my chest. I can't sleep unprotected and exposed. The spring nights are still chilly, but it will be fear, not cold that keeps me awake. If I tell Randy that my car is my home, that sleeping with a missing window could get me raped, or murdered, would he change his mind? But I can't tell him.

My pride won't allow it. Pressing my lips together, I say nothing, turning back to the kitchen as another order comes up.

I deliver two plates of sausages, eggs, and pancakes to a table near the window. They thank me with a nod, and I force a pleasant smile. My effort is minimal, unlike at my own restaurant. There, I worked the room, checking in and charming the diners. Here, I'm a delivery girl. At the next vacated table, I scoop a few coins into my apron and collect the dirty dishes. There's half a grilled cheese on a plate, temptingly untouched. I had a cheeseburger when I arrived, will have eggs before I leave, but this could be tomorrow's breakfast. Before I consider pocketing it, I tip the dregs of a cup of coffee onto it. I will not sink to eating the refuse off a stranger's plate. Not yet, anyway.

At the back of the kitchen, I drop the plates and glasses into the dish pit. And then I hear, "Hey, Lee."

The tone is friendly, conversational, and it takes me a second to realize I'm being addressed. I turn to see Vincent, the fry cook. He's a little younger than I am, taut and wiry, with a manic kind of energy. He might be a really bright guy, but his job prospects are limited by the tattoos on his face. A scorpion arches over his left eyebrow, and a small star adorns his right cheekbone. Unlike Randy's cold blue eyes, Vincent's are dark, intense, and unsettling. I don't like him, though I'm not sure why. We don't have much interaction that isn't food related.

"I hear you got robbed?" he says, moving toward me.

"Yeah."

He lowers his voice, moves in even closer. "You need a new phone?"

The thought of living without a smartphone would have been unthinkable even a month ago, but I obviously can't afford a new one. I'd tossed my original phone into the dumpster behind the restaurant, had picked up a new one as I drove across the country. But now the internet is a luxury indifferent to my survival. And it's not like anyone calls me. Though Randy might, to offer an extra shift. I *would* feel safer if I was able to call for help in an emergency.

"How much?"

"I can get you a dumbphone, two months prepaid on it. Thirty bucks."

These street phones are traded for favors, drugs, or money. Vincent clearly has unsavory connections; he's probably dealing on the side. The phone won't have internet, but it will let me make calls and send texts. I could call a few garages to check for a cheaper window replacement. I could book an appointment at the garage for the day after payday. And I could text my sister, just to see if she's okay. She won't recognize the number. She might even respond.

"Deal."

Vincent's eyes dart around the kitchen. "My friend will meet you out back after your shift," he says, and then he turns back to the grill.

The rest of the evening is steady, uneventful. There is one fight, but Randy and Lewis dispatch it quickly. At midnight, I clock out and Vincent slides me a plate of scrambled eggs and bacon. I eat in the back, at a small table near the staff bathroom. The all-night diner is still busy, the crowd drunker, louder. I savor my meal, hoping to linger, dreading the thought of retiring to my open-air car for the night. The side of brown toast goes into my pocket when Vincent and the other kitchen staff aren't looking.

Finally, I gather my two bags of belongings and catch Vincent's eye. He gives me a nod. His friend with the phone is waiting out back. I slip out the kitchen door.

The cramped parking lot is populated by four cars and a delivery truck. My damaged vehicle sits pressed up against the concrete block divider, an attempt to conceal the broken window. I see the glowing red cherry of a cigarette in the dark and move toward it. Vincent's friend stands at the edge of the lot, near the alley. He is small and nondescript in his hoodie and jeans. As I approach, he reaches into the pocket of his pants and withdraws a flip phone.

"Two months prepaid," he says, "Forty bucks."

"Vincent said thirty."

He looks me over, clearly considering bartering with me, and then he shrugs. "Fine. Thirty."

I hand him the cash—basically the night's tips, and he passes me the device. It feels greasy but I flip it open, and the digital face shines up at me. A lifeline. I drop it into my bag.

"Thanks," I mutter, turning toward my car.

The guy drops his cigarette on the pavement. "You looking to make some money?"

I know this will not be good, will not be legal, but I do need money, badly. I can't afford to ignore any offer.

"Maybe."

"I might be able to help you out," he says, and then he smiles, jiggles his hands in the front pockets of his jeans. "If you help *me* out."

I know what he wants; he doesn't have to elaborate. And for the first time, I see how easily it happens. If a person is desperate, if they have nothing else of value, they can always sell themselves. There is always someone willing to pay. I look at the lascivious glint in this guy's eye, and I realize...it would only take a few minutes, it would help my money problems, maybe even allow me to fix my car. But I am not there. I pray I never will be.

"Fuck off."

"Suit yourself." He shrugs. "Just thought I'd offer."

Like he was doing *me* a favor. Pulling his hood down over his eyes, he saunters off down the alley, and I hustle toward my car.

4

MY EYES DART FROM THE darkened highway to the gas gauge as I drive north on I-5. This is farther than I'd normally travel, but my tank is almost half full. I'm headed for the tony seaside neighborhoods populated by tech entrepreneurs, doctors, and lawyers. I will be safe there—at least from the criminal element. The danger in this upper echelon is the private security guard, or the eager cop trying to impress the higher-ups. They can't allow the disenfranchised to sleep in their cars among the mansions and pools and luxury SUVs. They won't arrest me, though...will they? More likely, they'll just ask me to move along, to park somewhere less desirable.

I exit off the highway carefully, keeping well within the speed limit. My driver's license is gone, so I don't want to get pulled over for even a minor infraction. How will I replace it without my social security number? Or any proof of Washington residency? How will I even prove who I am? But I'm too exhausted to worry about it now. I drive toward the coast; I've always wanted an oceanfront home. This wasn't exactly what I had in mind, but it will do. The area is unfamiliar, like the entire city, but I wind through quiet streets, the stately houses dark. It's almost two in the morning and these professionals, these captains of industry, need their shut-eye. You can't run the world unless you're well-rested.

The foliage is thick here, large trees and lush greenery concealing the residences. I keep driving and the homes dwindle as I move toward protected parkland. The road ends in a secluded pullout and it's perfect, sheltered by giant cedars, surrounded by thorny blackberry bushes. In the daylight, I imagine a family parking here, picking their way through the thick brush to the rocky beach a few yards below.

Parking the car, I move quietly to the trunk to collect my sleeping bag and my whisky. While I'm there, I stuff the remainder of the night's tips—just eight bucks—into a paper sack I got with my day-old muffin. I will keep my cash in different locations, to foil any more thieves. But there won't be random thugs roaming around in this neighborhood. Settling into the driver's seat, I revel in a moment of peace and security. Why didn't I think of this before? In each new town, I have gravitated toward others in my situation. The community of nomads I thought would offer me safety. But this is better, smarter.

Sipping the whisky, I wipe the flip phone with my sleeve. The battery has plenty of juice, but I'll need to get a cheap charger off the street tomorrow. I still know my sister's phone number by heart—I used to call her from the restaurant's house phone. My fingers hover over the keys…but what could I say?

There are only two words: I'm sorry. But Teresa will never accept my apology. How could she? What I did to her was too cruel, too self-serving. It doesn't matter that I was desperate, afraid for my safety, even my life. I'm no longer her sister. Those were the last words she spoke to me.

I take another pull from the bottle, trying to swallow down my self-loathing. Dropping the phone into the console, I put the knife in my lap. Just in case. Soothed by the sound of the ocean through my broken window, I drift away.

For the next few nights, I drive north after work, the busy I-5 desolate in the wee hours. This leafy community becomes my bedroom. I still wake up stiff and sore, sometimes mildly hungover, but my head is less clouded, my eyes less sandy. It's so quiet, so sleepy that it would be easy to believe that the surrounding homes were empty. But there are a few signs of life: a dog—large and aggressive—barking in the night, guarding his property; the occasional luxury vehicle purring in the distance; an early morning gardener firing up a lawn mower.

But on the third morning, I hear something unusual. It is soft but distinct against the lapping of the waves on the beach. What time is it? The sky is pale and pink, telling me dawn is about to break. It's probably 5:00 or 6:00 a.m. Another hour or two of sleep are necessary to assuage my bone-deep exhaustion, but I can still hear it. Sitting up in my reclined seat, I strain my ears to listen. It's a woman. And she's crying.

Opening the phone, I see that it is 5:52 a.m. *Go back to sleep,* I tell myself, reclining again. A strange woman crying on the beach at the crack of dawn is none of your concern. But she's not stopping. And the sobs are beginning to grate on my nerves. "I'm sorry," she cries. And then I hear a splash.

I sit up in my seat, heart pounding. Adrenaline courses through me and there's no way I can ignore this. What the hell is this woman doing? It's just April—the Pacific will be frigid. Climbing out of the car, I spot the path. It is overgrown, barely visible, but I scramble my way down it. I smell the beach before I reach it, brackish and briny. It's a rocky cove, seaweed and kelp coating the stones in shaggy green. I see her, the woman, standing hip deep in the water. She looks about my age, with shiny dark hair like I used to have. She's wearing a running outfit, formfitting and expensive. Her sobs are softer now, but her shoulders shake with emotion. She closes her eyes. And then she goes under.

Maybe she's swimming? But I know she's not—not in her clothes, not in this temperature. Still, I wait a few seconds, hoping she'll resurface, hoping I can slip back to my car and sleep for another hour before I need to move on. Hoping I don't have to intervene and draw attention to myself. But I'm already moving across the slippery rocks and kicking off my shoes. Because the woman does not come up.

I run into the water and feel the icy chill. It won't take long for her—or me—to go numb, to succumb to the cold. When the water hits my waist, I start to swim. She went under here, but she's gone. She must have swum out, farther, deeper. I take a breath and dive beneath the surface. The water stings my eyes, shocks my system. And then I see her.

She is moving away from me, but slowly. Her legs kick weakly, her arms barely move. She is fading, it's clear. And then she stops moving altogether, and her body goes limp. Her long dark hair floats around her like sea snakes. With a few strong strokes, I am on her.

I reach out and grab her jacket, drag her toward the surface.

5

MY FEET HAVE JUST TOUCHED the rocky bottom when she comes to. I feel her inert body surge with life, and suddenly she is fighting me.

"Let me go!" she screams, twisting from my grasp, flailing out at me. "What are you doing?"

"Saving your life," I yell back.

"No!" she shrieks. "Get the fuck away from me."

I let her go, but we're at the shore by then. We both stagger out of the water and collapse onto the rocks. I look over at the woman, gasping for breath beside me. Her skin is so pale, her lips tinged blue. She's probably hypothermic or very close to it. "Stay here," I say, firmly but gently. I scramble across the slippery rocks to the path.

My car is open, vulnerable, but the neighborhood is still asleep. Retrieving the sleeping bag and the whisky, I return to the beach. She's huddled there, arms clutching herself, forehead lowered to her knees. I drape the sleeping bag around her shoulders and open the bottle of whisky. I take a sip before I offer it to her.

She looks at it for a moment before she takes it and drinks, wordlessly. We pass it back and forth a few times, until I notice her shivering is less violent. The sun is coming up, the day slowly warming, but I am still frigid. The drowning woman notices and invites me under the blanket. It feels strangely intimate, but I'm too cold to refuse.

We huddle together in silence for a while, the warmth of our bodies, the whisky, and the sleeping bag raising our core temperatures. In swimming lessons, they taught us to remove wet clothing to battle hypothermia, but that would be too weird. And we weren't in the cold water long enough to warrant it. I take a sip of whisky and watch a boat pass by—an early morning fisherman. Would he have saved this woman if I hadn't intervened? But he barely seems to notice us, motoring by with his face turned toward the horizon. If I hadn't heard her cries, this stranger would have drowned. As she clearly intended.

"You should have left me," she says then, her voice hoarse from the shrieking and the alcohol. "I don't want to be here."

"It was instinct," I reply. "I took a lot of swimming lessons."

She smirks and gives me a side-eyed look. "Well, you fucked up."

"Why?" I ask. "Why were you trying to drown yourself?"

"I hate my life."

"So do I."

"You don't understand."

No, you *don't understand,* I want to say. There is no way that this woman, in her designer jogging suit and running shoes that probably cost as much as my car, has a life worse than mine. But I'm not about to show my hand. And this is not a contest.

"My marriage is…toxic. And sick. My husband is abusive."

"Get a divorce," I say. "You don't have to kill yourself."

She laughs darkly. "You don't get it."

She's right, I don't. My relationship history is dismal but anti-climactic. Work has always usurped relationships. In my twenties, I lived with a guy, André, for three years, but the romance petered out, due to neglect and indifference. When we split, it was cordial. He left me the couch. Since then, I've had lovers but few real boyfriends. There was never time; they were never a priority. It was easier to have no-strings hookups while I focused on my career.

"My husband is a criminal defense lawyer. He's rich. And he's powerful." She takes a swig from the bottle. "And he's a sadist."

It might be hyperbole—people call their partners horrible names all the time—but her words send a chill through me. Something tells me that her description is literal. That this woman's husband is turned on by abuse and humiliation. Hers.

She gets up suddenly. "I have to go."

I follow her up the trail that spits us out right next to my car. Can I pretend this isn't mine? That I, too, occupy one of the magnificent homes surrounding us? But when she looks at it, and then over at me, I realize it's clear. This is my Toyota. This is my home.

"Do you need a ride?" I ask lamely.

Her eyes roam over the plastic-covered window, the cold toast on the dashboard, my cheap phone in the console. The back seat is filled with clothes—some neatly folded, some tossed haphazardly. And then I see the knife, abandoned on the front seat. It had been on my lap when I scrambled from the vehicle. Has she spotted it?

"I just live up the street," she says, looking away, ashamed for me. "Eight thousand square feet, right on the water. But it's a prison."

"Better than living like this," I mutter, eyes on my home on wheels.

"No," she says. "It's not."

Without another word, she walks away.

6

I NEED MORE SLEEP, BUT I am soaking wet, with seaweed in my hair and green slime on my clothing and skin. The brackish smell of Puget Sound is strong on me, and I need to shower and change. Normally, I can go a couple of days without a proper wash, but I can't go to the diner like this. Working quickly in the low light, I peel off my wet jeans and struggle into a pair of black tights. They stick to my skin, forcing me to wriggle and jump into them. Yesterday's T-shirt is atop the pile in the back seat. It smells like grease, and there's a mustard stain—or is it egg yolk?—down the front, but at least it's dry.

Though my head feels thick and cloudy, I need to focus. Strategy is key to survival for the homeless. There must be a community pool in this area where I can scam a hot shower, but I have no idea where it is. If I still had my smartphone, I could have googled it, but the dumbphone won't help me. I decide to drive south, back to the lower-income, more familiar neighborhoods. Before I leave, I stash some of my belongings in the thick brush so I don't have to cart them with me. I will come back here tonight. I've been sleeping peacefully in this spot...except when there's a woman trying to drown herself.

She's stuck in my head as I drive past the sleeping mansions, out of the forested enclave, and merge onto the highway. The plastic on the window thwaps relentlessly, and I feel the tension build between my eyebrows. Her husband must be a monster for her to want to die, to give up her life of privilege and luxury. And why drowning? Aren't there more efficient, painless ways to do yourself in? But the poetic nature of an abused woman walking into the icy ocean cannot be denied. If only I hadn't stopped her.

There was something about her, though...Even after I dragged her from the water, when she sat shivering and dirty on the slippery rocks...she had an effortless elegance, a sense of refinement. As I sat beside her, the two of us soaked through, passing that bottle back and forth, I felt captivated by her.

I'm desperate for connection, I think. As my life spiraled down the drain, my friends scurried away like rats. And my best friend, my sister, hates me. That's what I miss—that closeness, that bond, that I took for granted until it was gone. I destroyed it. It's all my fault. But that doesn't mean I don't yearn for it.

As I near the city, traffic starts to thicken. I drive past the heart of Seattle, heading toward familiar territory. I try not to use the same shower too often—their goodwill will only stretch so far—but I'm driving on autopilot, my thoughts muddled by exhaustion. Suddenly, I find myself in the same parking lot. The lure of the hot water and soap is too strong, and I go inside.

"Hi," I mumble, all too aware of my slimy appearance. "I lost my pass."

It's a man this time, with heavy brows and a shock of gray hair. His face is hard, etched with his history. I can already tell...there is little room in his heart for compassion.

"This pool is for paying customers," he says, his words gruff.

"I'll pay," I say, reaching into my pocket for my tip money. "No problem."

"No," he barks, waving me away with a gnarled hand. "You're not here to swim. Get out."

I don't have the energy to pretend. "Please," I say, feeling tears welling in my eyes. "I'll just shower and go."

He looks me over with a disgust that borders on loathing. "This isn't a shelter. We don't allow vagrants here."

Two women enter then, chatting brightly, but they stop as they near me. Their clean hair is scraped into ponytails, their morning skin dewy with moisturizer. Not so long ago, women like these would have come into my restaurant. They would have admired the aplomb with which I ran it, marveling at my rapport with staff and customers, the obvious joy I took in it. I'd have come by their table to check on their satisfaction and offered a digestif on the house. They might even have envied me. But now I see the wary look in their eyes. And the pity.

It is worse than the man's disdain.

I hurry out of the building.

Eventually, I find a YMCA with a gym and pay to use the shower. Afterward, I go to the laundromat, where I doze in a chair as my clothes and sleeping bag wash and dry, and then I go to work. I force a cheerful demeanor, but it doesn't increase my tips. By the end of the shift, I've stopped trying. With the night's meager earnings in my pocket, I drive back up north, to that upscale community, to the secluded alcove. In the dark, I struggle to find the bags I stashed in the bushes, but they are still there, untouched. I put them in the car, recline my seat, and sleep. Hard and deep. Until I hear it.

A sharp tapping on the glass beside my head wrenches me into consciousness. I lurch forward, hands groping for the knife in my lap. I grasp it, just as I make out the face framed in the window, backlit by the rising sun. It's not a cop or a thief or a rapist. It's her.

The drowning woman.

7

TENTATIVELY, I OPEN THE CAR door and step out. The morning sky glows a promising shade of peach, and there's already a whisper of warmth in the crisp air. The woman is in another expensive jogging outfit, dark hair pulled back from a flawless, makeup-free face. But she looks different now, softer. Smiling.

"I realize that I never thanked you," she says. "For saving me."

"It's fine."

"I thought I wanted to die. But I don't. I'm grateful that you found me when you did."

I shrug because there is really nothing to say.

The woman removes a small pack from her back and unzips it. "I brought you something. To say thanks." She presses a small object into my hand. It's smooth and white, a hole through its center.

"It's a netsuke," she explains. "Traditionally, Japanese men used them as toggles on their kimonos. It's carved from bone."

I look at the figurine: an intricate figure of a coiled snake. "My husband collects them," the woman says. "This one's from the early nineteenth century."

I'd have preferred a package of bagels. Or a latte. "Thanks."

"It's quite valuable. I'm not sure what it's worth but it's signed."

Turning it over, I see the artist's name in Japanese characters. "Sell it if you want. Or keep it. Put it somewhere in your new place, once you're back on your feet."

What is it worth? I wonder. It would be rude to ask. But if I can get even a hundred bucks for it, I'm selling it. I appreciate the sentiment, but money is more important than a trinket right now.

"And...," she says, digging deeper into the pack, removing a brown paper sack, "breakfast."

That's more like it. My stomach churns with the promise of food. Free food.

"Shall we eat on the beach? Watch the sunrise?"

Before I can answer, she's moving toward the path. She calls over her shoulder, "Your car is safe. I jog here every morning. No one ever comes by."

I trail her down to the ocean.

We settle on a driftwood log, bleached soft and gray, and the woman unpacks the paper sack. "I'm Hazel," she says as she passes me a roll covered in seeds. "I baked these a couple of days ago. I couldn't make anything fresh without Benjamin noticing."

Benjamin. The husband. The sadist.

"So, what's your story?" she asks, setting a shiny red apple on my lap. "Why do you live in your car?"

Do I tell her that I was a successful restauranteur? That I'd finally manifested my dream when COVID hit? That I'd done everything in my power—legitimate and then illegal and finally immoral—to keep my business going? But I can't. "Pandemic," I mutter, biting into the bun. It's light and moist and filled with peanut butter and honey. It's the taste of my childhood and my throat clogs with longing for a simpler time.

"It hit a lot of people hard," she says, eyes on the horizon. "But Benjamin made even more money."

"What's *your* story?" I ask. "What do you do?"

She turns to face me then. “I do what I’m told.”

“By Benjamin?”

Her eyes return to the sea. “Yep.”

“Surely you have your own life.”

Her response is a question. “What’s your name?”

For some reason, I hesitate, consider giving her a fake. But finally I say, “I’m Lee.”

“Well, Lee, my relationship doesn’t allow me to have my own life.”

“I don’t get it.”

She looks at the Apple Watch on her wrist. “Shit.” She scrambles to her feet. “I have to be home by six-thirty.”

“Why?”

“I’ll be punished.”

“That doesn’t sound like a marriage, Hazel. It sounds like a master and a slave.”

“That’s exactly what it is.”

She is already scrambling over the rocks toward the path before I can ask her if she means it.

8

THE NEXT DAY IS PAYDAY. It's also my day off, but I go into the diner early to collect my money. I'd hoped that Hazel would come by again with a pilfered breakfast and a few minutes of companionship, but she didn't. Maybe Benjamin only lets her jog on certain mornings? Or maybe one free meal and a Japanese figurine are thanks enough for saving her life.

Randy slides me an envelope and I feel the lightness of it. I'm an illegal worker, so he can pay me what he wants. We'd agreed on a wage, though, so this should be more than enough to repair my window. I have an appointment at a glass place a few miles from Uncle Jack's diner. The man on the phone promised same-day service for a price. I would give all the money I've saved to fix my car. The nights are too cold to sleep outside, and it's not safe. I'm too frightened to go to a rooming house where I'd share a wall with an ex-con, a drug dealer, or worse. My pride still won't allow me to go to a shelter.

I'm the first customer at the autobody shop. Four mechanics in coveralls loiter in the office, drinking coffee and shooting the shit. "I called," I say as I enter. "I need my window fixed. Today." I hold out my keys, and an older man with a thin, gray ponytail steps forward, takes them.

"I can do it, but it'll cost you."

"I know."

His watery eyes roam over me, and his eyebrow arches skeptically. "You've got the money?"

My poverty is apparent in my ghostly complexion, my uncombed hair, my rumpled clothing. Over time, my air of competence, confidence, and capability has dissolved. Now I look weak, desperate, and broke. "I've got it," I snap.

He sets his coffee cup down. "Right. You can pick it up at the end of the day."

"I'll wait."

"Okay." He nods toward a coffeepot, a stack of paper cups, a jar of powdered creamer. "Coffee's free for customers."

The men reluctantly disperse, my presence an irritant. I pour a cup of coffee, shake in the creamer, and stir it with a wooden stick. It tastes awful but it dulls the hunger pangs. On my days off, I get no free food, so I must strategize the cheapest way to eat. At least the waiting area is safe and warm, and no one will chase me away. I'm a customer. I'm allowed to spend the day here.

It comes on slowly, after my third cup of coffee. A tickle in the back of my throat that I attribute to the noxious liquid. But when it's followed by a chill, and an ache deep in my bones, I realize I'm sick. It's a cold, or more likely a flu. It's not surprising I'd catch a virus. I'm malnourished and exhausted, and when I rescued Hazel, I'd gotten a nasty chill. But I can't be ill. Survival is hard enough when I'm healthy.

I need chicken soup, and tea, and cold medicine. I need twelve hours of uninterrupted sleep in a comfortable position. But I don't know where to find supplies in this area and I must stay upright and semi-alert. This is a place of business. I huddle into myself, wrapping my sweater tight around my ribs. Just for a moment, I close my eyes and let self-pity wash over me. The universe is punishing me for what I've done. I deserve this misery.

At some point, a mechanic enters, trailed by a customer. They move to the counter to discuss quotes for a cracked windshield. I keep my eyes down, focused on my tepid cup of coffee. The two men don't seem to notice me, though I am subtly shivering now. I hug myself tighter, rubbing the backs of my arms. Is the air-conditioning on? Why am I so cold?

The mechanic moves back to the workshop, and the customer heads for the door. I allow myself a quick glimpse of him as he passes. He's average height but noticeably fit, wearing faded jeans and a thin T-shirt that shows off a muscular body. His ropy forearms are decorated with tattoos, and I spot a skull that looks hand-drawn. The man is my age, or perhaps a little younger. Once, I might have smiled, even flirted with a guy like this. But when he glances my way, I drop my eyes, shift uncomfortably. I must look as bad as I feel, if not worse.

When he's gone and I'm alone, I pull my knees up to my chest, rest my head on them. My body throbs, and there's an insistent pressure building in my sinuses. I haven't eaten since last night, but I don't have much of an appetite. Still, some food might make me feel less nauseous, less dizzy.

My head pops up as the front door opens. It's him, the customer who just left. He's back and he's looking right at me, his brows knitted together, his mouth set in a grim line. He holds out his hand to me. In it is an orange.

Our eyes meet and his are not filled with pity or condescension, just human decency. I can't help but notice the color: hazel, flecked with green and gold. I accept his offering. It's just an orange, but my throat clogs with emotion.

"Thanks."

He gives a slight nod and then he leaves.

It's not a particularly good orange—a bit stringy—but I eat ravenously, juice running down my hands, stinging the scratches on my wrist. I can almost feel the vitamin C coursing through my body, and I pray for a miraculous recovery. When I'm finished, I find a restroom that says employees only, and slip inside. My haunted reflection stares back from the chipped mirror. I run the water until it's warm, then wash my sticky hands, the area around my mouth. My teeth are full of orange pith, but my toothbrush is in my car. I pat at my hair, try to flatten it, but there's no use. Giving up, I slip back to the waiting area.

By the time the ponytail mechanic returns, I am weaker, sicker, colder. My throat feels like it's closing, and my sinuses are throbbing. "Your window's fixed," he says, dropping my keys on the countertop.

"Great." As I walk toward him, the floor tilts under my feet. Luckily, I reach the counter before I stumble.

"You okay?" But he doesn't care about me. A woman collapsing in his lobby will be bad for business.

"Yeah. Fine."

He punches the buttons on an outdated cash register and gives me my total. I reach into the pocket of my cardigan for my pay packet and withdraw the cash. I count it out with shaky hands. The man recounts it quickly, then scoops it into the till. I put the few remaining bills back in my pocket, thank him, and leave.

My car is secure now. I can park anywhere and be safe. In this largely industrial area, I'll be able to find a side street where I can rest, undisturbed. I should find some soup and then go to sleep. I have to work tomorrow. I can't afford to miss a shift. Turning the key, I pull out of the parking lot but pause as I get to the street. I think about that hand punching through the window, clutching my wrist, stealing my purse. I look at the scratches on my arm, still puffy and red. And then I think about Hazel.

I head toward the northbound interstate.

9

THEY SAY A RESTAURANT IS like a baby. It demands your constant attention, occupies your mind when you're away from it, and even in the worst moments, when you want to cry with exhaustion and frustration, you wouldn't trade it for the world. That's how I felt about the Aviary. It was more than a business. It was my passion, my true love, my social life, my family.

Old friendships faded away, suffering from neglect and scheduling difficulties. As the boss, I should have kept myself aloof, removed from the rest of my team but at the end of each night, we'd eat dinner, drink tequila, and play cards. Like a party. Like a family. Often, I wouldn't get home until 3:00, even 4:00 a.m. Sometimes I wouldn't go home alone. It wasn't a healthy existence, but god…it was so much fun.

These were the people I worried about when I vanished, when I locked the door and walked away. I put together food kits for the staff, divvying up the rice and flour and beans, the cheese and butter and chocolate. In the office, I left an expensive bottle of red for my manager. My sous chef received his favorite tequila. Each item was tagged with a note:

With gratitude,
Lee

And then I vanished, before Damon could break my hand.

The Aviary was my identity as much as my business. I was the restaurant, and it was me. That's why I tried to hang on to it. That's why I betrayed my sister. Because I was afraid that I would lose myself without it, that I would disappear.

And I have.

It feels like a severed limb sometimes, an invisible ache for a lost lover or a cherished pet. Sometimes it's a physical pain. Or maybe that's the throb of the crushed bones in my finger. They have healed by now, but in the cold, damp climate the discomfort returns.

The tap on the window wakes me, but I don't start, don't reach for my knife. I'm too sick to care who is out there, what they might do to me. Murder might be a relief from my current state of misery. Kidding… Sort of. But the face peering in my window isn't dangerous. It's concerned, compassionate, and beautiful.

I open the door a crack. "Hey."

"God, Lee. You look terrible." Hazel rests her hand on my cheek. "You're burning up."

"What time is it?" I scrabble in the console for my flip phone. "I have to go to work."

"It's six-fifteen in the morning. Where do you work?"

"Uncle Jack's. It's a diner in Beacon Hill."

"Call in. Tell them to get someone to cover. You're too sick."

I meet her eyes, my voice deliberate. "I can't afford to miss work."

"This is my fault, isn't it?" She observes me, arms crossed. "You got cold and wet when you pulled me out of the water. And now you're sick."

I shrug. "There's a bug going around."

"I brought you a croissant." She hands me a greasy paper sack that I hadn't noticed. "What time do you start work?"

"Four."

She presses her lips together, thinking. "I have to go home now, but I'll try to come back later and bring you some supplies…soup, cold medicine, and vitamin C. Anything else?"

"Tea."

"Got it." She strokes my hair like an injured dog's. The affection, the human touch, is so nice. "Eat your breakfast, then go back to sleep."

I close my eyes, wishing beyond hope that she would invite me into her home. That she'd offer me a spare bed with a soft mattress and clean sheets, even for a couple of hours. But she doesn't. And I can't blame her.

I'm already drifting off as she shuts the door and jogs away.

10

WHEN I GET TO THE diner at three-thirty, I feel almost human. My throat is still sore, but the cold medicine Hazel brought me has cleared my sinuses and soothed my body aches. She had returned, as promised, in a black Mercedes. She was dressed in stylish jeans, cool white sneakers, a well-cut blazer over a T-shirt. She was carrying a canvas bag filled with supplies: the medicine, lozenges, vitamin C, a container of soup, a paper cup of tea, and a bunch of cosmetics.

"When you look good, you feel good," she explained. "Let me fix you up a bit."

What I needed was a hot shower and a blow-dryer, but Hazel wasn't daunted. She sat in my passenger seat and gently washed my face with a scented facial wipe. Then she moisturized my skin and applied some light makeup. Her ministrations were relaxing, maybe even healing. When she brushed my hair, I closed my eyes and thought of Teresa. My sister had braided my hair when we were girls, her fingers tickling my scalp as she worked through my dark mane. I had tried to braid hers, but the results were never as tidy. My throat felt tight with the memory.

When Hazel was done, she angled the rearview mirror toward me. "You're gorgeous."

I took in my face by section: contoured eyes, rosy cheeks, a glossy mouth. Gorgeous was a stretch, but I looked pretty. And more importantly, healthy.

Lewis glances up as I set a fresh glass of Sprite in front of him. Has he noticed my makeover? There is a flicker of acknowledgment, even appreciation in his eyes, but he turns away as the front door opens, all business. The man who enters isn't here for drugs, though. He takes a seat at the opposite end of the bar, and I slide a menu to him.

"Coffee?"

"Yes, please." He looks up and our eyes meet. His are intense, almost golden in the fluorescent lighting. It's him. The guy who gave me the orange at the garage yesterday. Does he recognize me?

As I retrieve the coffeepot, I feel strangely shy. This isn't a huge coincidence. The man was having his windshield fixed in the area; he probably lives nearby. But his small gesture of kindness had been so meaningful, so needed, and now he's here, in my diner. And I look better than I've looked in…well, a while. Something dormant stirs inside of me.

I pour him a cup of coffee. "What's good here?" he asks.

"It's all about the same," I say. "Stick with the basics. You'll be fine."

"So, avoid the Thai curry shrimp bowl?"

"Definitely."

He smiles and there's a twinkle in those hazel eyes. Does he remember me as the pitiful mess in the garage? If he does, he doesn't mention it. He orders a beef dip, fries, and a Coke.

"Good choice."

"Good advice."

After I submit his order to the kitchen, I attend to my other tables, but his presence is distracting. I find reasons to return to the counter, to busy myself with drinks and condiments, hovering around him. His eyes track me—at least I think they do. I can't look. I feel fluttery, like a teenager, my lips curled into a small, self-conscious smile. When his order is up, I place it in front of him.

"Thanks, Lee." He's read my name tag.

"You're welcome...?" I prod.

"Jesse," he says, and he smiles, revealing a dimple in his left cheek. "Nice to meet you. Again."

So, he does remember. "Thanks for the orange. I was pretty sick yesterday."

"I could tell. Feeling better?"

"Yeah."

"You look better. I mean, you look great. Not that you looked bad yesterday; you just looked...sick."

We're flirting. It feels stiff and awkward, like an unused muscle, but I'm still grinning, and my chest feels light. "That orange must have cured me."

"I should be a doctor."

"Lee!" Randy barks. "Table fourteen is waiting for their change."

"Busted," Jesse says with a conspiratorial wink. I wink back and then hurry to the waiting booth.

I force myself to focus on my other customers; losing my job is not an option. Randy monitors me as I move efficiently from booth to booth and back to the kitchen. Jesse is still at the bar, still eating his sandwich, still in my peripheral vision. Watching him is part of my job—refilling his coffee, offering dessert. Noticing the outline of strong shoulders in his thin T-shirt, the curl of his brown hair at the nape of his neck, is not. When he pushes his plate away, I hurry toward him.

"Anything else?" I ask.

"What time do you finish, Lee?"

"Midnight."

"I'll come back. We can get a drink somewhere."

I should say no. I'm sick, and on medication that should not be mixed with alcohol. And after my shift, I get a free meal that I need to sustain me through the next day. But I'm pulled toward this man like a magnet. He makes me feel like the old me. Like an attractive woman again.

"Sounds good," I say. And I smile.

11

THE PILLOW IS SOFT AGAINST my face, and I snuggle under the blankets. I'm tempted to go back to sleep, but a slip of spring sunshine filters through the blinds, telling me it's morning, that I should get up. My throat is tender, and my mouth feels parched from mouth breathing. I roll over in search of my water bottle and my back twinges. It's used to sleeping in a slightly reclined position; I haven't lain flat in so long. Suddenly, I sit bolt upright, grasping for my bearings.

I'm alone in a masculine bedroom sparsely furnished with a battered four-drawer dresser and a wobbly bedside table. In a corner are several dumbbells and an acoustic guitar case. Clothing litters the parquet floor: faded jeans, T-shirts, a couple of flannels…I recognize my own jeans and black T-shirt in the disarray.

It comes back to me then: Jesse. We had gone for a drink at a dive bar a few blocks from the diner. I'd left my car parked behind Uncle Jack's; he'd driven us in his Audi. I should have ordered a Coke or a bubbly water, but I was nervous and excited. I thought the whisky would calm my nerves, make me charming and witty. Surely my tolerance was up from my nightly indulgence. But combined with the cold medicine and my illness, it had nearly put me to sleep.

Scrambling from the double bed in my bra and panties, I gather up my clothes and struggle into them. I need to find a bathroom, to pee and freshen up, before Jesse sees me. We didn't have sex, or even kiss—*that*, I'd remember—but I'm embarrassed, subtly ashamed. Who nods off on a first date? After one drink? And though there's no mirror in his bedroom, I know I look terrible.

I open the door a crack and peer into the apartment. The charcoal-colored couch is vacant but there's a pillow at one end, a jumbled blanket at the other. So, that's where he'd spent the night. The rest of the living area is dominated by a massive TV and a bunch of gaming consoles. A small alcove off to the right presents as a den, housing a cheap single-drawer desk, a laptop, a few books on kinesiology. It's a typical bachelor pad. But Jesse is not typical. The way he'd insisted I couldn't drive last night was so caring. And the way he'd brought me home, gently helped me out of my clothes, settled me into his bed, before kissing my forehead and slipping out of the room, was beyond. Where is he now? Before I go searching, I notice the bathroom door slightly ajar and scurry toward it.

The room is small and dated like the rest of the apartment. The pink appliances, the scuffed hardwood, and the yellowing paint are incongruous with the expensive Audi Jesse drives. But it is not unheard of for a guy to sink more money into his car than his home. I relieve myself and then hurry to the mirror above the sink. Ugh. The makeup Hazel applied yesterday is smudged and smeared. I wash it away with a spa-brand facial cleanser (Jesse apparently spends money on skincare, too). My skin feels tight, but I look better. I squeeze a glob of toothpaste onto my finger and finger-brush my teeth. There's a hairbrush on the counter—perfect for a wavy mane like mine—and I run it through my hair. I find an elastic in the pocket of my jeans and I scoop my hair into a high ponytail.

When I emerge, I listen for my host, but the place is silent. The only sounds are the clatter of pipes above me and the distant hum of traffic outside. Peeking through the living room blinds, I notice the heavy steel bars on the window. The apartment is on the ground floor and looks out onto a dismal alley. Clearly, break-ins must be an issue in the area. Still, it is infinitely more secure than living in a car.

I move into the small galley kitchen where a large evergreen tree blocks the light of the only window. At least it eliminates the need for security bars. Jesse has virtually no appliances. The chipped laminate counter is lined with supplements and protein powders. With the free weights in his bedroom and Jesse's muscular physique, I'm getting a picture of a fit, health-conscious guy. What was he doing in a greasy spoon like Uncle Jack's? Unless…it had been more than a coincidence. Had he been looking for me? The possibility evokes a flutter in my chest, and I smile into the emptiness.

I peek into his fridge. It's rude to help myself, but I'm a little queasy from last night's whisky on an empty stomach. There are more vitamins, almond milk, a plastic box of spinach, and two apples. Can I take one? Will he mind? But I'm already reaching for it, running it under the tap, and biting into it. It's crisp and juicy, and I close my eyes, savoring the sweetness. This moment, in a warm kitchen, with a fresh piece of fruit, is something I would have taken for granted in my old life. Not anymore.

On the sofa, I curl up under the blanket and eat the apple. I wait. And then I wait some more. As I nibble at the core, I feel a tinge of panic. What if Jesse's not coming back? Maybe he's gone to work and won't return for eight or nine hours? I don't know where I am. How will I get back to my car? How far am I from the diner? Seattle is still unfamiliar to me, and without a smartphone, I'm lost. Do I have enough money from last night's tips to pay for a cab? Even if I do, I don't know the number. I'm on the verge of freaking out when I hear a key in the lock.

Jesse enters carrying a cardboard tray with two disposable coffee cups and a paper bag. "You're up," he says, moving toward the couch. "How are you feeling?"

"I'm fine." It's almost true. "Sorry about last night."

"Tea." He hands me a cup. "Lots of honey. Good for the throat." He sits beside me. "Why are you sorry?"

"I don't normally pass out on the first date." *Date.* It was just a drink, not a date-date. I feel like a fool.

But Jesse takes a sip of his drink and I smell the strong coffee. "You were sick. It's understandable." He digs into the paper sack and removes a muffin the size of my head. "Banana walnut okay?"

I take the muffin, breaking off a piece and shoving it into my mouth. It's sweet, greasy, more like cake than a breakfast food but it's delicious. With effort, I eat slowly, casually. "I stole an apple," I admit.

"Just leave a dollar on the table when you leave."

He's joking but I realize I've probably overstayed. "I should get out of your hair."

"Relax. I don't have a client until eleven."

"What do you do?"

"Personal trainer." The body. The supplements. The weights. It makes sense. Would the old Lee have dated a personal trainer? She would have been concerned about conflicting schedules, a shortage of common interests, and probably a certain superficiality. But now, all that matters is that he is good and kind.

"I want to write music," he adds, "but it's a tough business."

God, he's a poet. A poet with a killer body.

"What about you?" he asks. "You like working at the diner?"

A derisive snort erupts from me. "It's fine. It's a job."

"But you'd rather be doing something else?"

"I used to own my own restaurant. In New York. But that was another life."

"Maybe you can again?"

He doesn't know I'm homeless, that I'm barely surviving. But even if I wasn't, it's a huge leap from waitressing at Uncle Jack's to being a restauranteur. "I don't think so." I scooch forward on the couch. "I really should go."

"Okay. I'll drive you home."

"I left my car at the diner. Can you take me there?"

As he maneuvers the Audi through the streets, I try to pay attention to my surroundings, to get my bearings, but I'm hopelessly lost. Seattle plays tricks with its huge lake mimicking the ocean.

"This is a nice car," I say.

"It's a lease," he admits. "A business write-off. Most of my clients are wealthy and kind of stuck-up. I have to play the part." He hangs a right into an alley and suddenly we're behind the restaurant, idling near my Corolla.

"Thanks." I unclip my seat belt. "For letting me crash. And for taking care of me. And for the tea and the muffin."

"Let's try this again." He angles his body toward me. "When you're feeling better."

"I'd like that. Should we exchange numbers?"

"I know where to find you."

Our eyes meet and I wonder if he'll kiss me. The chemistry is there, I'm not imagining it, but I'm still sick, probably contagious. Jesse leans in and presses his lips to my forehead.

"See you soon, Lee."

I climb out and stand in the alley, watching his car drive away.

12

THE I-5 STRETCHES OUT BEFORE me, now-familiar fast-food joints and strip malls zipping by my window. I have four empty hours until my shift starts. For once, I am rested and nourished, and despite this cold, I'm filled with a giddy energy. I've met someone, someone thoughtful and considerate and hot as hell. Even with the mess I've made of my life, my desperate circumstances, I feel a sense of optimism. The potential of romance is startling in its power. I'm still homeless, my future is still bleak, but I can't quell the buoyant feeling in my belly.

In my past life, my real life, I would have called Teresa. My sister would have let me gush about Jesse, shared my excitement, while asking probing, protective questions. For years, she'd wanted me to find a solid guy to ground me in my frenetic existence. Although…I'm not sure Jesse would qualify in my sister's eyes. Would a personal trainer with a basement apartment and a leased car be up to her standards?

Teresa had found her guy. Clark was—still is—a plastic surgeon: older, stable, attractive in his academic, leather-and-tweed way. She'd moved into his spacious home on Long Island, taken to her role as mom to his two chocolate Labs. I only met Clark three times—once for coffee in midtown, once at their elegant engagement party, and once when he walked into my restaurant with another woman.

He'd had no idea that he was bringing this *girl*—she was barely legal—into his future sister-in-law's establishment. Teresa had to have mentioned the Aviary, but men like Dr. Clark Bailor didn't pay attention to such details. I'd watched from the kitchen, my stomach churning as my sister's fiancé openly pawed at this young woman. Something about her age, her outfit, and her plucky demeanor made me wonder if he was paying her. I reached for the house phone, about to call Teresa, when I froze.

A dark, ugly feeling descends as I remember what I did next. I try to shake it off, but it creeps into my psyche. My business was struggling by then. I was already falling behind on bills and payments; Damon was already circling. Still, the choice I made in that moment was self-serving, ugly, and just plain wrong. I hung up the phone and pulled my cell out of my back pocket. Surreptitiously, I photographed Clark and his side-bitch as they kissed and cuddled at their secluded table. And then I tried to blackmail him with the photos.

My plan was to get the money and then tell Teresa about the cheating anyway. I still wanted to protect my sister. But it backfired. Clark fell on his sword, confessed his transgressions to his fiancée, promised to go to therapy (he was a sex addict, apparently). What he had done was forgivable: What I had done was not. Instead of saving my only sibling, my best friend, I had tried to save myself. Teresa didn't believe that I would have told her the truth after Clark paid up. What I had done was sickening; she had every right to excise me from her life. Our parents took her side, of course. They didn't overtly cut me off, but their judgment and disdain were palpable. That's why it was so easy for me to vanish. No one cared enough to look for me.

Is that why I'm driving back toward the beach, toward Hazel?

She is the closest thing I have to a friend or confidante. Perhaps she is a second chance for me. I will not hurt or betray her. I won't put my own selfish interests before hers. And I have already saved Hazel's life. The bond between us is profound.

Exiting off the highway, I navigate through the old-growth fir and cedar trees toward the ocean. Hazel is probably worried about me. Yesterday, she'd found me trembling and feverish. This morning, when she went for her run, I wasn't there. She might think the worst—that I was too weak to drive to my usual camp, that I am in the hospital, or even dead. If she comes to check on me this afternoon, I want to be there.

I've just parked in the secluded spot when I realize it's Saturday. Hazel's weekend routine is unfamiliar to me. Her husband will be home from his high-powered job. Perhaps he won't let her leave the house? This makes me wonder how he controls her. Is the abuse strictly physical? Does he withhold affection or money? Whatever he does, it's bad enough that she wanted to drown herself.

Securing my belongings in the trunk, I make my way down the steep trail to the beach. The rocky cove is deserted, as it always is. The residents of this tony neighborhood are at the gym, or the yoga studio, or on the massage table. They're out for brunch, or seeing their dermatologist, or on a beach in Hawaii. If they are at home, they're clearly content to watch the white-capped ocean from the comfort of plush sofas, through massive picture windows. But they can't hear the roar of the waves, feel the ocean breeze on their faces, smell the briny scent of the sea. If I lived in such luxury, would I give this up? I settle onto that same driftwood log, rub the soft silvery surface with my fingers. No. When I have a comfortable home again, I will still come to the beach.

A shiver runs through me and I rub the backs of my arms, but it's not a chill. Jesse has wormed his way back into my mind, a pleasant touch of memory: his handsome face, his kindness, the chemistry between us… Will he come to the diner tonight, or is that too soon?

I don't want to play games, don't want him to wait until tomorrow or the next day so he doesn't appear too keen. If he doesn't come until Thursday, I'll have the day off. The possibility that I might miss his visit, that he might not come at all fills me with panic. It is stupid to be so enamored with a man I just met, but this morning, having tea and a muffin in his warm apartment, the way he'd kissed my forehead in his car…it's the happiest I have felt in months.

It is then that I spot her. Hazel is picking her way across an outcropping of rocks farther down the beach. There must be another access point farther south. She hasn't noticed me and seems lost in thought. I stand and wave.

"Hazel!" I call, the wind grasping my voice, pulling it away, but she turns. A small smile chases away her haunted expression, but not before I clock it. She continues across the rocks toward me.

Her greeting is a hug. "I was worried about you," she says, holding me at arm's length. "Are you feeling better?"

"Yeah." My chest warms with her concern. "That's why I came back. I didn't want you to worry."

We settle onto the driftwood log. "Where were you last night?" Hazel asks.

"I stayed at a friend's." It comes out giddy and girlish.

"Oh?" She arches an eyebrow at me. "Who's the friend?"

"His name's Jesse." I tell her about the orange, how Jesse found me at the diner, how we'd gone for a drink. "I was too groggy to drive, so he took me home. But nothing happened. He slept on the sofa."

"You like this guy." It's a statement, not a question.

"We've just met, but he's really nice. And thoughtful. And so sexy."

"What's his last name? Have you googled him?"

Without a smartphone or a computer, that simple universal background check has become a hassle for me. And I never thought to ask his last name. "Not yet," I say.

"You need to be careful, Lee." Hazel's pretty face is dark. "Sometimes people aren't who they say they are. I should know."

This isn't about me. And this isn't about Jesse. "What happened with you and Benjamin?" I ask.

Her head is lowered, eyes fixed on the rocky beach. "Do you know what Total Power Exchange is?"

"No."

"Neither did I." She looks at me then, her dark eyes shiny. "It's a type of dominant/submissive relationship. Normally, couples have *scenes*, you know, *moments* where they play those roles. With TPE, it's twenty-four seven."

"God..."

"It's usually consensual. If it works for both partners, then great. But it stopped working for me a long time ago. And Benjamin stopped caring what I wanted."

I'm without words, still unsure of what it all means, but Hazel continues.

"When we first got together, we had a Master/slave contract. I outlined my limits, things that I would and wouldn't do. He agreed to keep me safe, to never go too far. Aftercare was important to me. Cuddles and reassurance. But then... Benjamin broke the rules. He hurt me out of anger. He manipulated me and bullied me. And there was nothing I could do about it. My lack of consent made it more exciting for him."

My throat feels swollen, the words come out a croak. "Does he abuse you?"

In response, she pulls down the back of her pants. I can just see the black and blue lashings on her buttocks.

"Oh god, Hazel. I'm so sorry."

"The physical abuse isn't the worst of it. It's the mental torture. The constant fear. If he saw me right now... talking to you. I'd be locked up."

"Locked up where? How?"

"There's a soundproof room in our basement. It has no windows and a fortified door. That's where he puts me when I've displeased him. That's where he flogs me."

"That's horrific! You have to leave!"

"I can't. He'd kill me. And our house is a fortress. There are cameras everywhere. He watches me all day from the office; he controls everything I do. I'm allowed to go for a run each day. To the gym or yoga a few times a week. Sometimes he lets me go for lunch with friends. But only women he approves of."

"You should go to the police, then."

She snorts. "Benjamin is powerful and connected. The police won't take my side in this." She swivels toward me, her eyes searching mine. "How did you do it? How did you disappear?"

For me, there was no forethought or strategy. And it's simple when no one cares about you. "I just…walked away."

"It's not going to be that easy for me." She reaches for my hand, grasps it so tightly it hurts. "Will you help me?"

"Of course," I say, but the words tremble. How can I help her when I'm barely surviving myself?

"I'm so glad we met, Lee. When you saved me, I knew…We were meant to find each other. Does that sound corny?"

It should but it doesn't. It feels true. I shake my head.

She checks her Apple Watch and stands. "Shit. I have to go. I'm only allowed twenty minutes on the beach." She sprints for the trail, turns back at its mouth. "See you tomorrow?"

I smile through my trepidation. "Of course."

13

WHEN JESSE WALKS INTO THE diner on Tuesday near the end of my shift, my first feeling is relief. In the three days since I last saw him, I'd begun to worry. If he'd discovered that I was homeless, on the run, he'd want nothing to do with me. I couldn't blame him for it. And Hazel's words of warning had sifted through my thoughts. Perhaps Jesse wasn't the tender, considerate guy I thought he was. Maybe he didn't care about me, after all. My friend had planted a seed of doubt, and Jesse's failure to appear had let it fester. Every day I'd made the effort to shower and apply the makeup Hazel had given me, for nothing. But now he is here, looking casual and sexy and happy to see me.

"Hey," he says, sliding onto a stool at the bar. "Are you off at midnight?" I tell him I am. "Want to grab something to eat? There's a great late-night ramen bar a few blocks from here. Or we could go somewhere closer to your place?"

"Ramen sounds great."

Jesse orders a coffee, nurses it as I finish my shift with one eye trained on the clock. A table of drunk college kids is rude to me, and I see Jesse's posture stiffen, feel him watching the situation. It's nothing I can't handle, but his protectiveness warms me. It's been a long time since someone looked out for me. I drop off their bill, jittery with anticipation. We're about to go on a real date. A date-date. With food. And I'm not going to nod off on him this time. If I end up back at Jesse's apartment, it will be because I choose to go.

When I've clocked out, Jesse suggests we walk. "It's a nice night. And I'll walk you back to your car after."

It's respectful, even chivalrous, but part of me is hoping I'll spend the night with him. His soft bed, the coffee and muffins. And now that I'm feeling better, I can't deny my attraction to him. My sex drive had been extinguished by the stress of running away, of surviving without a home. But as I stroll the streets with Jesse's body mere inches away, it returns with a vengeance. Pheromones are at work. And I'm hungry for physical affection, starved for that connection.

The restaurant is tiny with rough-hewn wooden booths, the windows coated with steam from the boiling vats of soup. We are led to a cramped table near the kitchen where we order two bowls of the special and two frosty Japanese beers. As our waitress leaves, Jesse speaks.

"I would have come to see you sooner, but I knew you were sick. I thought I should let you recover. Did you take some time off?"

So, he hadn't forgotten about me. "I bounced back pretty quickly," I say. "Thanks to that orange."

He chuckles, though the joke is overdone now. Two brown bottles of beer are plunked on the table. We clink them together and drink. The liquid is cold and sharp and delicious. The first sip of alcohol settles my nerves, but I must take it in slowly.

"Where did you grow up, Lee?" It's a normal first- or sort of second-date question, but I've grown used to being guarded. I can't see any harm in talking about my background now, though. Jesse is a safe space.

"In upstate New York. I moved to the city for college and stayed."

"And opened your restaurant," he says, remembering our last conversation.

"What about you?" I ask.

"Spokane," he replies. "I never went far. My mom still lives there. And my sister and her kids. It's nice to be close to family."

"Mmmm." It's ambiguous but implies agreement.

"You must miss yours."

"Yeah," I say, and it's true. "But we're not that close."

The ramen lands in front of us before Jesse can ask me to elaborate. We doctor our bowls with garlic paste and furikake, a Japanese seasoning made with toasted sesame seeds and nori. As I stir the soup with my chopsticks, I steer the conversation away from me.

"I'm worried about a friend of mine." It's a dark topic for a date, but I like how it sounds. Normal. Like a girl who lives in an apartment and has a social life. "I think she's in an abusive relationship."

"Oh no," he says, and his handsome face contorts with empathy. "She needs to leave."

"She says it's complicated. She wants me to help her."

"Help her how?"

Over the past few days, Hazel and I had plotted her escape. Most mornings, she had tapped on my window, dressed in her jogging outfit, carrying whatever breakfast she could pilfer from her kitchen. We'd moved to our silvery log and eaten our fruit or rolls or granola bars, the morning sky pale and promising as we hatched a plan.

"You'll need cash," I told her a couple of days ago. "Credit cards can be easily traced."

Her hands worried at the zipper of her hoodie. "I don't have my own bank account. But there's cash in a safe in Benjamin's study, if I can get into it. I could sell some jewelry. Or another netsuke. What did you get for yours?"

I still haven't sold it. The truth is…I've attached sentimental value to the smooth bone carving. It's silly, but part of me feels that if I let it go, I'll lose Hazel. But I'm going to lose her anyway. That's what saving her means. "I haven't had time to sell it," I fibbed.

"What about fake ID?" she asked. "How did you get yours?"

"I didn't think that far ahead," I admitted. "I just…left. And then all my ID was stolen."

"I'll figure it out," she promised. "I'll get documents for both of us. A whole new identity." She paused for just a breath. "If you want that."

She was offering me a chance to start over, as a new person, unabashed and unafraid. To put all my failures and mistakes behind me, to wipe the slate clean. It meant giving up any hope of reuniting with my sister and my parents, but after what I'd done, there was no hope. They would never forgive me.

"Yeah, I want that."

"Okay." She stood. "Thank you, Lee."

I'd smiled. "Of course." But I didn't know why she was thanking me.

Jesse's next question brings me back to the room. "Does she want to stay with you?"

"My place is really small." Emphasis on the *really*. "She needs cash. And documents."

"Can you help with that?"

"I hope so. I mean…I'll do what I can."

"My mom was abused by my stepfather," he says, sadness in those golden eyes. "No woman should ever have to live that way."

He's right. Hazel's situation is unbearable, and I'm in a unique position to help. If anyone knows how to disappear, to live an anonymous life, it's me. And it's a chance to make up for the way I hurt my sister. Even if it means losing my only friend.

The conversation takes a lighter turn as we eat our soup with porcelain spoons, twirling noodles on chopsticks. Jesse orders another beer, but I abstain. When the meal is finished, I fish for the night's tips, but Jesse insists on paying.

"I asked you out," he says. "It's on me."

"Thank you." Our eyes meet and I'm drawn in by his warm gaze. There's a flutter—subtle, like butterfly wings—in my low belly.

We stroll back toward the diner, savoring the time together. At least I am. But while our progress is slow, my mind is racing. Would it be too forward to suggest a nightcap at his place? I've already slept over, so it's not out of the question. But I don't want to come on too strong. One-night stands were common in my old life, but this feels...different. It feels like *potential*.

We approach Uncle Jack's. The fluorescent lighting and noise of late-night diners—most of them drunk—spill into the street. As we pass, Jesse's hand slips into mine and I like the way it feels. Like we are together, a couple even. When we reach the alleyway, we turn. It is dark, strongly scented with cooking and garbage. Behind a dumpster there are two men—smoking something? shooting up?—but Jesse's presence, his strong hand in mine, makes me feel safe.

"Here we are," he says, stopping near my Corolla.

I swallow, all the words I want to say stuck in my mouth like glue. Finally, I manage to speak. "How about—" But his lips come down on mine. His mouth is warm and soft and tastes of beer. I melt into him, my arms sliding around his waist. I haven't been touched, held, caressed in so long. His hands are in my hair, cradling the back of my head, and my knees weaken. My desire is like hunger, like thirst, startling in its intensity. I press myself against him, hands tugging at his hips. Abruptly, he pulls away.

"I should go."

My cheeks burn. I feel embarrassed by my own lust. "Yeah," I mumble. "Me too."

His fingers tilt my chin up so our eyes meet. "I like you, Lee."

"I like you, too."

He kisses me again—once, softly—and steps back. It's my cue to get into my car and leave. I move robotically to the driver's side and open the door. As I'm about to get in, he says:

"Have a good sleep."

He thinks I'm going home to a warm bed, to cuddle under soft blankets, to think about him. He has no idea that I'll be cold and alone, frightened and on edge. That I'll sip whisky to numb myself, that I'll cradle a hunting knife in my lap.

"You too," I say, and my voice wobbles. I slide into the car and close the door.

14

IN THE MORNING, HAZEL IS there, tapping gently at my window. It takes me a few moments to gather my bearings, to focus my thoughts through the dull throb between my eyebrows, the furry feeling in my mouth. The near-empty whisky bottle sits in the console next to me; last night, it had been almost half full. After I left Jesse, self-pity had consumed me. My time with him had felt so normal, so promising, but as I sat alone in my car, the tattered sleeping bag pulled up to my chin, my optimism had abandoned me. I felt hopeless and ashamed. How could I build a relationship with a man who had no idea who I really was? The horrible secrets I was keeping? If I told him, he'd be disgusted. He'd end our relationship before it even began. If I hid it, and he found out later, it would be even worse.

Righting my seat, I open the door and climb out of the car. My body aches, as it does every morning, and my bladder is full to bursting. I am glad to see Hazel, but this morning, her squeaky-clean presence serves only to highlight my misery.

She smiles at me, seemingly oblivious to my hungover state. "I brought homemade granola and bananas," she says brightly, indicating the small pack on her back. "And coffee."

"Thanks," I mutter, heading for the bushes. "I have to pee." I'm too blurry to feel embarrassed.

When I emerge, Hazel has moved to the beach, to our usual driftwood log. I stumble across the smooth rocks toward her. She is pouring steaming coffee from a thermos into the plastic lid. I sit beside her and gratefully accept the cup, sipping the strong hot liquid. With eyes closed, I feel the ocean breeze on my face, hear the gulls squawking overhead, and I begin to feel normal again. She turns to face me.

"I found someone to make us fake IDs."

"How?" Hazel's life seems to revolve around yoga and society lunches. Where did she meet a person with that capacity?

"Online," she says. "Reddit. I connected with this guy and he helped me. I had to go on the dark web!" She sounds thrilled, even proud. "We have to send passport-quality photos. It's not cheap but they'll be totally legit."

"I don't have much money," I say, thinking of the stash in my trunk that never seems to grow.

"It's fine," she says, handing me a small plastic bag filled with cinnamon-scented oats, nuts, and seeds. "I sold some jewelry. By the time Benjamin notices, I'll be long gone."

"I'm sorry you had to do that."

"I was glad to get rid of it," she says, venom in her voice. "They were makeup gifts, all of them. After Benjamin took things too far. After he hurt me. There was always some shiny expensive trinket."

"I'll pay you back," I say around a mouthful of sweet granola. It will take time, but I will not welch on any more debts.

She waves her hand dismissively. "You saved my life, Lee. You're still saving my life. It's the least I can do."

I smile, embarrassed by the compliment but also relieved. I need to save every penny.

"Have you ever been to Panama?"

It comes out of left field. "No. Why?"

"Benjamin will expect me to go to Europe. France, probably, because I speak a little French. Or Italy. Somewhere he's taken me before. He won't look for me in Central America."

I swallow the cereal, now a tasteless paste in my mouth. "Why Panama?"

"I've heard that if you have cash, you can build a life there. No questions asked."

"Sounds like a good place to disappear."

"I think so, too."

My voice is hoarse. "When will you go?"

"The passport will take a couple of weeks. And then I need to plan my escape. It's not going to be easy with the security guard at our front gate. And the cameras."

"Right." My throat hurts now, raw with emotion. "I'll miss you," I mutter.

"I'll miss you, too." Her smile is sad. "I wish you could come with me."

She's being flip, of course. We barely know each other. And my presence would surely complicate her getaway. And then there's Jesse. Our future may be uncertain, but I'm not ready to give up on it yet. "I wish," I say with a chuckle. "I could use some sunshine."

We move on to the logistics of obtaining our new identities. Hazel tells me about a nearby drugstore where I can get my photo taken. I'm to deliver it to her in the morning; she'll take care of the rest. I don't ask her how she'll do it when she is under constant surveillance. She's clearly adept at fooling Benjamin.

"I've got to get back." Hazel stands. "Stay. Finish the coffee. I'll pick up the thermos tomorrow."

I thank her, watch her slim form skip across the rocks to the mouth of the trail. She looks lighter than I've ever seen her before, more carefree. I realize she's excited for her future, anticipating a life of freedom and opportunity. I hope her emancipation will not look like mine.

She's only gone a few steps when she turns back. "What's going on with you and that guy? Jesse?"

This is the first time she's asked about him. I'd assumed she'd forgotten. But I can't tell her how he kissed me last night, lit me up inside, how I wanted more. I can't tell her that he likes me, *really* likes me, and maybe, if I can keep my secrets, we could have something. Not while Hazel is still under the control of a violent man. It would be cruel.

"We went for ramen last night," I say casually. "He's nice. But we're just friends."

"That's probably for the best. I mean... until you're back on your feet." Her smile is bright, optimistic. "Which will be soon."

"Yep."

She turns and hurries back to her master.

15

THE PAWNSHOP IS AT THE edge of Pioneer Square, a historic neighborhood of cobbled streets, turn-of-the-century lampposts, and trendy bars, restaurants, and boutiques. This block has none of the charm and all of the seediness of the district. A group of vagrants stands smoking on the corner, their clothes filthy, their energy hostile. I smell them as I pass—body odor, stale nicotine, sour booze. I was unable to shower this morning. I'm wearing slept-in jeans and a hoodie fraying at the wrists. My appearance is subpar, but I am not one of them. I have not fallen that far.

An electronic sensor dings as I enter the cluttered shop. It specializes in rare coins, watches, and jewelry. I'd spent the morning at an internet café researching pawnshops that might appreciate the value of the netsuke. This one, while out of my way, seems the most likely. There is a man behind a plexiglass shield with a shiny bald pate and a small pair of glasses perched on his nose. He doesn't look up as I approach, busy with paperwork. I slide the white bone snake through the small opening.

"How much can I get for this?"

He holds it with his fingertips, peering through the glasses. "A netsuke," he says, more to himself than to me. Turning it over, he inspects the signature on the bottom.

"I'll give you two hundred bucks for it." He meets my eyes for the first time. "But honestly...if you sell it to a collector, you could get more."

"How much more?"

"I'm no expert but five hundred. Maybe a thousand?"

A thousand dollars could change my life. It's enough for a deposit on a small apartment. With the fake ID Hazel is getting for me, I'll be able to fill out a lease application. And I'll be able to get a better job. A legitimate job. For the first time since I left New York, I'll be able to live like a normal person. A new person.

"How do I find a collector?"

"eBay."

It's not easy with no computer and only a dumbphone. But I can go back to the internet café. "Thank you," I say sincerely. This man could have bought it and resold it himself. I appreciate his honesty. I slip the smooth figurine back into my pocket.

My car is in a concrete parking garage deep in the touristy district. It costs a small fortune to park there, but I couldn't find any street parking. Despite the potential upturn in my financial prospects, I am conscious of the time. I hurry to the garage, not wanting to pay for an extra minute. A light rain is falling, so I pull the hood of my jacket over my head, grateful for the cover. And the concealment. I'm passing by a row of high-end restaurants and stylish boutiques that serve to highlight my bedraggled appearance. The before-me would have blended right in, completely at home, but now I don't belong. I slide by the chic patrons: A bum. A vagrant. Invisible.

I am exhausted—I am always exhausted—but I feel a sense of accomplishment. My time at the internet café had been productive. In addition to finding the pawnshop, I had done some personal research. Because, as Hazel suggested, it is only prudent to google the guy one is seeing. Jesse's last name, I'd learned over ramen, is the unfortunately common Thomas. Over twenty

Jesse Thomases had appeared in my search results, including a successful athlete and a character actor. But I had found *my* Jesse eventually: his personal trainer profile on a gym's website. His online presence was minimal, but it was enough. He was exactly who he said he was.

The other search I'd done had yielded more relevant results. Hazel's husband, Benjamin Laval, was a partner in a high-profile law firm. His portrait on their OUR PEOPLE page was stern but handsome. He was younger than I'd expected—or maybe he'd had work done. His face was lightly lined, dark hair silver around the temples. He was undeniably good-looking, but I saw the hard glint in his gray eyes, the capacity for cruelty. My friend claimed this man treated her like a slave, and I believed her. There was never any doubt, only curiosity. This is what a sadist looked like.

Benjamin Laval had defended a number of high-profile criminals. He was interviewed on numerous news sites, held various press conferences. I muted his voice and watched him speak, controlling the conversation, dominating the room. I thought about him controlling and dominating Hazel.

As if conjured, she materializes before me. Hazel is there, wearing a blush-colored dress topped with a cropped leather jacket. Her hair is down, dark and lustrous, her face flawlessly made up. She's got a large leather tote over her shoulder, and she's fumbling to open an umbrella in the spring drizzle. Hazel looks cool, beautiful. And happy.

My feet stop moving and I feel a strong urge to turn away. Hazel has another life, of course she does. She told me that Benjamin allows her to go out for lunch, to go shopping, to keep up appearances. Seeing her out of context is jarring; that's all it is. I press forward, approach her.

"Hi, Hazel."

Her pretty face pales. Her mouth opens but no words come. The glass door behind her opens—it's an oyster bar—and two women emerge. They're with Hazel; I know it instantly. They are three of a kind: sleek, shiny, and expensive. Hazel's eyes dart to them and then back to me. As they sidle up beside her, I clock her terror.

"Can we help you?" one of the women says. She is a little older, small and blond and hard. Condescension drips off her. Disdain. Even disgust.

"It's okay," Hazel says quickly. And then to me. "I'm sorry, I almost didn't recognize you." Her features soften. "How are you doing?"

She's talking to me like I'm a small child. Or perhaps a lost dog. My response is guarded. "I'm fine."

"Good. That's good." Her smile is gentle. "Are you staying at a shelter in the area?"

I see what she's doing now. Being kind to the homeless woman. *Noblesse oblige.* "No. I was at a pawnshop." I realize, too late, that I've played right into her narrative.

As the other women open their umbrellas, Hazel digs in her giant purse. She extracts a bill and holds it out to me: a fifty. "Why don't you get some lunch? On me."

My face burns with humiliation and anger. How dare she? I saved her goddamn life! I've listened to all her ugly secrets, helped her plot her escape, and now she is treating me like a beggar. A nuisance. Tears sting my eyes.

I snatch the bill from her—because fifty bucks is fifty bucks—and push past the well-dressed gaggle. As I hurry along the sidewalk, the haughty blonde's words follow me.

"You're welcome!"

16

I DON'T GO BACK TO the beach that night. Or the night after. I sleep in the corner of a mall parking lot—until a security guard shoos me away—and on a quiet suburban street east of the city. My hurt and anger simmer. Hazel conned me into thinking we were friends, confidantes, and then she treated me with such condescension, with such fucking *pity*. It was uncaring at best, cruel at worst. Because over the past few weeks, I have grown to need her.

When Jesse walks into the diner that evening, I almost don't recognize him. He is unshaven, wearing a ball cap and sunglasses. The look works for him, though, and his presence lifts my spirits. In a normal relationship, we would text each other or talk on the phone between dates. But my circumstances are not normal. And maybe his aren't either? As long as Jesse keeps showing up, I am pleased.

He slides onto a stool at the bar and removes his glasses. God, he's sexy. "Want to grab a bite after your shift? Or a drink?"

I feel a glimmer of my past boldness. "Let's go to your place. Watch a movie or whatever?"

In the beat before he replies, my breath catches. If Jesse turns me down, tells me I'm moving too fast or that he's not actually into me, I swear I will burst into flames. But he smiles, thank god, revealing that dimple in his cheek. "Sounds good."

I follow him in my car. It would be too forward to ride with him, too presumptuous. I fully plan on spending the night with him, but some old-fashioned sense of decorum has me playing coy. Or maybe it's just fear of rejection. I'm still unsure of his feelings for me. And I'm still brittle from Hazel's dismissive treatment.

The apartment is just as I remember it—tidy but sparse. We settle on the dark gray sofa with two beers and the remote. "What should we watch?"

He has to know the movie was a ploy to get here, a euphemism for what I really want to do. I cock an eyebrow and shrug. "I don't care."

His smile is slow but knowing. He sets the remote on the coffee table and turns toward me. His arm is on the back of the sofa, his knee raised so it rests against my thigh. I swallow a mouthful of beer: liquid courage.

"How's your friend doing? The one with the abusive husband?"

I hadn't planned to go there tonight, but I find I'm eager to talk about it. "We had a bit of a falling out, actually."

"How come?"

I can't tell him that Hazel is ashamed to know me. That she offered me money like a panhandler. "She acts a lot differently around her other friends," I say. "She treats me badly."

"Do her other friends know about the abuse?"

"I don't know. I doubt it."

"My mom got really good at keeping up appearances." His fingers travel to my shoulder, touch the ends of my hair. "My sister and I knew what went on behind closed doors, but she'd act like everything was perfect with her friends. It drove me crazy. But it was a survival mechanism."

His words resonate. Hazel was playing a part with those other women. They don't know what I know. Why didn't I think of that before?

"I'm sorry you got hurt, though."

"I'm fine," I say, because suddenly, I am. Jesse's fingers are playing with my hair, his knee is pressed against my leg, and I've had just enough beer to make the first move. I lean in and kiss him.

It is slow and soft at first but quickly gathers force. My hands rove over his strong chest, his muscular arms, the stubble on his jaw. As it was with our first kiss, my desire for him is powerful. It's sexual but also physical. It's a need to touch him, to be close to him, to be connected. I've been drowning in loneliness and Jesse is oxygen.

And then he pulls away. "Lee. Stop."

For a moment, I am left panting and confused, and then the humiliation descends. He doesn't want me. I should have known. He is out of my league now. Because I am worthless. The lowest of the low.

"I'm sorry," I say, my voice hoarse. "I'll go."

He grabs my hand as I try to get up and pulls me back to the couch. "Don't," he says. "I just want to make sure that you're okay with this. Things are moving so fast between us."

I stifle a snort. I could tell Jesse that I am a sex-positive woman, comfortable with my body, my desires, my sexual agency. I could tell him that this is, technically, our third date, so far from moving "so fast" in my opinion——in *most* opinions. I could tell him about my years as a restauranteur when casual hookups were all I had the time and energy for, when sexual gratification came quick and dirty with bartenders and waiters and occasionally customers. But I don't.

"I'm okay with this," I say, pushing him back on the sofa and straddling his lap. "I've never been more okay with anything in my life."

17

OF COURSE, I'D HEARD ABOUT the physical and emotional benefits of human touch. I knew that it released oxytocin, the hormone that creates feelings of trust, warmth, and well-being. I'd read that physical connection lowers stress, heightens compassion, increases immunity. Still, I am surprised at how the night with Jesse transforms me. I know it sounds syrupy, cliché, but it's true. The way he kissed me, touched me, held me…It made me feel seen again. Valued. It has given me back my confidence. I am more than my circumstances. I am more than my mistakes.

I am freshly showered, the scent of Jesse's vanilla shampoo lingering in my hair. My clothes are clean, washed in Jesse's basement laundry room. At work, the tale of his mother's abusive relationship runs through my mind as I refill coffees and pour beers, shuttle plates of food to and from the kitchen. Like Jesse's mom, Hazel is afraid, ashamed, hiding the truth. I am likely her sole confidante. So, she put on a show of perfection for those glossy women, pretended I was a virtual stranger, a charity case. It still smarts but I am willing to give Hazel a chance to apologize. After the way I treated Teresa, I would be a hypocrite if I wasn't.

After my shift, I drive back to the beach and park my car in that wooded alcove. I recline my seat, close my eyes, and listen to the waves crashing against the rocky shore, the knife cradled loosely in my grip. This is not a home, but the spot gives me a sense of familiarity, of belonging. I'd much rather be with Jesse, pressed against his smooth, warm back in his double bed, but this is second best. With thoughts of our recent night together in my mind, I drift off to sleep.

The tapping at the window startles me, though I am half awake, half expecting it. I fumble for the knife, but it has slipped down, perhaps under my seat now. Early morning sun filters through clouds, revealing Hazel's face—pretty, contrite—framed in the window. I'm relieved. She came. And I wonder... Has she come every morning since our awkward encounter in front of the oyster bar? It was days ago, and yet, she is here, her features contorted with remorse.

"Thank god you came back," she says when I open the door. "I'm so sorry."

I climb out of the car and stretch before I mumble, "It's fine."

"I should never have treated you that way, Lee. I panicked. I didn't know what to say. I fucked up."

I don't respond. I'm enjoying her groveling, just a little.

"I brought breakfast. And coffee." She indicates the familiar little pack on her back. "Shall we go to our log?"

When we are seated, side by side, Hazel offers me the thermos. "Those women are not my friends," she says, digging in the backpack. "They're married to Benjamin's colleagues. He insists I see them for lunch a couple of times a month. They're shallow and horrible." She hands me a brown paper bag. The scent of sugar, butter, and flour hits me.

"Peach and brown butter scones," she says with a rueful smile. "I made them."

Has Hazel baked each night, hoping to win me over with

pastries? I bite into the buttery scone. It's delicious. I'd forgive almost anything for this.

She picks up the thread of her explanation. "If I'd introduced you as my friend, those women might have mentioned you to their husbands. And then they might have said something to Benjamin. He'd stop me from seeing you, Lee. He vets all my friendships. I couldn't risk it."

"It hurt," I tell her around a mouthful of scone. "A lot."

"I feel sick about it. That's not who I am." Her chin trembles with emotion. "And you didn't deserve it. You've been such a good friend to me."

I decide to put her out of her misery. "Fear and desperation can make you do terrible things. I should know."

She doesn't press but her body language is open and receptive, her brow piqued with curiosity. I feel a strong pull to unburden myself. Maybe it is my renewed confidence, the regained sense of self. Or maybe I want her to know that I truly understand.

"I betrayed my only sister," I admit. "And she'll never forgive me."

"What happened?" she asks. And, after a deep breath, I tell her.

I expect disapproval, or at least distaste, but she says, "You were under so much pressure. Can't she understand that?"

"She'll never get over it. Not as long as she's with Clark." I look down at the remnants of scone in my hands. "They'll be married by now."

"How could she forgive him and not you?" It's a rhetorical question. She gives my forearm a gentle squeeze. "You've lost so much."

Tears well in my eyes, but I blink them away. Self-pity is an indulgence I don't have time for.

"Let me take you for a spa day," Hazel says brightly. "Massage, facial, haircut—the works. On me."

"No," I say automatically. "I couldn't."

"I was an utter bitch. You *have* to let me make amends. I insist."

A smile curls my lips at the thought of a day of pampering. "Are you sure?"

"God, yes! I want to do it. When's your next day off?"

"Thursday."

"There's a great boutique spa in that little complex across from Trader Joe's. I'll book everything and meet you there at ten. Sound good?"

"Sounds *amazing*."

She holds her hand out. "Give me your phone."

I pull the flip phone from my back pocket. She doesn't comment on the antiquated technology as she adds her number to it. "Call me if anything comes up."

Nothing will come up. This is the best thing that's happened to me since I left New York—other than Jesse. "But what about Benjamin? Won't he want to know who's calling you?"

"I'm not allowed to have my phone on when he's home. I'll only answer if I'm alone." She stands up, brushes scone crumbs from her lap. "I'll book a massage, haircut, mani-pedi..."

"Could you book me a bikini wax?" My cheeks are hot and, I'm sure, bright red. "It's been a while."

"I thought you and that guy were *just friends*?" She's teasing me, like girlfriends do, but I feel awkward.

"We're more than that now." I shrug, look down at the rocks, my lips curling up.

"I'm happy for you." She's smiling, but her eyes look troubled. Maybe concerned. Maybe envious. But her voice is bright as she turns to go.

"See you tomorrow. I'll make rhubarb muffins."

18

"WHAT'S GOT INTO YOU?" IT'S Randy, his tone cold and accusatory. Although...he always sounds like that. Default mode: *asshole.*

"What?" I ask, filling a glass with Coke from the fountain. "What am I doing?"

"You're cheerful," he says, pulling a toothpick from the dish near the cash register and peeling off the paper. "And nice. It's not like you at all."

I snort and roll my eyes, hurrying away with the glass of soda. Randy's not wrong. I'm happier than I've been since I came to Seattle. My prospects are slowly but surely improving. Hazel is getting me new identification. When I sell the netsuke, I'll have a thousand bucks. And I have a spa day to look forward to. More importantly, I have a friend. And a boyfriend. Or a lover. Whatever Jesse is.

He hasn't come to see me since I spent the night with him, but I'm not concerned. It's only been a few days. And I didn't imagine our connection, the closeness between us. This sense of vulnerability is new to me, though. I'm used to having the power, holding the strings. I've never felt this way—not with André, my boyfriend of four years, not even in high school. I'm raw and needy.

Is it because I've been stripped of my identity and everything I valued? Has my downfall opened me up, torn down my emotional walls? It is an odd feeling: heady, exciting, and terrifying.

After my shift, I eat a burger in the kitchen, toying with my flip phone. It has been virtually useless to me. I've only made a handful of calls to auto glass repair shops. The phone has never rung. Not even once. Flicking through the contacts, I find Hazel's number. And Teresa's. I added it a couple of weeks ago, afraid I might forget it. But I'll never call her. I know that now.

I don't have Jesse's digits, but I know where he lives. I could show up at his apartment. It's late, but he might appreciate the booty call. Or he might think it's creepy. That *I'm* creepy. Because a *call* implies using a phone, not showing up in person. The old Lee would have gone to him, wouldn't have worried about rejection, but I am different now. Softer. More fragile. The next time I see Jesse, I'll ask him for his number.

With a wave to the kitchen staff, I shuffle out the back door. The alley is dark, and quiet. A single bulb in a metal cage burns over the parking area. I am tired tonight, and the drive to the beach stretches long ahead of me. As I reach my car, I become aware of a figure in the shadows. I stop, my heart rabbiting in my chest. The knife is inside my car, next to the driver's seat. Do I open the door and grab for it? Or run back into the diner? The figure is coming toward me, growing familiar.

"Hey." It's Jesse, his voice husky. "Did I scare you?"

"Uh…yeah."

"Shit. Sorry."

"Why didn't you come into the diner?"

"There's no parking out front. I found a spot back here and decided to wait for you."

"I'm glad you did." I slide into his arms and it feels warm and comfortable and right. My heart rate slows as endorphins flood through me. With him, I feel like I'm home.

"I wanted to see you," he says, his voice muffled by my hair. "My sister and her kids are in town. They're staying with me."

That explains his absence. It's too soon to meet them. Obviously. But if he asked me to, I would.

He lifts my chin so our eyes connect. "I miss you."

"Me too."

He kisses me and it is deep and hungry. The chemistry between us is so potent, so magnetic, that it just takes over. Last time we were together, I was the aggressor, but now it is mutual. Our hands run over each other's bodies, our hips pressing together. Jesse wants me—I hear it in his panting breaths, feel it in the pressure of his erection against my thigh. His lips travel from my mouth, down my neck to my collarbone. Soon, his hands are fumbling with the button of my pants.

"You make me so hot." The ache in his voice, the need, renders me weak with desire. I grab at his belt, undoing it with trembling hands. This is a bad idea. Randy or Vincent or anyone could come out for a smoke at any moment. I'd be humiliated. I could be fired. But Jesse pushes me up against my car and I gasp as he enters me. I wrap my legs around him, bury my face in his neck as he moves inside me. Soon, he climaxes.

"God, Lee." His body collapses against me. "You do something to me."

I suppose it's a compliment, but I'm not sure how to respond. "Thanks?" I mumble.

"I'd better go." He zips his pants and then smirks. "I told my sister I was running out to get milk."

"She'll think you've gone searching for a cow."

He kisses my lips, a quick peck. "They're leaving tomorrow morning. You can come over later, yeah?"

"Sure," I say. "I'll cook for you." But he doesn't respond. He is already hurrying away.

I button my pants with shaking hands. I feel strange, almost light-headed, unmoored. I didn't come—it was too quick, too frenzied—but that's not why I feel empty, dissatisfied. What I have loved about being with Jesse is the tenderness, the closeness, the *normalcy.* Fucking me up against my car in a parking lot, the scents of grease and garbage around us…it felt dirty. It felt demeaning. But this is my issue, not Jesse's. He doesn't know that I am broke, homeless, and running away from my past. He doesn't know that I need tenderness, warmth, and care.

"Hey."

I turn toward the voice. It's Vincent, from the kitchen. Did he see what just happened? My face burns with humiliation.

"Hey."

Farther down the alley, the Audi starts up. Vincent's eyes follow the sound, but they give away nothing. Without a word, he turns and heads back inside.

As the car drives off, I realize I forgot to get Jesse's number.

19

THE SPA HAS GLEAMING WHITE walls lined with pine shelving, each one displaying an array of beautifully packaged products. The bright scent of citrus lingers in the air, melding with the ambient electronic music that plays softly in the background. It has a Scandinavian feel to it, clean and modern and luxurious. As I walk to the reception desk, I feel out of my element. I used to get waxed and buffed and polished. Not often, but I had personal grooming standards then. Such treatments are a luxury I could never even consider now.

A young woman with dewy skin greets me with a smile.

"I'm Lee Gulliver," I say. "I have an appointment?" It comes out a question. Hazel had promised to book my treatments, but I haven't had a chance to confirm with her.

The woman taps at an iPad screen for an interminable length of time. Like she's scheduling a flight. Or surgery.

"It might be under Hazel Laval," I say, growing concerned.

Hazel was meant to join me so that we could spend our day of pampering together, but she'd thought better of it. "Benjamin gets my credit card bills. If the spa charge is double, he'll ask questions." She was forgoing her monthly spa session for me. I felt badly, but Hazel had insisted.

"Here we are." The woman finally looks up. "We've got you booked for a bikini wax, a massage, and a mani-pedi, followed by a cut in the salon."

Relief—and anticipation—flutter inside me. "Thank you."

She leads me to the changeroom, a steamy space full of mirrors, showers, and sweating jugs of cucumber water. Opening a locker, she hands me the key dangling on a wristband. "Your robe and slippers are inside. Your esthetician will meet you through those doors when you're ready."

Hurriedly, I strip out of my clothes, donning the fluffy white robe. It's an equalizer. Without my worn and rumpled clothing, I am just another woman getting pampered on a Thursday. I pour a glass of cucumber water and take it with me into the hall. The esthetician, about my age, wearing a white medical top, greets me.

"I'm Nadia. I'll be taking care of you today." She leads me down a dimly lit corridor. "Let's get your bikini wax out of the way and then get onto the good stuff."

The entire process is heavenly—except for the wax, which is necessary torture. Nadia hands me off to Ryan, the masseuse, and the massage relaxes me, makes me feel oddly weepy. But I gather myself enough to make small talk when Nadia returns to trim, file, and paint my nails a pale sheer pink. Like me, she works six days a week, but she is supporting elderly parents and a ten-year-old daughter who is a promising pianist. Her husband works at a meatpacking plant. I volunteer no information about myself to this hardworking woman. I'm ashamed of my tumble from privilege, of the things I've done, the choices I've made. While my nails dry, I move into the salon.

The stylist, whose fair hair and skin matches the Nordic vibe, stands behind me, taking in my reflection. He lifts a hank of hair from my shoulder. "Let's cut off these dry, brassy bits, give you some light layering at the ends for movement. Maybe a few subtle highlights through the crown?"

"Sure." I shrug. This is Hazel's stylist. I feel safe in his hands.

When he is done, my hair is gorgeous. He has straightened my natural wave and the style and color look a lot like Hazel's. I feel pretty, and I'm thrilled that I have plans to see Jesse tonight. I've missed him. And I want him to see me looking my best.

I dress slowly, savoring the last moments of serenity, taking in my reflection, drinking more infused water. Eventually I return to the lobby and the front desk where another glossy woman stands sentry. I've been here so long there's been a shift change. "Did you enjoy our treatments?" she asks.

"Everything was wonderful," I say, because it was. "Thank you."

"Will you be needing any products today?"

I wish. "No thanks."

"All right, then." Her eyes dart to the iPad screen. "That'll be five hundred and sixty-five dollars, please."

My eyes widen with momentary panic, but I quickly recover. "It was prepaid. By my friend who made the appointment."

The woman leans closer to the screen, her Botoxed features inscrutable. "No. There was no prepayment made."

"My friend is Hazel Laval," I explain. "She comes here all the time."

"Okay..." It's clear this woman doesn't know Hazel. "I don't know who booked these services. I just know that they need to be paid for."

There is an edge to her pleasant tone, and my armpits feel damp. "Of course," I mumble. "It's just... Hazel said she was treating me."

"Perhaps you could put it on your credit card and settle up with her later?"

She doesn't understand. It's not that I can't afford it—I literally *can't* pay. I don't have enough cash, and I no longer have a credit card. "My credit card was stolen," I tell her, my voice wavering. "Let me call Hazel."

I step away from the desk and open my phone. Finding Hazel's number in my contacts, I dial.

"Hello?" Her voice sounds small, far away.

"Hazel, it's Lee." I feel awkward and embarrassed, but I have no choice but to press on. "I'm at the spa. They're saying—"

The line goes dead.

Panic sets in for real now. Hazel hung up on me. Or we were disconnected. I dial again.

"Hi. You've reached Hazel Laval." It's her voice mail. *"Please leave me a message."*

"Hazel, please. Can you come to the spa? Or call them? They're saying I have to pay for these treatments, and..." My voice cracks. "I can't."

I hang up. Maybe Benjamin is there, monitoring her. That means that Hazel is not coming to my rescue. That means I owe this spa over five hundred dollars that I do not have. I dial again, just in case.

"Hi. You've reached Hazel Laval."

Fuck! The woman at the counter is watching me, the weight of her gaze heavy. I feel anxious as I hit redial. I know it is hopeless, but I am stalling for time, trying to figure this out. Hazel's cheerful recorded voice answers again.

Jesse. He is my only hope. He will help me out of this mess. If only I had gotten his number last night, but at least I know where he lives. I return to the counter.

"Hazel's not answering," I tell the receptionist. "But I can go to my boyfriend's place and come back with a credit card. Or cash."

"Can't you call him?" Her tone is suspicious and rightly so. I can't admit that I don't know my boyfriend's phone number.

"He's working," I say, which might be true. "I can leave something. So you know I'll come back."

She breathes out heavily, exasperated with me. "I guess that's fine."

But I have nothing. My flip phone is not worth the cost of a painted fingernail. And then I remember...

"I have a netsuke in my car. It's worth a thousand bucks."

"I have no idea what that is." She's no longer trying to sound pleasant. "I think I should call my manager."

"Let me show it to you," I say quickly. "My car is right there." I indicate the battered Toyota through the window and realize it doesn't instill confidence in my ability to pay. But she lets me go to my vehicle, rummage through my belongings for the netsuke. I am moving slowly, hoping beyond hope that Hazel will rescue me.

When I return, I hold the bone carving out to the receptionist. "I had this appraised," I say. "It's worth a thousand dollars." I read the skepticism on her face as she looks at it, and I glance desperately at the parking lot. And that is when a sleek black Mercedes pulls in. It is her! Hazel. Relief floods through me like a drug.

"She's here." I say it more to myself than to the frustrated girl behind the counter. I watch Hazel get out of the car, her hair dark and shiny and so like mine now. She's wearing a long cardigan and huge sunglasses and has a stylish leather bag over her shoulder. She is the epitome of style, of cool, but there is a grim set to her mouth, and her movements are rushed and frazzled.

"Sorry," she says as she hustles to the counter, already pulling the wallet out of her purse. "Her treatments are on me."

"Thanks." My throat is thick with relief, gratitude, shame. The woman swipes the proffered credit card, her demeanor slowly returning to polite, even obsequious in Hazel's presence. I wait patiently, awkwardly, until the transaction is complete. And then I trail Hazel out the door.

We stop next to my car and Hazel addresses me for the first time. "I'm sorry. I fell asleep. Last night was…a lot."

"Are you okay?" I ask, though she is clearly not.

Without a word, she removes her sunglasses. Under her left eye is a half-moon of dark purple bruising.

"I have to leave," she says softly. "Before he kills me."

20

WE SIT IN MY CAR, parked behind a fast-food restaurant a few blocks from the spa. We've left Hazel's Mercedes there, in the lot. She says we will be safer, less conspicuous in my Toyota. I'm not sure what she means, but I do know that her luxury vehicle is less likely to be towed away than my old Corolla.

Hazel touches her eye gingerly. "It's my own fault. I knew what Benjamin wanted from me, but I just couldn't do it. I couldn't degrade myself again. So, he hit me."

"You have to get away from him." My voice is pleading. "Now."

"I know," she says. "My passport came. I got your ID, too. I meant to bring it, I just…I blanked."

"It's fine," I say, though I wish she had. I'm excited to see my new persona, to try it on and walk around in it. What will my new name be? I've already planned to tell people that Lee is my middle name. It's an easy sell. Lee is probably the most ubiquitous middle name in North America.

"I've got the cash and the ID," Hazel continues. "I'm just afraid I won't make it to the airport."

"Why not?"

"The cameras. Benjamin knows when I come and go. If I don't

return from a yoga class or the gym on time, he'll have his men after me."

"His *men*?"

"Security. He's defended all sorts of criminals. He's had death threats. Attempts on his life. These men look out for him and keep an eye on me. He says it's for my protection." She snorts mirthlessly. "But that's not what it's about."

It's even worse than I thought. Hazel truly is a prisoner. I don't know what to say to her. I don't know how to help her.

I feel her gaze on me. "You look beautiful, by the way."

"Thanks." I smile. "I look a bit like you."

"You do." She touches my hair. "Maybe Karl only knows one haircut?"

"I love it." I shake my head. "And I'm flattered that there's a resemblance."

Hazel bites her lip, her eyes still on me. I see a light in them, a spark even. "My god…," she says softly. "You could pass for me. We're about the same height. And size. And now we have the same hair."

"I guess," I say warily.

She reaches for my hand, grips it. "All I need is a head start, Lee. Time to get to the airport and get checked in. Even an hour. Two would be better."

"What are you suggesting?"

Her words come out in a torrent. "I'll go to the gym and you can meet me there. We can exchange clothes. Then I'll get a cab to the airport, and after about an hour, you can drive my car back to my place."

"Are you serious?"

"It'll work, Lee. You can drive past security, no problem. And then let yourself into the house with my keys, make yourself a cup of tea or a snack. Benjamin will see you on camera and think you're me. He'll barely look at you, I promise. And I'll have time to get to the airport and get on the plane and leave. And then you can go. Dump my car, get back in yours, and disappear."

Anxiety flutters in my belly. Does Hazel really expect me to let myself into her home? To risk an encounter with a violent man? To try to fool her husband and his security team?

"I'll make it worth your while," she adds, reading my reticence. "I've managed to get quite a bit of money together. I'll leave you fifty grand. And the new ID. That's enough to start over, Lee."

I blink at her for a moment, struggling to process her proposal. An hour ago, I was in a state of relaxed bliss. Now I'm being asked to impersonate my friend, to risk my own safety to help her flee an abusive marriage. And she's offering me money. A lot of money. A life-changing sum.

Hazel is watching me, holding her breath. I see the hope on her face, the desperation. And I see that dark crescent of bruising under her pretty eye.

"Okay," I say softly. "I'll do it."

She bursts into tears then, wrapping her arms around my shoulders. Her face is pressed to mine, her relief and gratitude dripping down my cheek, dampening my neck. "You're the best," she murmurs.

My throat is too knotted to reply.

21

"JESUS CHRIST, LEE. IS THAT SAFE?"

I wasn't going to tell Jesse about the plan, but he could tell something was troubling me. We are on his sofa, my feet in his lap, sipping red wine. I'd cooked for him tonight, bustling around his kitchen like it was my own. Coq au vin, an old standby. Peeling the delicate pearl onions, browning the chicken, and flambéing the dish with cognac had felt familiar and comforting. After we'd eaten, Jesse insisted we leave the mess and take our wine to the living room. He'd been recounting a cute story about his nieces, Ella and Olive, playing a torturous rendition of "Hot Cross Buns" on their recorders. I'd smiled along but I couldn't focus. My mind was trapped in Hazel's escape and my role in it. When he questioned me, it had all come pouring out.

"I'll only be in the house for an hour or so," I tell him. "And her husband will think it's her. We're the same height. We have the same hair."

"That's breaking and entering."

"It's not. Because I'll have a key. If her husband comes home—which he won't—I'll just say I was meeting Hazel. He's not going to call the cops on me."

"What if he hurts you?"

"He won't," I say quickly, though my mind flits to that soundproof room where Hazel has been abused and tortured. "I have to help her. He could seriously injure her. Or even kill her."

"You really care about her, don't you?"

My voice is husky. "Yeah, I do."

He sips his wine. "When are you doing this?"

"Tomorrow."

"Christ." He sets the glass on the coffee table. "Why so soon?"

"When I saw her yesterday, she had a black eye." Jesse winces, but I continue. "And she's ready. She has her documents and cash." I swallow. "She's leaving money for me."

"Really?" He cocks an eyebrow. "How much?"

"Fifty grand."

He lets out a low whistle.

"That's not why I'm doing it, though. Hazel has been a really good friend to me." *My only friend,* I do not say. *My only comfort, companionship, and support.*

"I know." He squeezes my socked feet in his lap. "You're a good person."

I am not a good person, but Jesse doesn't know that. He doesn't know that helping Hazel is an attempt to atone for past sins. The money is nice, I'd be a fool to turn it down, but this is about saving my friend. And it is about my karma.

"It's a lot of money," he says. "She must be really rich."

"She is. Her husband's a criminal lawyer."

"Promise me you'll be careful."

"I'll be careful."

He pulls me toward him for a kiss. It's gentle at first, but as always, it escalates quickly. Ever since that night in the alley, Jesse's hunger for me seems almost rabid. Our first night together had been tentative and tender, but as our relationship has developed, our sex life has become more... athletic. I'm fine with it. I enjoy it.

But I can't help but miss the tender, romantic lovemaking of that first time.

"Let's go to bed," he growls in my ear.

We get up off the couch, and I grab the canvas bag near my feet. In it, I have a toothbrush, some makeup, a clean T-shirt, and panties. I never know when Jesse will be waiting for me after a shift, when I'll end up following him home in my car and spending the night. All my belongings are stuffed in the trunk, but I've taken to being prepared with my mini overnight bag.

The sack feels suspiciously light, and I peer inside. My keys. I was sure I'd dropped them in here after I'd parked on the street. I root around in my belongings, but they're not there.

"What's wrong?" Jesse asks, sidling up beside me.

"I thought I put my keys in here."

He buries his face in my neck while his hands explore my body. "We can look for them after."

"I'd rather find them now." I try to sound casual, but my voice is tight. I can't admit that my car is on the street containing all my worldly possessions. If someone found my keys and opened my car, they could clean me out.

Jesse shifts away from me. "Okay. Check your pockets."

The keys are not in my pants. My khaki jacket is hanging near the door. I move to it and stuff my hands into each pocket. Nothing.

"Could you have left them in your car?" Jesse asks.

"I couldn't have," I say, but panic burbles up in my chest. If my car is stolen, my entire life will be gone. "I'd better check."

Jesse stops me with a hand on my arm. "I'll go. I don't want you out there alone at night."

He doesn't know I spend virtually every night out there, alone. That I sleep with a knife in my lap. That I will use it, I will protect myself, if I have to. "Thank you," I murmur.

After he leaves, I hurry to the small den space and push open the window. Jesse's apartment is on the ground floor, facing the alley, but if I lean out slightly, peep through the blinds, I can see my car on the side street. Not stolen at least. Relief washes over me with the cool night breeze. It's not surprising that I would misplace my keys tonight. I am nervous about tomorrow. More than nervous—I'm afraid. I'd put on a brave face for Jesse, but what I am about to do for Hazel terrifies me.

I see Jesse, Adidas slides on his feet, approach my car and peer inside. It is tidier now; I've left a few toiletries and clothes here in the apartment. But will he know that I live there? After a moment, he turns back toward the building. The keys are not inside, evidently. Shit. I pull my head back inside, mind racing. If my keys are gone, I cannot execute the plan. I'll have to call Hazel and tell her to wait while I go to a dealership and get a replacement key. We'll have to put it off over the weekend because Benjamin will be home. What if he hurts her again? Or worse?

I am at the apartment door when Jesse enters. He's smiling. And holding my key ring.

"Thank god," I say, taking it from him. There is a single car key on the chain, a tiny key from the safe in my office at the restaurant, and a plastic letter *L*. "Where did you find them?"

"On the grass by the front walkway." He steps out of his slides. "I guess you dropped them. There's only a car key on here, though. Where are the keys to your apartment?"

My face flushes involuntarily. "I keep them separate. In the trunk."

He gives me a quizzical look. It's a little odd to keep two key rings, but he won't suspect that I am homeless. And after tomorrow, I will add apartment keys to that ring. Hell, I might even get a new car. I move toward him, slide my arms around his waist. Despite my anxiety, his presence comforts me, calms me, and excites me.

"Thank you," I mumble into his neck. "Now, where were we?"

22

IN THE MORNING, WE CLEAN up the mess in the kitchen. Last night's red wine pounds between my eyebrows and my stomach churns at the congealed food left on the plates. I hadn't meant to overindulge, but I'd been trying to settle my nerves, to blunt the edges of my fear. But how much of this awful feeling is a hangover and how much is anxiety? Trepidation? Full-blown panic over what I am about to do?

Jesse has a client at 11:00 a.m., so I kiss him goodbye, drive to a coffee shop, and treat myself to a latte. With my steamy cup, I find a quiet table, only noticing its wobbly leg after I am seated. I don't relocate, though. I sip the expensive coffee, watching people come and go with practiced efficiency. They are going to work, to appointments, running errands. One day soon, my life will be as mundane.

At 11:45, I return the empty cup and get back in my car. As I drive north, I realize that the extra caffeine was a bad idea. My hands are jittery on the steering wheel, my heart thuds at the base of my throat. Jesse's words from last night flicker through my mind as I take the exit. "Promise me you'll be careful."

I will be, of course, but I am just a pawn. Hazel has orchestrated the whole thing and it feels surreal. Like a spy movie. A thriller. A getaway film with a plucky heroine and her stalwart sidekick. As instructed, I park on the street, a half block away from Hazel's gym. I don a ball cap over my straightened hair and grab a small gym bag that is buried in my trunk. I walk casually to the entrance of the gym, past Hazel's black Mercedes in the parking lot. There could be eyes on me right now, I realize. Sweat drips between my breasts.

Signing in, I pay the $7.50 drop-in fee. I use my own name: Lee Gulliver. It's untraceable. And in a few hours, I will be someone entirely new. I decline the bored receptionist's offer of a gym tour but ask her to point me to the changeroom. No one pays me any attention as I hurry toward it.

Hazel is there, seated on a wooden bench, scrolling through her phone. When I enter, her head snaps up. She is pale under her makeup, her eyes red and watery. The bruise above her cheekbone peeks through the concealer, reminding me of why I am here. I give her a weak smile, meant to convey my support, my gameness, but she doesn't return it. She just stands and starts to remove her clothes.

I set my bag on the bench, drop my hat, and shrug out of my jacket. A shower is running in the background, but otherwise we are alone in the cool, tiled space. I slip out of my jeans and hand them to Hazel. She passes me her black leggings and her fitted workout top and I struggle into them. They are clingy and unforgiving. I am slim but soft from diner food and lack of exercise, not toned like Hazel. I pray no one—Benjamin—will notice the difference.

When we are dressed, we catch our reflections in the bank of mirrors running above the row of sinks. Hazel is wearing my jeans, T-shirt, jacket, and cap. Only the shoes are her own, expensive black trainers two sizes too small for me. I am dressed in pricey spandex, an oversized hoodie, worn black running shoes on my feet. The resemblance is astonishing. From a distance, we are virtually interchangeable.

Hazel turns to face me. "Thank you, Lee." I hear the tremor in her voice. "I…I've never had a friend like you."

My response is a small smile. I'm too moved to respond.

"The envelope is in the kitchen." She is referencing the money and my new ID. "It's in the first drawer. Beneath the blender."

"Got it," I manage to croak. She has already taken me through the layout of her house, the rooms that are monitored, the ones that are not. Only the bathrooms and Benjamin's study are free of cameras. The kitchen surveillance equipment is mounted above the cupboards, a birds-eye view. From that aspect, it will be impossible for Benjamin to determine that I am not his wife. I will enter, slip the envelope into my bag, and busy myself at the fridge. After a workout, Hazel often makes a salad. I will do the same. When the microwave clock displays 2:00, I will gather her designer purse and car keys, get into the Mercedes, and leave.

"Drive to Trader Joe's," Hazel had advised me as we faced each other in my car. "I'll drive your car there and catch a cab to the airport."

"What if I'm followed?"

"You will be," she stated calmly. "But Nate, the security guy, will just think you ran out of avocados or something. He won't panic. Until you don't come out."

I will come out, of course. But Hazel won't. At Trader Joe's, I will go straight to the public bathroom. There, I'll ditch Hazel's hoodie, car keys, and her oversize purse. Inside it, she will leave me a jean jacket, a newsboy hat, and a smaller bag. With my new accessories and my hair pulled back, I will buy a juice and then go directly to my Toyota. The key will be on the back left tire. I will drive away, unnoticed.

"That's when Benjamin will get the call that I'm missing," she'd said. "And by then, I'll be in the air. I'll be safe." She smiled. "And you'll be on your way to starting your new life."

The shower turns off in the background. Soon, a woman will join us.

"I should go," Hazel says, her face paling even more. "Maybe you could visit me someday? In Panama?"

"How?"

Her eyes mist over as she realizes…there is no way. This is goodbye. Forever. She grabs me in a tight hug. When she releases me, we trade car keys, and she hands me a large pair of black Burberry sunglasses. I slip her a pair of drugstore aviators.

Hazel looks about to say something else, but a muscular woman wrapped in a towel emerges from the shower. Before the woman can spot us together, Hazel is gone.

23

IT IS NOT UNTIL I am in the black Mercedes, driving toward Hazel's waterfront home, that the magnitude of my mission hits me. If something goes wrong, I could be arrested. Or assaulted. Maybe even shot. I am a homeless person impersonating a wealthy woman. If I am found inside her home, it will not go well for me. And Hazel won't be around to back up my story. Will they think I've done something to her? Kidnapped her? Disappeared her? Panic billows in my chest, but then I remember her bruises, her tears, her tales of Benjamin's twisted sexual games. I know I have to risk it. I have to set her free.

I am setting myself free, too. In just over an hour, Lee Gulliver will be gone. Her debts, the anger and grievances against her, will vanish. I push thoughts of my family from my mind, the finality of this goodbye. They let me go. They chose Teresa. As I wind my way through the tall cedars and firs, I breathe slowly through my nose. I can do this. I must do this. For Hazel and for me.

The driveway to the Laval home is black, freshly paved. With a brief wave of my fingertips, I pass the security guard parked at the end of it. As Hazel instructed, I ease into a parking spot to the right of the garage. I don't see a camera here, but when I move toward the door, I spot it and lower my gaze. The back of the house facing the road is rather unassuming, but I know the home is spectacular. Hazel has pointed to it from the beach. One night, I'd picked my way across the rocks and logs to get a better view. It is an architectural masterpiece of glass and steel, clinging precariously to the cliffside. The lights were on and I could see the high-end furnishings, but no one was inside.

As I approach the entrance now, I look down, pretend to fumble with my keys. Hazel has marked the front door key with a small red dot, and I slip it into the lock. My hands tremble, but it turns easily. I open the door and step inside.

It is tempting to gape at the open-plan splendor of this place. A two-story wall of glass displays the navy-blue Pacific, a backdrop to sleek white furniture, low-slung and modern with dark wood accents. But I am Hazel. She would not gawk in wonder at her own home. I casually drop my car keys into a glass bowl on the teak sideboard and move into the living room.

With a casual stride, I approach the windows. Surely Hazel does this—stares out at the glorious view. I won't attract Benjamin's attention if I take a moment to drink it in. Whitecaps stipple the dark water and rays of sunshine filter through the scrim of gray. In the distance, the sky grows menacing and angry. It will rain later. I turn away to admire the room that Hazel decorated: the low lacquered coffee table strategically covered in books on architecture and archaeology; a sterling silver bust of a woman—something ominous in her limbless form—perched on a marble plinth. For a moment, I imagine I really am Hazel, the tragic heroine caught between beauty and ugliness. Between privilege and abuse. A woman so desperate that she would walk away from all this.

On a side table, a black and white photo in a silver frame catches my attention: Hazel and Benjamin at their wedding. It is candid but perfect. The groom stands behind his bride, arms wrapped around her slim waist. He wears a dark suit; she is in a simple, strapless sheath. Hazel is laughing, her head thrown back, Benjamin's face nestled in the crook of her neck. Their happiness radiates from the frame. Was it real then? When did it all go wrong? Before I stare too long, I move to the kitchen.

I am greeted by more white: sleek handle-less cupboards, quartz countertops, built-in Thermador appliances. I open the first drawer below the restaurant-quality blender that would have cost a couple grand. The envelope is there, nestled on top of the cutlery. I snatch it up, feel the heft of it, at least two inches thick, then slip it into Hazel's purse. Setting the bag on the counter, I move to the fridge.

Inside, I find a jumble of food, leftovers, bottles of wine and condiments. It's a messy normalcy I hadn't expected in this pristine palace. Pulling out the salad ingredients, I set them on the center island. With my back to the camera mounted inconspicuously in an upper corner, I begin to chop a tomato. Is Benjamin watching me right now? Is he noticing the slight tremble in my hands, the way my ass doesn't fill out these pants the way Hazel's does? Will he send in security? But he is a busy man. Surely he doesn't have time to watch his wife make a salad. *I am safe,* I tell myself. I keep my eyes on the produce, on the knife slicing methodically through each item.

When I have filled a salad bowl with vegetables, the clock on the microwave reads 1:28. Hazel had begged me for a two-hour head start. I'd loitered in the gym changeroom for forty-five minutes. The drive to her home had taken twelve. I have been inside this mansion for almost half an hour. In roughly twenty minutes, I can leave. Sitting down and eating is out of the question, so I grab a dishcloth and wipe the counter, scrubbing at an imaginary spot. When I am done, I check the clock again: 1:30.

The bathroom. There are no surveillance cameras in the main floor powder room. According to the detailed floor plan Hazel shared with me, it's located between the kitchen and Benjamin's study. I stroll toward the privacy of the toilet.

It's spacious for a powder room, with a pedestal sink, a toilet, and a small velvet chaise longue that is completely decorative. Obviously, no one lounges in a bathroom, but I sit on it, run my hands over the deep garnet fabric, stimulated by the tactile surface. When I have my own apartment, I will buy a velvet sofa. With the money Hazel has given me, I will fill my home with pretty things. Sumptuous fabrics. Feminine designs.

At the sink, I lean my hands on the porcelain and take in my reflection. Other than the hair, I don't look much like Hazel. My coloring is fairer, my bone structure less defined. If my face is exposed to the camera for more than a second, Benjamin will know I'm not his wife. My chest constricts, making it hard to breathe. This is too risky. I want to leave. But Hazel needs a few more minutes.

With a gentle click, I open the door. What time is it now? I could go back into the monitored kitchen and check the clock, but I am right next to Benjamin's study. Hazel had mentioned the lack of cameras in his sanctuary. "Benjamin likes his privacy," she'd said, though he afforded her none. And I am curious to know more about the man Hazel is fleeing. What books does a sadist like to read? Does he collect anything other than netsukes? Will his home office provide any clue to his cruelty? His perversions?

On silent feet, I slip down the hall toward the open door. I have just reached the entryway when I hear it: a *crack*. It could be a bird dropping a shell; a deer breaking a stick underfoot; the wind knocking a cone from a tree. There could be any number of benign sources, but the sound sends a jolt of electricity through me. Someone is coming. Panic grips my throat. I have to get out of here. Hazel has had enough time to get away. But as I turn to go, something catches my eye.

A hand.

The sound I make is something between a gasp and a scream. I stumble backward, away from the motionless appendage, terrified that it will animate. That Benjamin Laval will come lunging out of his study toward me. But no one comes. The hand, resting on the arm of the office chair, doesn't move.

I should turn and run, but I am gripped to the spot. There is a man sitting quietly in that chair. It has to be Hazel's husband. But why is he home? And why hasn't he heard me moving through his house? There's probably a simple explanation. Perhaps Benjamin had papers to retrieve from his office, and while there he'd decided to take a nap. He is clearly a sound sleeper. So still. So silent. Or is something else wrong?

Tentatively, I move around him for a better look. My eyes travel from the hand, up the arm, to the torso, and what I see clutches at my throat. Benjamin wears a gray button-down shirt but the front is red, soaked with blood. I can see the stab marks in his chest, puncturing the fabric—four of them at least. His face is turned away, the dark hair matted and bloodied and I feel dizzy, faint. This man is not asleep. He's dead. Murdered. I don't realize I am standing in a small pool of blood until I slip, going down on one knee, one hand.

Bile rises in my throat as I clamor to my feet, the metallic scent sharp in my nostrils. I wipe the blood on my pants, Hazel's pants, but there is so much of it. Benjamin has been killed angrily. Violently. And then...I notice the tattoo peeking out of the rolled cuff of his sleeve. It appears to be a hand-drawn skull. With my foot, I turn the chair around and the face—slack, gruesome—is revealed. I scream, a guttural shriek of terror and pain.

The man in the chair is Jesse.

Part Two

HAZEL

24

I WAS WARNED ABOUT BENJAMIN Laval before I even met him. Marielle and I were sitting at the mahogany bar in the Balmoral. It was a swanky lounge across from the law courts, a known hangout for wealthy attorneys. We were there to meet rich men, which sounds shallow and mercenary, and I guess it was. But if I was a gold digger, I paid for it dearly.

He was staring at me over the rim of his bourbon, his eyes slate gray and sexy. I sipped my flute of bubbles and met his gaze. Marielle's voice was close to my ear. "Not him."

I set the flute down. "Why not?"

"That's Benjamin Laval," Marielle said. "He's a big-shot criminal lawyer. My friend Ashley hooked up with him last year. He's a total freak in the bedroom."

I'll admit I was titillated. This distinguished attorney, in his expensive suit, exuding class from every pore, had a secret kinky side. "I'm game," I said with another glance in his direction.

"No, you're not," Marielle said. "He's a psycho. Into the rough stuff."

This information should have dissuaded me, but it didn't. I wasn't into kink, per se, but I was sexually adventurous, curious. I envisioned harmless *Fifty Shades of Grey* stuff: bondage, blindfolds, playful spanking. And when I went home with him that night, that's exactly how it was. Marielle's friend was just too vanilla for a man like Benjamin Laval. I was more fun, more exciting.

He called me a week later and took me to dinner. "What do you do?" he asked after he'd ordered for us: Wagyu steaks, though I didn't normally eat red meat. I was twenty-six then, a sometime model, most-time office temp. "I'm a model."

His eyes roved over me appraisingly. "You're too beautiful to be anything else."

I chose to take it as a compliment, though it wasn't one. Beauty and brains are not mutually exclusive. But I'd struggled with an undiagnosed learning disorder most of my life. By the time I realized I wasn't stupid, it was too late. I'd chosen my looks as my defining characteristic, my ticket. I would ride the pretty train as far as it would take me.

"I'd like to open my own bakery one day," I told him, my cheeks flushing with the admission. "Baking is really therapeutic for me. And I'd design the space, too. Wainscoting. Floral wallpaper. Traditional meets modern."

"Sounds adorable." I didn't pick up the dismissiveness in his tone then. I should have.

On Benjamin's arm, I was exposed to a life I'd only dreamt of as a girl. My parents had divorced when I was young. My mother and I moved into a cramped apartment in the University District, while my dad moved south for work and eventually built a new family. My mom had a decent job as a dental hygienist. After hours, she sold whimsical sex toys at boozy parties to make a little extra. It should have been enough—*just*—but my mom had a taste for the finer things, treated shopping as therapy. I was no better, spending far more than I earned at my fast-food job in a crusade to keep up with the cool girls. And so we lived beyond our means, in an atmosphere of unrelenting financial anxiety.

And then, when my mom was fifty-four, she started to forget things. We laughed it off at first: the keys in the fridge, her phone left at the coffee shop, the hour spent trying to remember where she'd parked her car... She was far too young for it to be anything serious. But she became moody and withdrawn. At work, she was obstreperous and eventually got fired. Finally, when she found her life savings stashed in a shoe box in her closet and had no memory of withdrawing it from the bank, she went to her doctor. She was diagnosed with early onset Alzheimer's.

I cared for her for as long as I could, but we couldn't afford the medications meant to slow the disease, so it progressed rapidly. In the night, Mom would get up and try to cook, setting off the smoke alarm. She'd wander away from the home care nurse and forget her way back. Sometimes she was angry at me or frightened of me. When she threw a lamp at me in terror, I knew I was in over my head. My mother needed round-the-clock care.

Unfortunately, Washington State has some of the most expensive memory care in the country. Because Mom had left her job prior to her diagnosis, there was no insurance. I was forced to put her in a state home. It was all I could afford and even then, just barely. I did temp work, waitressing, modeling when I could get it. Even with my shared accommodation, I was broke.

Benjamin never worried about money. He took me to the finest restaurants, introduced me to foie gras, real champagne, and taught me how to eat oysters. We spent weekends in Sonoma and Carmel and Big Sur. There were two glorious weeks in a bungalow over the turquoise waters of Bora Bora. We stayed in jaw-dropping luxury at Le Negresco, on the Promenade des Anglais in Nice. I took to it like I was born to it.

The sex was fun then. Benjamin took his time with me, escalating slowly, methodically. I didn't realize I was being groomed because he could be tender, too. And he was so generous. His sexual proclivities seemed a small price to pay for the life he offered me. It was all manageable... until he proposed.

"I want you to look at this contract," he said about a week before our wedding.

I assumed a prenup. He was a successful lawyer with a glass house, two luxury vehicles, and a boat. I brought nothing to the union. I didn't blame him for wanting to protect his assets. And we were so in love then. I couldn't imagine a future where he wouldn't look after me.

"I want to move our relationship forward. From D/s to M/s," Benjamin explained.

I knew the acronyms by then. We were in a dominant-submissive relationship: He wanted us to become Master and slave. My stomach twisted sharply, and I felt myself pale. As a submissive, I was allowed to set limits and boundaries. Our dynamic played out in scenes, usually confined to the bedroom. As a slave, I would submit my will to him 24/7. Permanently. I'd obey or I'd forfeit the relationship.

"What's wrong with how things are?" I asked, my voice tremulous.

His response was succinct. "I need more, Hazel. Total control. *Total Power Exchange.*"

"And if I don't want to?"

"Then we won't be getting married."

We had two hundred guests joining us for an extravagant cliff-side ceremony. Thousands of dollars had already been spent. That meant nothing to Benjamin. He would get what he wanted from me, or he would cut me loose. My face burned at the thought of explaining the breakup to my family and friends. And I felt sick when I considered leaving this luxurious life, returning to the damp basement apartment I'd shared with two roommates, stressing and struggling to make ends meet. And I couldn't do it to my mother.

Benjamin had relocated her to a private facility that specialized in her condition. My mother was housed in a bright, spacious home, surrounded by serene, landscaped gardens. They offered art, music, and canine therapy. There was a vegetable garden, a high-end chef, a small movie theater, and a crafts room. My mother no longer knew who I was, but she was happy. She was comfortable. It was all I had wanted.

So, I signed Benjamin's TPE contract. I made a few stipulations to protect myself, but I agreed to give him complete control. The prenup he later presented was even simpler because I had only one request. My husband was to look after my mother for the rest of her life.

"As long as we're married," Benjamin negotiated, "your mom will be taken care of."

The words didn't set off any red flags for me. Not then, anyway.

A few days later, when we stood up before that crowd of well-wishers, I promised to love, honor, and obey him.

25

CONSENSUAL NONCONSENT IS NOT UNCOMMON in sexual relationships: pretending to resist and protest while prior consent has been given. Plenty of normal, loving couples play this way. For the first few years, it was all a game. But I wasn't a good enough actress to please Benjamin. Eventually, my pain and humiliation had to be real. He had to break me. The physical abuse was sporadic, but the mental and emotional torture were constant. I was criticized and disparaged. If I displeased him, I was sent to *the room.* It would be hyperbole to call it a dungeon, but it was in the basement. There was no furniture, only a small rug and a rough woolen blanket.

A true submissive would have reveled in the punishment, but it did not arouse me or provide me any kind of satisfaction. I used the time alone to dwell on my isolation, my alienation, my misery. And to hate myself. Since I was a girl in the suburbs, struggling at school, I had dreamed of something more. But not this. Never this. I'd sold my freedom for a life of privilege and luxury. And I had agreed to an arrangement that was destroying me.

Outside of the bedroom, our marriage resembled a fifties-style relationship. My role as Benjamin's wife was to meet his needs.

I did his laundry, ironed his shirts, and kept the house clean (with the help of a weekly housekeeper). He told me what he wanted to eat for dinner, and I dutifully shopped for ingredients and prepared the meal. In the evenings, I dressed to greet him—sometimes in a pretty frock, sometimes in a schoolgirl costume, other times naked except for a black leather hood. Whatever Benjamin dictated I wore.

When we went out, we had "in the world" protocols. I had to walk slightly ahead of him, to his right, never straying farther than three feet from his side. If I needed to use the restroom, I asked his permission. If he said no, I suffered. He ordered for me at restaurants—halibut and pinot grigio, a cheeseburger and a Coke, or a green salad and a glass of water. I always ate it. I always thanked him.

"You'll call me Chief," Benjamin said. "It's innocuous enough to use in public, but still shows your respect."

"Okay."

"Okay, what?"

"Okay, *Chief.*"

Around others, he called me *Missy.* It was outdated, a little condescending but it didn't raise any eyebrows. Except once. We were at a cocktail party hosted by a female colleague of Benjamin's, a shark of an attorney called Miranda.

"That's a little patriarchal, isn't it?" she'd commented.

"A little." He'd smiled at her. "But Missy likes it."

No one ever guessed that it stood for *submissive.*

Old friendships faded away from lack of attention. Marielle tried to hang on, but we were in different places. She was still single, still going out, still having fun. Eventually, she gave up on me. New friends were not allowed. Acquaintances were fine, they were necessary, but they had to be approved by Benjamin. The women I was allowed to associate with were the spouses or girlfriends of his colleagues. He preferred to be present when I was with them, but he allowed lunches or shopping trips. He needed all the details: who, where, and for how long. Sometimes he would call me away in the middle of a visit, just to test my obedience. I became adept at making excuses on the fly.

When the pandemic hit, the governor issued stay-at-home orders. For two months, my husband worked from his home office while I tried to stay out of his way. Domestic abuse rose worldwide during lockdown and my household was no exception. Benjamin took his fear, his sense of powerlessness, and his frustrations out on me. And with no one to see the bruises, the violence escalated. I took it—I had no choice—but my resignation seemed to increase his disdain. By the time we emerged back into the world, my husband had grown to hate me.

The use of surveillance in our marriage escalated then. Benjamin had a private security team financed by his firm. He'd represented dangerous people, and not always successfully. Threats on his life were common, on my life sporadic. "Nate will keep you safe." Benjamin explained the security guard posted at the end of the driveway. "But he's watching you. And he'll report back to me if you don't do as you're told."

That's when I began to run. Our street abutted a heavily wooded state park. The security guard could not follow me in a vehicle, and I was far too fast for him on foot. To my relief, Nate, a massive man with a shiny bald head and hint of warmth in his brown eyes, was a lackadaisical minder. Perhaps he knew that I needed this small taste of freedom. That I would eventually return because I had no other options. When I was running along the forest trails, I was unencumbered and uninhibited. For a while the endorphins kept the depression at bay. But after a while, I succumbed.

"You're going to see a psychiatrist," my husband announced one morning. "He's a friend of mine."

I dutifully agreed, but it was a sham, of course. I couldn't tell Dr. Veillard the truth about my marriage. He would have reported it directly to Benjamin. Instead, the shrink asked me about my mom, my self-isolation, my lack of motivation. He'd recommended a hobby. Prescribed sleeping pills and Xanax. When Benjamin inquired about our sessions, I pasted on a smile.

"I'm feeling a lot better."

But at night, when I lay awake next to my Master, the pain descended, dark and heavy. The abuse was escalating, slowly but surely, and one day he would go too far. I would not survive the relationship for long, but leaving him, filing for divorce was impossible. Benjamin would kill me; he'd told me as much. And my mother would be as good as dead. He'd stop paying for her deluxe care facility and she'd end up withering away in a state home or even on the street. My mom's comfort and care were more important to me than my own life.

And so, I stayed. I could see no way to get away from him.

26

Benjamin controlled my grooming habits: French manicure, full wax, spray tan in the winter months. He chose my shoulder-length hairstyle and my subtle makeup palette. I had some freedom with my wardrobe; I'd always had a flair for fashion. If I stayed within allotted parameters, I could usually wear what I wanted. In public, at least.

My running addiction made me lean and sinewy, and Benjamin didn't like it. He insisted I cut my daily jogs from five miles to three and join a gym to build muscle. I consulted with a nutritionist to try to create the body type my husband desired: curvaceous, with hips and boobs, but it was impossible with my build. And I was addicted to exercise. It was my only outlet, my body the only thing I could control. Almost.

When we'd been married just six months, he made the announcement. "I've made you an appointment for breast implants."

I'd laughed, completely incredulous, but Benjamin wasn't joking. After a brief consult with a plastic surgeon friend of his, a date was set. I wept as I was rolled into surgery, disturbed and afraid. It felt like Benjamin was invading my body, getting under my skin. The implants he'd selected were slightly too large for my frame; not overly conspicuous, but heavy and cumbersome. They would cause me back problems one day. I felt like his Barbie doll, a plastic version of myself designed to please him. I lived in fear that he'd insist on a Brazilian butt lift next. I spent most of my time at the gym doing squats.

That's what I was doing when I met him. He was just a voice behind me, critiquing my form. "Keep those knees out," he said.

I dropped the twenty-pound dumbbell I was holding at my chest and turned to face him. "Who are you?"

"Jesse. I'm a trainer here."

"I don't need a trainer," I snapped.

"Of course not." Our eyes locked and his were golden. Like a lion's. "But I don't want you to get hurt."

There was no way he could have known how much I got hurt—physically, mentally, and emotionally—every day. Or that his choice of words would break down my walls, make me instantly receptive to him. I allowed him to correct my posture. His touch was professional, gentle, and tentative. But it lit me up.

At my next workout, he asked me out for coffee. "I'm married," I said.

"It's just coffee." His smile was bemused. "We can talk about your training."

"I can't."

But the chemistry between us was impossible to ignore, and soon I opened up to him. I told him that I was being watched. That my husband had a security guard tailing me—supposedly, for my own protection. Jesse came up with a solution. His Audi was parked behind the building in the staff lot. We could slip out the back door and drive off together. As long as my Mercedes remained parked in front of the gym, I was safe.

We went to his apartment. It was masculine, bare-bones, like he hadn't lived there very long. It was on the ground floor, facing the alley, the windows barred. It was a dump, frankly, but to me it was a sanctuary. That's where I explained the Master/slave dynamic in my marriage. I felt weak and ashamed, but the words poured out of me. Jesse listened, his face transformed by compassion and pity. When he touched my cheek, it felt so comforting. And when he kissed me, it felt loving and right.

Things escalated quickly. I was starved for tenderness, affection, and good old-fashioned sex. Three to five days a week, I'd arrive at the gym, lift a few weights, and then we'd slip out the back door and into his Audi. I would slouch low in the seat as we raced to his apartment, my hair covering my face, my lips pressed into a smile of anticipation. I didn't care that our relationship was a cliché.

As soon as we closed the apartment door behind us, we were tearing at each other's clothes. Sometimes we fucked right there on the parquet floor of the entryway. Maybe I should have felt cheapened by the urgent, almost animal sex. But to me it felt pure and beautiful.

"I think I love you," I told him after one particularly ardent session of lovemaking. It was far too soon, and my stomach twisted with fear. My words would scare him away. He'd think I was needy, pathetic, crazy. But Jesse pulled me close to him.

"I love you, too."

Relief flooded through me. "I wish we could be together. I wish I didn't have to go back."

"Then stay."

"I can't." I lifted my head, looked up at him. "He'd find me. Find us."

"So? What would he do?"

"He'd kill me. And you. He'd throw my mom out in the street. He's dangerous."

Jesse must have read the gravity and fear in my tone because he didn't press. He didn't ask me how Benjamin would destroy us. He took my word for it.

"You'd have to disappear," he said softly.

"How?" I scoffed. But he didn't answer. Not then.

About a month after our affair began, I broke down. Benjamin had been particularly cruel that morning, and I was desperate, despondent, terrified to go home. We were lying in Jesse's double bed, my head on his strong chest, my tears slicking his skin. "I don't know how much more I can take."

"I've been thinking about it," he said, his voice steady. "Maybe there's a way you can leave him."

My response was instant. "I told you, he'd kill me."

"Not if you're already dead."

The suggestion shocked me, but not as much as it should have. A kernel of an idea had already been planted. "I can't leave my mom," I said.

"But Benjamin doesn't even let you see her."

My husband had banned my visits, saying they were a waste of time. And it irritated him that I often returned from them emotional and morose. She was comfortable and cared for, he said. My presence was pointless. My mom didn't know who I was anymore. But I still felt that somewhere, deep in her soul, she knew that I was there. That I was her daughter. That I loved her.

"And he has to take care of her. Even if you're dead, right?"

I had made sure of it. "Yes. As long as we're still married when I die."

"Wouldn't your mom want you to be safe? And happy?" Jesse pressed.

My voice was soft, but curious. "How?"

"An accidental drowning." He propped himself up on an elbow. "Bodies disappear all the time off the coast up here. There are rips. Deadhead logs that would smash a person to pieces. Sharks."

"Suicide," I countered. "I want Benjamin to think he drove me to it. I want him to be shamed."

"Sure." Jesse's golden eyes were unreadable. "That'll work."

My throat closed with emotion: gratitude, hope, love. "Can we really do this?"

"I want to be with you more than anything, Hazel." He reached out, cupped my chin with his strong fingers. "I'll make it happen."

27

WE PICKED A DATE: A Tuesday in early April. I would take off on my early morning run as usual. Once I was past the security sentry, I would head down to a secluded beach and enter the chilly water. Jesse's friend had a boat he could borrow. He'd scoop me up and give me dry clothes, a blanket, and hot tea. We'd cruise north, dock in Bellingham, and then head to the airport. Jesse had bought us plane tickets to Panama City with a stop in Dallas. Benjamin would never find me there.

"I'll get you a fake passport," Jesse offered.

"How?"

"Dark web." He sounded unfazed, like he was comfortable in that murky underworld. "I just need your headshot."

He was taking care of everything. Taking care of *me.* Not since I was a little girl had I felt that kind of security. There was only one thing he asked me for.

"Can you get money?" Jesse asked. "I have some, but a little extra would help."

Naturally Benjamin controlled my bank accounts and credit cards. But there were valuable items in the house that could be sold or pawned. And a safe in his study that I could probably get into if I put my mind to it. But all I wanted was to be with Jesse and to be free. Maybe I was unrealistic, overly romantic, but I didn't want Benjamin's money tainting our fresh start. And my greed had impacted my choices for too long. So, I told him no.

"It's too risky. I don't want to do anything to tip Benjamin off."

Jesse's face darkened, but only for a second.

"I'll get a job in Panama," I promised. "And when I've saved a bit of cash, I'll open my own bakery. It's always been my dream."

"Sure," he said. "We'll be fine."

I kissed him. "We'll be amazing."

When I was alone in my bathroom (one of the only rooms in the house without a camera), I wrote a suicide note.

> Benjamin,
>
> To say you have made my life hell for the past six years would be an understatement. I can see no way out and no way forward. Your cruelty and abuse have driven me to this. I can't live another day as your slave.
>
> Goodbye.
> Hazel

My husband would be enraged. It was the ultimate betrayal. The ultimate humiliation. And the ultimate loss of control.

The weather was mild that morning, but as I slipped out of bed and into my running gear, I was shivering. Benjamin slept deeply, soundly, rising at seven. He wouldn't hear me leave, and if he did, he wouldn't suspect anything. I was just going for my morning jog, as usual. But I couldn't stop trembling as I placed the note in the drawer of the teak credenza. I couldn't have him find it until I was long gone.

I had jogged past the battered Toyota the last couple of mornings, assuming it was abandoned, stolen maybe. I didn't see anyone in it, didn't notice the reclined seat. Naturally, I wasn't paying it much attention that morning. My head was reeling with nerves and excitement. With the promise of freedom. A life with the man I loved.

On the beach, I was suddenly overcome with emotion. A jagged sob ripped through me and I realized I was crying. I was leaving my mom behind, forever. Even though my visits were rare, even though she no longer recognized me, she was still my mom. And the person I loved was still in there, somewhere, trapped by the horrible disease. But I had to say goodbye to her. Forever.

"I'm sorry," I said out loud. And then I walked into the water.

It was even colder than I'd expected, but I wouldn't be in it for long. I just had to walk out to the end of the sandbar and swim a few yards so that Jesse could collect me. I'd suggested leaving my jacket on the beach, tossing a shoe into the ocean before he picked me up in his car and drove me to the marina. But that was too risky, Jesse said. People could see us. And he couldn't beach the boat here because of the sandbar. So, I would go, fully clothed, into the Pacific. A tragic figure. This had to look real.

My legs were numb, and my teeth were chattering, but I dove into the water, kicking and clawing my way forward. Hypothermia could set in quickly, but Jesse would be there with blankets and tea. He would rescue me, warm me, whisk me away.

I felt weak, my strokes barely moving me against the current. I was a decent swimmer, but the cold water and the weight of my clothes were dragging me down, deeper, my head slipping under. Where was the boat? Why wasn't Jesse coming? Blind panic gripped me for several seconds, followed by an overwhelming weariness. It would be so easy to stop fighting, to just let go. To allow myself to sleep, to finally rest.

And then a hand dragged me to the surface.

28

"WHERE WERE YOU?" I ASKED, my voice choked with emotion.

"I was five minutes late," Jesse said, drying my tears with his thumbs. "Maybe ten. My friend didn't get to the marina on time."

"I could have drowned."

"You didn't, thank god." He pulled me close, kissed the top of my head. "But this woman has fucked up everything."

We were in his apartment, where we'd plotted our escape. I rested my head against his chest, curled my feet beneath me on the charcoal sofa. "We can try again."

Jesse didn't respond for a moment. "Who was she?" he said. "What does she know?"

"She's nobody. She's homeless, living in her car." But my voice sounded reedy. Was Benjamin on to me? Had he planted that woman near the beach to thwart my plan? I'd jogged home after, torn up the suicide note, and flushed it down the toilet. Then I'd thrown my wet clothes in the washer and jumped in the shower. When I emerged, I made my husband breakfast, as usual. And then I met Jesse at the gym as if nothing had happened. But I'd learned not to underestimate my husband.

"I don't want to try again until we know who that bitch is." Jesse's tone was angry, and rightfully so. We'd be in Bellingham by now, headed for the airport, if not for that woman. Still, I winced inwardly at the misogynistic term.

"So, what did you tell her?" Jesse continued. "What did you talk about?"

I extracted myself from his embrace. "Nothing." My cheeks were hot, and I hoped he didn't notice. "I basically told her she should have minded her own business." My memory of the encounter was hazy, but I'd felt comfortable with the woman who'd saved my life. Comfortable enough to drink her whisky, to sit with her under her sleeping bag. To open up to her about my abusive marriage. Just a little, though. I hadn't told her too much.

"Go see her tomorrow," Jesse said. "Find out what you can."

"Okay."

He looked at his watch. "We need to get back to the gym soon." His hands reached for my hips, pulled me toward him.

I didn't want to have sex; I still felt shaky and fragile and frightened. But I knew my boyfriend had a high sex drive, and I'd been programmed to please men. So, I let him slide my tights off, allowed him to lay me back on the sofa and enter me. His physical proximity calmed me, somewhat, and I buried my face in his neck. Because I needed to be close to him, and I needed him to want me. My whole future depended on him.

A gift seemed the most obvious reason for me to return to the scene of my near-drowning. I would thank the woman for saving my life, tell her I'd reconsidered ending it. And then I would find out why she was really sleeping in the park at the end of my street. Our home was filled with expensive objets d'art, but I had to choose something that wouldn't be missed. The living room pieces were curated and expensive, so they were out of the question. But Benjamin's study was chock-full of books and trinkets. At the back of a lower shelf, dusty from being ignored by our weekly cleaner, was his collection of netsukes. I scanned the ancient Japanese figurines and found the appropriate one: a coiled snake. Intricate scales had been carved into the smooth bone, two sharp, precise fangs. If the woman's presence in the park was benign, she could sell this for five hundred bucks, maybe more. If she was working for my husband, the gift was symbolic. I was onto her, and I would strike.

That morning, I tiptoed into the kitchen and packed a simple breakfast for her: a roll I'd baked filled with peanut butter and honey, a crisp red apple. I placed them in my backpack next to the netsuke; then I slipped out the door and jogged toward the park.

She was asleep when I arrived, her seat reclined, her brow troubled even in slumber. I observed her for a moment, taking in the bottle of whisky in the console and the large knife across her lap. It was clear, beyond a doubt, that her presence here was entirely innocent. This woman was vulnerable and afraid. She wasn't working for my husband. She wasn't here to spy on me. I almost turned and left, continued my jog, but something—Empathy? Pity?—propelled me forward. I tapped on the window, watched her startle awake, groping for her knife. My heart twisted in my chest.

We sat on that soft gray log and watched the sunrise. She ate the bun I'd brought her like it was eggs Benedict with smoked salmon and caviar, savoring each bite. I tried to engage her in conversation, but she was circumspect. To fill the void, I told her even more about my marriage to Benjamin. My secrets had piled up, festering inside me. And this woman wouldn't judge me. She had fallen farther than I had.

When I saw Jesse, I relayed what I'd learned. "Her name is Lee. She went broke during the pandemic. She's homeless and she's scared. She drinks herself to sleep each night with a knife in her lap."

It wasn't much, admittedly, but it was enough. "We don't have to worry about her," I assured him. "We can reschedule our escape."

"Okay," he said, but I heard the doubt in his voice. "I'll see when I can get the boat."

29

THAT SHOULD HAVE BEEN THE last I saw of Lee, but it wasn't. She was stuck in my mind like a song, and nothing I did could dislodge her. I felt sorry for her, of course, but there was something more. A sort of kinship. Because none of my friendships were real, all forced upon me by my husband. I played a part with everyone in my life. Even Jesse. But with Lee, I could be open. I could just be Hazel.

I jogged to her car with a buttery croissant in my backpack and found her shivering and sick. Really sick. She probably needed a doctor, but she obviously didn't have health insurance. And when she said that she had to go to work, that she couldn't afford to take a sick day, my chest hurt. This was life for so many people. Despite my toxic marriage, I was privileged.

I promised to return with medicine and tea because her illness was my fault. After my frigid dip in the ocean, I'd gone home to a hot shower and dry clothes. Lee had sat chilled in her car, her immunity lowered, and she had picked up a virus somewhere. With an exhilarating sense of purpose, I sprinted back home, ensuring I returned suitably sweaty and out of breath. When Benjamin emerged fresh from the shower, I greeted him brightly.

"Morning, Chief."

"Good morning." He was in a crisp white shirt and light gray pants, his suit jacket slung over his arm. "I want eggs. You'll have two slices of toast."

"Yes, Chief."

In the kitchen, I prepared his scrambled eggs the French way—stirring constantly with a pat of butter. Benjamin was on his laptop at the breakfast bar, but we didn't chat. The silence had less to do with our M/s agreement, and more to do with his disinterest in me. I couldn't blame him. My universe had dwindled over our years together and I had little, if anything, of interest to contribute.

When I set the plate in front of him, he spoke. "I'm worried about you."

"Me?" My voice was tight. "Why?"

"I think you have an exercise addiction."

"I don't," I said breezily. "I just like to stay in shape for you."

His gray eyes appraised me over a forkful of eggs. "You've gotten too thin again. You know I don't like it."

"I'm going to build up my lower body," I said. "Get more muscle on my thighs and booty."

"You can go to the gym for one hour from now on. Not two."

I couldn't question his dictate; that was our agreement. I followed his rules or there were repercussions. But one hour was not long enough for me to sneak out the back and go to Jesse's apartment. We would barely arrive when we'd have to turn around. Again, I worried that Benjamin knew about the affair, but passive-aggressive punishment was not his style. If he knew I was cheating on him, I would feel it.

"David Vega's wife is planning a breast cancer gala. I told him you'd help out."

"Of course," I said, though I already had a charity case. "May I go to the drugstore today? I need some vitamins. And a few toiletries."

"You may." He swallowed the last forkful of eggs. "You need to find a way to contribute to society, Hazel. It's embarrassing to have a wife who does nothing but jog and lift weights."

My face felt hot with humiliation, though I should have been used to it by now.

"What about your little bakery idea?"

I'd told him my dream in the early stages of our relationship, when I thought he was kind and nurturing. It resurfaced on occasion—as a way to demean me and my puny goals.

"You're obviously not an entrepreneur." He slid his empty plate toward me. "But you could design a menu, decorate the place. It would give you some profile at least. And then I'll find someone to run it."

"Thank you, Chief."

"Do some sketches. Look into some locations. And call Vanessa Vega," he said, standing. "She's expecting to hear from you."

Later, I drove to Walgreens, then to the deli for soup and tea and returned to Hazel. She was weak but I dosed her with medicine and fed her. Something about her miserable state brought out a maternal side I hadn't known existed. I'd purchased a few cosmetics for her—when you look good, you feel good—and I applied them gently. She relaxed under my touch. I knew she lived in a constant state of fear and anxiety. Even more than I did. When I finished the makeover, Lee didn't look sick anymore. She looked beautiful.

My chest warm from my good deed, I returned home. I tried a few half-hearted sketches for the bakery, but there was no point. It had been my dream, but not the way Benjamin was controlling it. And it would never happen; my escape was imminent. With Benjamin cracking down on my gym time, Jesse and I needed to leave. Soon.

Finally, I gave up and seasoned the steaks that my husband had demanded for supper. I made a salad with fresh tomatoes and burrata and dressed in the figure-hugging jumpsuit he'd instructed me to wear. At 7:00, my husband returned from the office. While he went to change, I poured him a glass of cabernet sauvignon that I'd been decanting for an hour. At 7:15, I set his steak and salad before him. He cut into the rib eye—revealing the perfect medium-rare pink.

"How was your day?" I asked, my eyes on the plump tomato on my fork.

"It was fine." He chewed the steak. "Did you call Vanessa Vega?"

The fork slipped in my hand, but I caught it before it clattered on the edge of the plate. I'd completely forgotten about the breast cancer gala. "I…I didn't."

"Why not?"

"I thought I was supposed to call her tomorrow."

"I told you to call her today."

"It was a busy day. I guess it slipped my mind."

He set his utensils down gently, without noise, and finished chewing before he spoke. My heartbeat filled the silence. I knew what was coming.

"You had a *busy* day?" he asked rhetorically. "What did you do?"

"I went to the drugstore. A-and I did some sketches. For the bakery."

His anger was there, bubbling under the façade of calm. He'd made a simple demand and I had disregarded it.

"How could it slip your mind, Hazel? Your mind is completely empty. It's a void. A vacuum. Just like your zombie of a mother."

The words were cruel enough on their own, but I knew there was more abuse to come. If we were in a true BDSM relationship, the repercussions would have been agreed upon in advance. But Benjamin was not a dominant. He was a bully. A manipulator. An abuser.

"Go to the room."

"But the steak…," I said weakly.

His plate flew at me, the cutlery clattering to the table. I brought my forearm up to protect myself, the plate glancing off it sharply. The bloody piece of meat landed in my lap.

"Go!" he roared.

I stood and stumbled obediently down the stairs.

30

"WE HAVE TO LEAVE," I said. "Soon."

Jesse's eyes remained on the road ahead as he piloted the Audi through sparse Saturday morning traffic. "What happened?"

"This." I twisted in my seat to reveal my lower back, black and blue from the beating. Benjamin used a leather cat-o'-nine-tails, a common instrument of BDSM play. But the way he used it was not playful. It was brutal.

"Christ," Jesse muttered.

"And I'm only allowed to go to the gym for one hour now. It's not long enough for us to be together."

I saw his jaw clench. "That fucking prick."

"I have to get away from him, Jesse. He's going to kill me one day."

"I can't get the boat. It's chartered for the next month."

"Shit." I swiped at my eyes and the tears welling there.

His voice was gentle. "Don't cry, Hazel."

But I couldn't stop. The hopelessness of my situation was overwhelming me. I hated and feared my husband, but I couldn't leave him. He would find me, and he would kill me. And then he'd go after my mother. I winced as my bruised backside brushed against the seat belt buckle.

Jesse's voice cut through my meltdown. "I met her," he said without looking over.

"Who?"

"Lee. The homeless woman." Something in my chest clutched as he continued. "She works at a diner in Beacon Hill. It's a dive. Full of illegal workers. I sort of know the owner."

"But why did you want to meet her?"

"There's a strange woman living in the park near your house, Hazel. And she has a knife."

"She wouldn't hurt me," I said quickly. "She's harmless. She's nice actually."

"I'm not worried about her hurting you." Fat raindrops began to mottle the windshield and Jesse flicked on the wipers. "I think we could use her."

An unpleasant tremor ran through me. "Use her how?"

Jesse turned the Audi down a random side street. We were driving aimlessly. There wasn't time to go to his apartment. "This is going to sound like a lot but hear me out." He glanced over at me. I kept my face blank, receptive, but my heart rabbited in my throat.

"We could get rid of Benjamin. For good. You could keep everything: the house, the money, the cars. And we could be together."

The school system, my peers, and most of all my husband had convinced me I was stupid. But I wasn't. I knew Jesse was not simply a personal trainer. He had a past he wouldn't talk about. Tattoos on his body that looked suspiciously unprofessional. His home was not the home of a man who'd been living free all his life. Still, what he was suggesting shocked me. Because I'd assumed Jesse had spent time inside for dealing drugs, maybe breaking and entering, car theft at the most. Nothing violent. Otherwise, he'd still be in jail.

"You wouldn't do that." My voice was a whisper.

He turned and met my eyes. "For you, I would."

"There's no way," I said quickly. Because I'd fantasized about living in my beautiful home, free of the constraints and abuse and the malignant presence of my husband. "I'd be the prime suspect."

"Lee has a knife," Jesse continued. "If it's the murder weapon, she'll be arrested."

I was speechless, incredulous. In a heartbeat he'd gone from murder to framing an innocent woman.

"Think about it, Hazel. There's a desperate woman living in the woods watching you. She's lost everything. You have so much. It makes sense that she'd become obsessed with you."

I had no emotional response to the suggestion of my husband's murder. Most days, I thought about him dying: a car crash on the way to work, a heart attack on the golf course, a lump of steak lodged in his throat. He was evil and didn't deserve to live. But Lee was harmless. Innocent. "We can't do that to her," I said softly.

"Why not? She'll probably get off on some sort of mental health plea."

"She's not crazy. She's just poor."

"Prison's not that bad," Jesse said, articulating his experience for the first time. "She can get an education if she needs it. Learn a trade. And her life is hell right now. In prison, she'll get a warm bed, three meals a day, and support programs after her release."

He made it sound like we were doing her a favor.

"I can't stand to see that bastard hurt you anymore." The wipers scraped against the window as the rain slowed. "One day, I'll snap and kill Benjamin myself. Then I'll go down for it. And I won't get off easy." He flicked the wipers off. "They might think you were in on it, too."

Was there a threat in his tone? But when I glanced over at him, he was just driving.

"Go see her," he said. "She'll be at the beach soon."

"How do you know?"

"She crashed at my place last night."

I felt cold all over. "She *what*?"

"I took her for a drink. She passed out from the medicine you gave her."

My mouth tasted bitter. "Did you…?"

"Of course not. God, Hazel. I put her in my bed, and I slept on the couch."

"That was nice of you." There was an edge to my voice.

"You can trust me. And I'm not even attracted to her."

"She's attractive."

"She's like a low-rent version of you. Why would I downgrade?"

"You think she looks like me?"

"A little. She's about your size. You have similar coloring. She'd need a haircut, though." His eyes left the road, found mine. "I'm willing to kill to be with you, Hazel. Don't doubt my devotion."

"I…I don't," I stammered, suddenly fearful of losing him. "I'll do it."

"Tell her you're going to leave. Tell her you need her help to get away."

"Okay…"

And so I turned off my guilt, pushed it down so deep that I couldn't feel it, and I went to the beach as instructed. Lee was there, just like Jesse said she'd be. I listened as she told me about the guy she'd met, watched her face light up. And then I told her how Benjamin treated me, showed her my bruises. I didn't even have to lie to her. I asked her to help me escape.

The plan was in motion.

31

OVER THE NEXT FEW DAYS, I jogged to the beach to see Lee each morning, bringing her pilfered food and hot coffee. We sat together on our driftwood bench, watching the sunrise and strategizing. When it rained, I joined her in her car, trying to ignore the lived-in smell of it. Lee's current situation couldn't be any worse. She woke each morning in pain from sleeping cramped and upright. She urinated in the bushes. When she showered, it was at a public pool. Her dignity was already gone. She couldn't fall any lower.

Sometimes she wanted to talk about Jesse. She was smitten with him, a smile dancing across her face when she recounted their time together. I told her to be careful, to look into his past, but she brushed me off. I tried to plant a seed of doubt so she could save herself, but she chose not to. When a person is falling in love, they ignore the warning signs.

"Have you sold the netsuke?" I asked her one day.

"I haven't had time."

It was a key piece of evidence against her. It played into the narrative of the obsessed woman stalking me, breaking into my home, taking a souvenir. Why did she hold on to it? She clearly needed the money. Maybe her circumstances kept her from thinking straight. She was exhausted, stressed, drinking every night. She was playing right into our hands.

I promised Lee new identification. A new start. As the grieving widow, I would no longer need to reinvent myself, but I pressed forward with the fake ID. I sent her to get a photo, just as Jesse had sent me. She had to believe I was helping her.

At home, I played my doting slave role to perfection. Any hint of rebellion would tip Benjamin off to my plan, so I went along, meek, obsequious, and fawning. The punishments he doled out were rote, tolerable. I contacted Vanessa Vega and arranged a lunch. This would throw suspicion off me. How could a woman plotting her husband's murder simultaneously plan a gala fundraiser?

I wore a dress that day, a pale pink chiffon skirt despite the rain clouds brewing. I threw a cropped leather jacket over it to add some edge. Vanessa had suggested a trendy oyster bar in Pioneer Square, so I left early to avoid traffic. If I turned up late, word might get back to Benjamin and I'd be punished, for real.

When I arrived at the restaurant, all brick walls and high ceilings, Vanessa was already seated at a central table with Laurie Gamble. My stomach danced unpleasantly. Vanessa was polished and perfect, but she had a certain warmth, unlike her BFF. Laurie was an icy blonde with an innate ability to be dismissive and condescending. I'd met her on several occasions, but she had consistently looked me over, then overlooked me.

"Hello, gorgeous." Vanessa rose and kissed both my cheeks in a European greeting. Laurie's hug was perfunctory. I sat down across from them, instantly feeling outnumbered, subtly excluded. We made small talk—about hair, skin, and clothes mostly—as we perused the menus. Once we'd ordered oysters and salads, a bottle of wine for the table, Vanessa got down to business. "I'm so glad you agreed to help with the gala."

Like I had a choice. "Of course." I smiled. "Put me to work."

Laurie leaned forward. "We'd like you to take the lead on the silent auction. I've put together a list of vendors you can visit to ask for donations."

Begging for freebies was a miserable job. But once my husband was found murdered in my own home...well, surely, they'd let me off the hook. And the task would also afford me some freedom. Benjamin couldn't deny me my charity work. I'd be able to see Jesse.

"Great." I smiled again, took a sip of pinot grigio. "I'm on it."

As we ate, the conversation segued into spas, a trendy new wine bar, a trip Laurie had taken to Sedona. They both had children, so private schools were discussed, dance and art classes. I smiled, nodded, feigned interest. If Vanessa and Laurie told their husband that they saw me today, the worst they could say was that I was dull, a little vapid. But they'd never suspect that I was unhappy. That I was desperate. That I was plotting.

It was raining when we left, a light spring patter, but I was wearing leather. I dug in my tote for my compact umbrella, fumbled to open it. The spring was a little rusty, so I was struggling with it when I heard my name.

"Hi, Hazel."

The voice, familiar but out of context, made me start. I gaped wordlessly at Lee. What the hell was she doing in Pioneer Square? It wasn't that far from the diner she worked at, but she clearly hadn't been visiting a trendy restaurant or boutique. She wore a hoodie pulled up over her head, baggie jeans, and sneakers. She looked rumpled and unwashed...indigent. Which she was.

Laurie and Vanessa soon flanked me. "Can we help you?" Laurie snapped.

They thought Lee was a panhandler, or a drug addict. "It's okay," I assured them, feeling somewhat protective of my friend. "I'm sorry, I almost didn't recognize you. How are you doing?" I asked as I mentally scrambled to explain our relationship.

"I'm fine." She sounded cagey, her eyes darting to my companions.

And then I recognized the opportunity of this encounter. It was a chance to plant the seed of Lee's obsession with me. When my husband was found dead, stabbed with Lee's knife, Vanessa and Laurie would be all too eager to share this run-in with the police.

"Good. That's good. Are you staying at a shelter in the area?" I asked gently.

"No," Lee snapped. "I was at a pawnshop."

I nodded, kept my expression placid as I reached in my bag for the pièce de résistance. "Why don't you get some lunch? On me." I held out a fifty-dollar bill.

I saw rage in her eyes. And shame. And I hated myself, I did, but my life was at stake. I was committed to this plan, and I wouldn't back out. I couldn't back out. She snatched the bill from my hand and scurried away.

"You're welcome!" Laurie called after her with a humorless snort.

"Who was that?" Vanessa asked, her lip curled with distaste.

"Her name is Lee," I said, diving in. "She sleeps in her car in the park near my house."

"Oh god." Laurie was appalled. Revolted.

"I jog by her every morning," I elaborated. "Sometimes I take her some fruit or a muffin."

Vanessa pressed her palm to her chest. "You're so kind, Hazel."

"You are," Laurie echoed. "But that woman could be dangerous."

"I don't think so," I said with a dismissive laugh.

"Did she follow you here?"

"Oh my god..." The fear on my face must have looked genuine because Laurie continued. "She could be scoping out homes in your neighborhood. Or she could be deranged."

"I never thought of that." Concern fluttered across my face. They clocked it, just like I wanted them to.

"You should call the police," Laurie said.

Vanessa added, "Be careful, Hazel. You can't be friends with someone like that."

We hugged efficiently and went our separate ways.

32

I WAS DELIGHTED TO TELL Jesse how I'd played the chance encounter with Lee. He nodded appreciatively as I recounted Laurie Gamble's concerns, Vanessa Vega's warnings.

"Quick thinking," he said, pulling me in for a kiss. We were nestled on his charcoal couch. I was supposed to be asking restaurants for gift certificates right now, but I'd driven straight to Jesse's apartment. We hadn't had time to be intimate lately, and I knew it was important. I knew I had to please my man.

"Does she have your phone number?" Jesse asked, touching the ends of my hair.

"No, why?"

"We're building a case against her, Hazel. She's approached you in public. She's got that Japanese ornament thing. It would be good if she called you. A bunch of times."

"Right," I said, brow furrowed. "I'll think of something."

"And we need to get her into the house. On the day."

The day of the murder, he meant. I swallowed thickly. "I'll figure that out."

"The knife will be the clincher. You'll have to get it out of her car so I can use it."

He sounded so efficient, so businesslike. Almost like he'd done this before. I felt a heavy weight on my chest, struggled to respond. "Okay."

"That's my girl." He tilted my chin so our eyes could connect, and there was warmth in his. "It'll all be worth it, Hazel. When we're together, for real. When Benjamin can't hurt you anymore."

"I know," I said, and I tried to believe it.

The next morning, Lee didn't come to the beach. Perhaps she'd found a new spot to park? Or she'd gone to a shelter. But when she didn't return the next day, or the day after that, I began to worry. I'd hurt her. Embarrassed her. I'd chased her away.

"She's gone," I told Jesse. We were at the gym. He was supervising my dead lifts while we talked in hushed voices. "I fucked it all up."

"She's not gone," he said. "I'll bring her back."

"Really? You can do that?"

He smirked, pleased with himself. "She'll do anything I say. She's falling for me."

"I know." My words were bitter in my mouth. "She told me."

"Don't be jealous," he said playfully. "I'm doing this for you."

It was true. Anything he did with Lee was in service to our plan. He was sending this woman to jail to free me from my abusive marriage. I couldn't be jealous. So, what was this feeling twisting in my guts?

I tried to keep my voice level as I asked, "Are you sleeping with her?"

"Of course not," he snapped. "Don't be so stupid."

"Look…" I dropped the weight and stood upright. "This doesn't feel good. Or right. Can we just go back to the original plan? Get a boat and leave the country?"

A muscle clenched in Jesse's jaw—irritation, frustration. Without a word he strode to the back of the gym and out the exit.

Obediently, I trailed after him. When we were alone in the staff parking lot, he turned on me. "Don't fuck this up, Hazel. We've come too far."

"I can get some money," I told him. "Enough to start over in a new country. Where things are cheaper."

"Why would we do that when we can live here, in perfect luxury? In a fucking mansion with art and fancy cars and shit?"

"I...I don't care about any of that," I said. "I just want us to be together."

"So do I," he said, his voice softening. "But the original plan won't work. I've looked into it, and something like eighty-five percent of drowning victims are found. Or at least parts of them are found. Benjamin won't believe you're dead without a body. And if he thinks you've run off, he'll never stop looking for you."

In my husband's line of work, he'd know how unlikely it was that my body would drift away, disappear. And he would hunt me down. He'd never give up.

"If he suspects you betrayed him, he'll kick your mom out of the nursing home."

That hopeless, panicky feeling was returning. Tears welled in my eyes, clogged my throat.

"This is the only way, Hazel."

"But Lee...," I croaked.

"Collateral damage," he said. "All that matters to me is you. And us."

He felt nothing for her. Less than nothing. I should have felt comforted. But I didn't.

"What time does Benjamin get home on Friday?"

My stomach dropped. We were setting a date. "He golfs on Fridays. He comes home at noon to change and get his clubs."

"Friday at noon. I'll be waiting for him."

I nodded mutely. It didn't feel real.

"And Lee will be at the beach tomorrow," he assured me. "Be ready."

He went back inside, leaving me alone in the alley.

I baked scones that night—peach and brown butter—and I plotted, worried, wondered. If Lee showed up, it meant Jesse had power over her. That she was emotionally, if not physically, involved with him. He'd assured me that they weren't intimate, but then how else had he cast such a spell on her? He and I rarely had sex anymore. There was no time. We were under so much stress. I told myself it was normal, but was it? Jesse was a passionate, sexual man. Was he having those needs met elsewhere? I shook off my petty jealousies. They would only get in the way. My focus had to be on Lee, on wheedling my way back into her good graces.

No woman could resist a spa day—especially a woman in her situation. I'd pay for her to be primped and pampered. I'd ask my stylist, Karl, to cut her hair, make it look like mine. And then I'd suggest she enter my house and fool the cameras. Would she do that for me? It would be terrifying for her. Lee knew my husband was violent. But if I offered her money and new identification, she might just go through with it.

Benjamin kept his golf clubs in the closet in his study. There were no cameras in that room. That's where Jesse would do it. Lee wouldn't even go in there. She'd be spared the blood and gore. She wouldn't even know my husband was dead, stabbed with her own knife, until the police came to arrest her.

The thought made me double over, and I worried I might be sick. But I pulled it together, righted myself, pushed the noxious guilt away. I directed my memory to Jesse's assurances that Lee would be okay, even cared for, that she would get the help she needed. And I set my mind on that bubble of hope. Of anticipation. Finally, I would be free. To be with Jesse.

The man I loved.

33

THE NEXT MORNING, SHE WAS there, as Jesse had promised she would be. My feet crunched on the loose rocks as I approached the car and tapped gently on the window. She opened her eyes, and they were cold when she recognized me. But she climbed out of the car, slowly, in pain, like she always was in the morning.

I begged her for forgiveness, literally begged. As I served her fresh-baked scones and coffee, I told her how I'd panicked when I saw her on the street. "Vanessa and Laurie are shallow and judgmental," I said. "If I'd introduced you as my friend, word could have got back to Benjamin. He controls all my friendships. He wouldn't let me see you."

I watched her soften. "Fear and desperation can make you do terrible things. I should know," she said. "I betrayed my only sister. And she'll never forgive me."

I listened, features composed in sympathy, as she told me how she'd photographed her sister's fiancé, how she'd attempted to extort money out of him. It was a shitty thing to do, but it seemed so trivial compared to my plot against her.

"You were under so much pressure," I said gently. "Can't she understand that?" But Teresa hated Lee. Teresa had gone through with the wedding, despite the cheating. The family had taken her side. I realized how alone Lee was then. She had no one…except Jesse and me.

"Let me take you for a spa day," I said as she blinked her tears away. "Massage, facial, haircut—the works. On me."

"I couldn't," she said, but she wanted to, I could tell.

So I pressed. "When's your next day off?"

"Thursday."

"I'll book everything and meet you there at ten. Sound good?"

Her face was glowing with anticipation. "Sounds *amazing*."

And then I saw an opportunity. "Give me your phone."

It was a casual request, but she looked slightly awkward. And when she handed me a cheap flip phone, I saw why. But I didn't comment as I added my name and number to her contacts. More evidence against her. Because I'd deny doing this, would tell the cops I had no idea how she got my number. She was a stalker. A psycho.

"Call me," I said. "If anything comes up."

"What about Benjamin? Won't he want to know who's calling you?"

"I'm not allowed to have my phone on when he's home." It was the truth. I stood to go. "I'll book a massage, haircut, mani-pedi…"

"Could you book me a bikini wax?" Her chuckle was self-deprecating, her cheeks pink. "It's been a while."

Did this mean Jesse *was* sleeping with her? That he had lied to me? Or was Lee planning a grand seduction? I felt my jaw clench, but I kept my tone light, teasing. "I thought you and that guy were *just friends*?"

"We're more than that now." She looked down but she couldn't hide her smile. They were lovers. It was in her voice and on her face.

Jealousy churned my stomach, sent a sick taste into my throat.

Jesse had lied to me. He had cheated on me. The infidelity hurt more than any of Benjamin's physical abuse. But when I looked at Lee, I felt something else. Self-loathing. Because I hated what we were doing to her, how we were playing her. And pity. She was as desperate to feel loved as I was.

Part of me wanted to tell her to run, to leave, and never come back. To stay away from Jesse. But she would never listen to me. She'd go straight to Jesse and tell him everything I said. And I would lose him. My lifeline. My only chance to get away.

It was her or me.

"I'm happy for you," I said, and it sounded sincere. But I turned to go before my façade slipped. "See you tomorrow. I'll bring rhubarb muffins."

34

JESSE AND I SAT ON his sofa, our knees touching, our fingers intertwined. It was essential that he didn't sense the shift in me. The hurt. The simmering sense of betrayal. And the doubt...After I'd left Lee at the beach, I'd replayed her admission over again in my mind. I believed her. She and Jesse were sleeping together. You couldn't fake the emotion I'd seen on Lee's face. And she had no reason to lie to me. Jesse, on the other hand, did.

At that moment, Lee was at the spa, getting her hair cut, her bikini line waxed, her tension massaged away. She'd be reveling in her treatments, trusting in the altruism of my gift. There was no way she could imagine what was in store for her. That tomorrow, it would all be over. If I was able to go through with it...

"What time will Benjamin get home?" Jesse asked.

I sat up straighter, focused on our plan. "He comes home at noon, changes, and leaves by twelve-thirty."

"I'll need to be inside, waiting, by eleven-thirty."

"I'll disable the back door cameras and unlock the door." I had thought this through, step by step. "Come up from the beach. No one will see you."

"I will. Make sure you're long gone."

"Of course."

"Lee needs to arrive at one. It'll be done by then." The coldness in his voice sent a chill through me. "How will you get her into the house?"

My mind had explored a multitude of ways to lure my friend into my home. I was sure I had figured it out. "I'm going to tell her I just need a head start to get to the airport. She only needs to come inside for an hour. She'll be perfectly safe."

"And you think she'll do it?"

"I'll promise to leave her money. And new ID."

"How much money?"

"A hundred grand, maybe? It has to be an incentive."

"Make it fifty. It's more realistic and it's still a lot of money for someone like her."

"Right." The figure didn't matter. It was just bait.

"And you need to get her knife."

"How?" I was beginning to feel panicky, overwhelmed. "I don't know how to break into a car."

"Calm down," he scolded me. "She's coming to my place tonight. I'll get the keys and toss them out the side window. You can get the knife, then put the keys in the bushes near the front door. She'll think she dropped them."

They had a date. Prearranged. Lee and her bikini wax. The information was like a sore I couldn't stop picking at. "She told me she's sleeping with you."

"She wishes," he snorted, pulling his hands from mine.

"I'd appreciate the truth, Jesse."

"Of course I'm not fucking her." His tone and his eyes were hard. "And I can't believe you'd take the word of that bum over mine. She's a drunk. She's a mess."

I had given him a chance to come clean, and he had chosen to lie. To attack Lee's character and credibility. It was so easy for him. So natural. I swallowed the sick feeling in my stomach. "Okay," I said softly. "I believe you."

"Good." He shifted away from me, ever so slightly. "Can you get away tonight?"

Benjamin always worked late on Thursday nights so he could take the next afternoon off to golf. I'd be able to slip out of the house and return before he did. I nodded.

"Hide the knife inside your house," Jesse instructed. "Where's a good place?"

"Near the back door," I said. "There's a laundry room there. I'll put it down beside the dryer."

"Perfect. I'll grab it and wait for him in his study."

The realness of what was about to happen bore down on me, and my stomach churned. I half stood, ready to move to the bathroom, when my phone rang out in the hushed space. Lee's name on the call display made my hair stand on end. It was like she'd somehow heard us. I glanced at the clock in the top corner of the screen. Lee would be done with her treatments by now. I'd promised to meet her there, to pay for everything, but I'd lost track of time. I picked up the phone.

"Hello?"

"Hazel, it's Lee. I'm at the spa. They're saying—"

Jesse grabbed the phone away from me and hung up.

"Why—" I started, but I knew what he was doing. Almost instantly, it rang again.

"Don't answer it." Jesse's voice was steely. We stared at the device, at Lee's name, as it rang out, went to voice mail. When it rang again, we did the same. Finally, it stopped. She had given up.

"Go to her now," he said. "Are you ready?"

I nodded and got up. Jesse did, too. We were moving toward the door when he touched my shoulder. "There's just one more thing..." I stopped and turned.

The punch came out of nowhere, smashing into my cheekbone, sending me reeling. Instinctively, I stepped back, covered my face, cowered away. But he was coming toward me, hands outstretched.

"I'm sorry, babe. It would have hurt more if I told you I was going to do it."

Tears were hot on my skin, though I hadn't realized I was crying. The pain was dull, throbbing, somehow far away. I couldn't speak. Couldn't move. I was in shock.

"I know Lee," Jesse said. "She won't go into your house just for money. We need to make her pity you. To think she's saving you."

I stood taller, found my voice. "Benjamin would never hit me in the face."

"Lee doesn't know that."

He reached out to wipe my tears, but I flinched away from his touch. The sudden violence had rattled me. And the ease with which he had hit me hurt more than the physical pain.

"Pull yourself together, Hazel." His voice was calm, controlled. "I know what I'm doing."

I nodded, blinked away the tears, and I left. When I was outside his building, I puked into the dry, brittle grass.

But it worked. When I removed my sunglasses in the spa parking lot, Lee was horrified by my injured face, my traumatized demeanor. When I asked her to come into my house, to set me free, she agreed. The money and the new identification were secondary. She was scared for me. She felt compelled to save me. And in return, I would send her to jail for a murder she hadn't committed. But it was the only way I could be free of one man to start over with another. A man who would do anything for me. Even kill for me.

The same man who had just punched me in the face.

35

LATER THAT NIGHT, MY HANDS pressed into the cool marble countertop as I leaned close to the bathroom mirror. The bruise was a deep navy blue, almost black. A small blood vessel had popped in my eye, leaving a red spot on the white surface. It no longer hurt, but it was hideous. I turned and lifted my shirt. The bruises on my back were fading, the skin an ugly shade of green and yellow. I looked at myself clinically and dispassionately. Who was this pitiful creature, so beaten and battered? How had she let it come to this? I turned away from the stranger staring back at me and focused on the plan.

Slipping out of the house that night was easy enough. While Benjamin controlled the surveillance cameras with an app on his phone, I simply angled the one over the back door to face the wall. Benjamin might notice, but he'd blame the wind. And by the time he got home from work he'd forget to adjust it. Tomorrow, Jesse would climb the steep, overgrown trail from the beach, creep through the forested backyard, and let himself in through this door. My husband didn't consider it a vulnerable part of the house. But he'd always underestimated me.

I scrambled down to the beach and walked around the rocky

point. The late spring sun still hung lazily in the sky, though it was almost nine. I clamored to the spot where Lee had often parked her car. It wasn't there, of course. She was spending the night at Jesse's. It was all part of the plan. And she'd be eager to show him her pretty haircut, her smooth skin, her sexy bikini wax...My mouth tasted bitter as I called and requested a taxi.

The driver picked me up in the secluded area without question (an Uber would have left a record) and zoomed past the black SUV parked at the end of my driveway. Nate, the security guard, dozed in the driver's seat. He had no reason to suspect I was not inside—the good wife, Benjamin's obedient slave. As long as I returned before my husband did, I could slip back inside, unnoticed.

The cab deposited me a block away from Jesse's apartment. "Can you wait?" I asked the driver. "Leave the meter running." He nodded, and I walked efficiently toward the six-story building. It was a drab, sturdy cube, lacking in character and in need of maintenance. As I approached it, I turned right, slipped into the alleyway. Jesse lived on the ground floor, at the back of the complex. Most of his windows had bars on them, but there were two on the side that opened freely. The stench of garbage hit me as I passed by dumpsters, and a creature scurried behind one, sending a shiver through me. The first time I'd visited, Jesse had explained that the place was temporary, just until he could get back on his feet. Soon he'd be living in the lap of luxury. If all went according to his plan...

The blinds were closed, but I saw the faint lamplight glowing from the living room. Jesse and Lee were in there, side by side on that sagging gray sofa. What were they doing? Making out? Making love? Lee was so into him. She thought their relationship was real. Jesse was such a good actor. I pushed the mental image of the two of them from my mind and pressed forward.

Creeping down the side of the building, I crouched below the kitchen window. It was slightly ajar. That meant Jesse had tossed the keys out already. It was dark now, and I worried I might have to use the flashlight on my phone, but when I felt around in the crisp grass and the pungent needles from that big fir tree, my hand touched something metal. The keys.

Dropping them into my bag, I stood and pressed my uninjured eye to the crack in the window. All I could see was the kitchen, the countertop cluttered with herbs, the papery wisps of onion skins, the red ring from a bottle of wine. She had cooked for him, something French and delicious. I heard low voices. Lee's gentle giggles. She was happy. She was in love. Jesse had handled her so well.

With the keys in hand, I soon found the Toyota parked on a nearby side street. It would be visible from the open kitchen window, so I crouched low and let myself in through the passenger door. Lee's Corolla was looking more like a car and less like a home on wheels. In fact, a couple of jackets on the back seat were the only evidence that Lee lived in it. Was she keeping things at Jesse's? I'd left my own shampoo there, some cleanser, and a hairbrush. I hadn't thought to look for Lee's belongings, but it was likely they were there. She spent more time at the apartment than I did.

Tentatively, I felt under the driver's seat for the knife, careful not to cut myself. When I retrieved it, I held it in my hand, felt the weight of it. I'd seen it before but hadn't realized its power. It was too sturdy for the kitchen. A hunting knife, probably. Where would an unassuming woman like Lee have gotten it? I traced the dull side of the blade with an index finger, wondering if she'd ever used it. I couldn't imagine it, but Lee had been surviving on the streets for months. She'd had to be tough and brave. Would a jury believe that she had plunged this weapon into Benjamin's chest? Jesse thought so.

An electronic beep sounded, sending my heart into my throat. My Apple Watch was alerting me to the time. Benjamin would be home in about an hour, and I needed to beat him there. Dropping the knife into my shoulder bag, I climbed out of the car. I hurried toward Jesse's building and tossed the keys and the letter *L* tag under a dying boxwood bordering the walkway. I turned and jogged away.

In the back of the cab, I gingerly touched the bruised skin of my cheekbone as we raced north on I-5. My mind replayed the scene of Jesse's fist plowing into my face and my insides twisted. I thought about him making love to Lee, manipulating her, tricking her into falling for him. As the car took the exit that curled toward the coast, the wooded road that led to the waterfront enclave, I felt the outline of my friend's knife in my bag. Abruptly, I sat forward.

"Stop here," I said. We were still over a mile from my house, the street dark and desolate. The driver glanced at me in the rearview mirror, mildly perplexed, but he turned on his indicator and pulled over. I paid him cash and climbed out into the chill night.

The trail toward the beach was overgrown and treacherous, but I made my way down to the ocean in the darkness. I was almost there when I stumbled, sliding on loose rocks, landing on my bruised back. But I did not cry out. I clamped my teeth together, gathered myself up, and pushed toward the sound of the gentle waves.

The ocean was black but for the lights of the mansions glimmering off the surface. A spit of craggy rocks jutted out into the Pacific, and I tentatively picked my way across them. It was risky in the darkness, but I wouldn't use my flashlight. I couldn't draw attention to myself. When I reached the final rock, I took the knife from my bag and with a strong overhand throw, I chucked it into the sea. A brief sensation of peace settled over me. I was protecting my friend. I still had a moral compass, however askew.

And then I climbed back up the trail and I walked home, slipping through the back door unnoticed.

I was safely tucked up in bed when Benjamin returned, my black eye pressed into the pillow. In the morning, I would have to address it, but I'd be ready.

"Are you asleep?" His voice was loud in the quiet room. It would have woken anyone, but I kept my eyes closed, breathing slow and steady. My husband knew I sometimes took a sleeping pill that would render me comatose. I pretended to sleep as I listened to him undress, use the bathroom, brush his teeth. Eventually, he crawled into bed beside me, rolled over, and went to sleep.

I lay perfectly still, my eyes closed, tears dampening the pillow.

36

"WHAT THE HELL HAPPENED TO your eye?" There was no concern, only outrage as Benjamin entered the kitchen. I poured him a cup of coffee, my hand barely trembling as I set it on the breakfast bar.

"I hit it with a dumbbell," I said with a sheepish chuckle. "I'm so clumsy." He took my chin in his fingertips, inspected the damage. "It was more embarrassing than anything," I continued. "The gym staff were fluttering around me like I was going to pass out."

"You can't go out like that."

"No, of course not." I was ready for this. "But may I please go to the gym? I mean, they all saw it happen. And if I don't show up, they might get concerned. They might want to check on me. They might be worried that I'll sue them or something."

I watched him process the possibility, find it reasonable. "One hour," he said.

That was all I needed.

I served him oatmeal and blueberries, as requested, and then I cleaned the kitchen after he left. Everything had to be normal. When the counters were wiped, the bowls in the dishwasher, I went into my bathroom and kneeled on the floor. Removing the top drawer, I found the manila envelope. With it pressed between my arm and body, I returned to the kitchen and slipped it into a kitchen drawer. Lee would collect it, believe it contained what we had discussed. She had no reason to doubt me.

When I'd dressed in my spandex workout clothes, I donned a pair of designer sunglasses and drove to the gym. I dug my member card out of my shoulder bag and swiped myself in. One of the trainers waved a greeting and I waved back, but I moved swiftly to the changeroom. It was empty, thankfully, and I sat on the bench, waiting anxiously. The door opened and I nearly jumped up, but it was a middle-aged woman, muscular and sweaty. She went to her locker, stripped off her clothes, and headed to the shower.

For only a split second did I consider that Lee wouldn't come. That she would realize that she was being used, or that her mission was far too risky. But Jesse and I had played our roles too well. And I knew how much she cared for me. When the door swung open and she entered, wearing a ball cap and a tentative grin, my throat knotted. I stood, and without a word, began to disrobe.

Lee's jeans were soft and worn, and only a little bit loose. I put on her jacket and cap, as she struggled into my clingy tights. When she was dressed, I stared at her reflection. Lee looked a lot like me. She would fool Nate, who was not the sharpest knife in the drawer (pun intended). But would our resemblance be enough to fool the cameras?

I turned to face her, saw the doubt and fear in her eyes, and I wished I could tell her everything. That Jesse and I had duped her, that we'd planned to send her into a trap. That he had used us both and that he didn't deserve either one of us. *When I'm gone, end it with him,* I wanted to say. *Promise me, Lee.* But Jesse had brainwashed her into loving him. She'd go to him, tell him everything I said, and he'd talk his way out of it. I had seen how easily he could lie. And then he would come after me. I now knew that he was dangerous. Ruthless.

So, I played my part. "Thank you," I said, my voice wobbly. "I've never had a friend like you." She thought I was sad to say goodbye to her and I was. But there was so much more behind my tremulous demeanor: guilt, shame, and fear. Real fear. Because after this, I will have no one.

As the shower turned off, I said, "I should go." When I saw the sadness in her eyes, I added, "Maybe you could visit me someday? In Panama?"

"How?"

It was impossible, of course. This was goodbye. Forever.

The woman emerged from the shower then, and there was no more time. Wordlessly, we exchanged keys and sunglasses, and I left.

And now I am driving aimlessly in Lee's Corolla, watching the minutes click by on the dashboard clock. Jesse will have approached my home by now, found the back door locked. Did he turn away? Or did he force his way inside? If he entered, he'd have reached down beside the dryer, searching fruitlessly for Lee's knife. What will he think when he can't find it? That I betrayed him? No, he won't believe that. I was his good girl: so helpless, so obedient, so dependent on him. He will think Benjamin stopped me somehow. And he will leave.

Jesse will expect me to go to the gym so we can regroup, discuss what went wrong. He'll want to try again. He's not going to give up the chance to live a life of wealth and privilege so easily. But I won't show up. I will spend the weekend at home with my husband, doing his every bidding. And I will rack my brain for another way to escape.

With Benjamin alive, I will need to fake my death. It's the only way to ensure my mother will be cared for when I'm gone. But can I do that on my own? Without Jesse's help? I've been controlled and manipulated for so long that the thought of hatching a complex plan, of carrying it out by myself, is daunting, even terrifying. But I must try.

And if I fail?

I won't live like this any longer. If I can't set myself free, then I will end my life. I will draw a bath, take a handful of sleeping pills, pour a glass of vodka over ice. I'll climb into the water and let the chemicals do their work. And then I will slip under and drown. Peacefully. Gone. On my own terms.

Finally, it is time. Jesse had instructed me to park the vehicle at the beach, close to my house. It would have played into the stalker narrative—the woman in the park who was obsessed with me. But that's no longer relevant. Ahead, I see the Trader Joe's where I told Lee I would leave her car. Flicking on the indicator, I pull into the busy lot.

I slide the car into a lonely spot away from the doors and climb out. Moving around to the back of the vehicle, I open the trunk. It is stuffed with all of Lee's worldly belongings. Carefully, I rummage through an overstuffed backpack until I find it. The netsuke is wrapped in a black T-shirt, but I remove it, stroke the snake's smooth head before stuffing it into my pocket. It is the last piece of the evidence against Lee. I have protected her as much as I can. Setting her keys on the back tire, I begin the long walk home.

My route takes me down side streets, through residential neighborhoods, along the gravel verge of a sparsely traveled highway. It will take me over an hour to get to my house this way, but I need the time to concoct a story. To explain why I am walking home. A lost key fob is the most believable. I'll grab the spare, collect my car in the parking lot where Lee will leave it. Benjamin will punish me for my carelessness, but I don't care. Soon, he won't be able to hurt me anymore.

As I trudge the last few yards to my home, I feel a prickle of anxiety. Nate is not at his post; the first sign that something is off. His black SUV is there, but it is empty. Did he catch Jesse coming in through the back door? Did he subdue him and call the police? My lover has a record, I'm sure of it. He could be charged with trespassing. Breaking and entering. Maybe even stalking. If caught, he'll go down for this. Would he try to take me with him?

My Mercedes is there, parked next to the garage. That means Lee was here, that she'd done as I asked. But she should have left by now in my car. My shoulders tense with worry. Was she confronted? By whom? She couldn't have encountered Jesse; the timing doesn't add up. But Nate could have intercepted her. Even Benjamin. Lee had a cover story, though. Our friendship. I swallow the thickness in my throat and put the key in the lock.

"Hello, darling!" I call out, putting on a show of normalcy. "Are you home?" No one answers and my heartbeat begins to slow. The house is still, empty. *Relax,* I tell myself. *Jesse did not come inside. Lee got away safely. Benjamin went golfing.* But my body remains tight and rigid with dread.

The netsuke is in my pocket, so I head to the study. I will put it back on the shelf as if it was never missing. As if I had never given it to Lee as a gift. As if we had never met. I move briskly toward Benjamin's office, but my feet slow of their own volition as a frisson of fear raises the hair on the back of my neck. Someone is in there. There is no sound, but the energy is palpable.

"Hello?" I call softly as I reach the doorway. No answer. Tentatively I peek my head inside.

He is there, at his desk, sitting perfectly still. The chair, a sleek Danish model, is turned away from me, but I recognize his hair, his shoulders, his hands. He is dressed casually, but he is immaculate, just like the rest of his office. Finally, he swivels around to face me.

"Hello, sweetheart." Benjamin's smile is cold, his eyes icy with anger. "Where have you been?"

PART THREE

LEE

37

SOMEHOW, I DIDN'T SCREAM. I stepped back, slipping in the blood again, but I didn't go down this time. Jesse. *My* Jesse. Why was he in Hazel's home? Why was he dead? His blood was still wet, which meant my boyfriend had been killed recently. But by whom? And then I heard that noise again. Something, *someone* was outside. A killer. A cop. The security guard. Whoever it was, I could not be there, at the scene of the crime. I was a homeless person, inside a mansion, with a dead body.

There was no way I could run out the front door, get in Hazel's car, and drive off. Saving her was no longer my priority. I had to save myself. She had mentioned a back exit, off the kitchen past the laundry room. As I ran toward it, I spotted the large purse still on the kitchen counter where I'd left it. Snatching it up, I scampered down the hall, past the washer and dryer, toward the door. Bursting through it, I found the trail toward the beach.

I scrambled down to the ocean, roots catching at my feet. The blood—Jesse's blood—was still on my hands and clothes and in my nostrils. When I hit the rocky shore, I kept moving north toward the forested park. I would be safe there. No one ever came down that far, especially not during the week. When I was far from Hazel's house, had ensured no one was following me, I waded into the ocean. The water washed the blood from my shoes and my pants. I scrubbed at my hands, the cold water turning them numb.

Only now, as I clamber onto the beach, does the shock begin to set in. I can feel it in my fluttering heart, my shallow breathing, my cold, clammy skin. But I mustn't let it overtake me. Because I am in danger. I walked into the scene of a crime, my lover's murder. And I am probably on camera. But what the hell was Jesse doing in Hazel's home? Who killed him? And why?

Despite my racing thoughts, I realize I am exposed and vulnerable here on the beach, so I push toward the bushes. The spot where I had slept so many nights would be safe. Unless…unless someone is looking for me. I scramble up the path and press farther into the forest, ears pricked for any signs of danger. My mind grapples with the bloody scenario I encountered as I crash through the underbrush. Why had my boyfriend gone into that house? I'd told him about my plan. Had he gone there to protect me? To intercept me? Had Benjamin Laval or one of his henchmen stabbed Jesse to death?

Or…did Jesse know Hazel somehow? Her husband kept her on a short leash. She was only allowed to go jogging and to the gym. But not Jesse's gym, surely. Seattle is a big city, with hundreds of workout options. What are the odds that the two had met, had developed a relationship? A relationship that had gotten him killed.

When I am safely ensconced in a forested thicket, I press the heels of my palms into my eyes. *Don't cry,* I admonish myself. *Don't fall apart now. You've survived this long on your own.* But my throat is thick with sadness, my heart tight and racing. Jesse is dead. His chest full of deep gashes, his face grotesque in its death mask. He was my lover. My comfort. My safe place. And someone has brutally murdered him. In Hazel's beautiful house.

Suspicious thoughts swirl in my head, snaking their way through my grief. Had my feelings for Jesse blinded me to the red flags? His sparse apartment and luxury car were at odds. He had never given me his phone number, leaving me waiting and wondering for days on end. Did Jesse have another life that I wasn't a part of? Another woman? And was that woman Hazel?

I had pitied her, tried to save her from a sick and toxic marriage. But now I wonder if she tricked me. Played me. All the while, she could have been involved with my boyfriend. But even if she was, why is he dead? And why the fuck did she want me to discover his lifeless body?

The purse. I'd had the wherewithal to grab it as I fled, but what is inside? Hazel was supposed to leave me a disguise—a jacket and a hat. I unzip the leather bag and search for the clothing. It's not there, of course it's not. Because now I know that Hazel's plan was just a ruse. My fingers alight on the fat manila envelope and I withdraw it. I'd been so optimistic when I'd first retrieved it. The thought of a new identity, enough money to live like a normal member of society had buoyed me. But it will be filled with useless paper, another cruel trick. My damaged finger throbs and my others are weak from cold, but I tear it open.

There is a note on top, handwritten. I pull it out and read it.

Lee,

You have to go. Start over. Rebuild your life. Jesse is not who you think he is.

I'm so sorry. You were always a good friend to me.

H.

An audible sob shudders out of me, and I press a fist to my mouth. What has Hazel done? To me and to Jesse?

I shake the envelope into my lap to see what else Hazel has left me. There is money. A lot of money. Stacks of hundreds wrapped in rubber bands like the proceeds of a robbery. My mind struggles to calculate the number, but it has to be fifty grand, just like she promised. I find a passport too. I open it up; my face, pale and serious, stares back at me.

Kelly Jane Wilcox

A new birthdate. Born in Portland, Oregon. But it is me. And it looks legitimate.

A small folder, navy blue with a white logo, is buried under the bills. It is from a travel agency. Inside, I find a paper plane ticket. It is made out to Kelly Wilcox, an unrestricted one-way fare. I can travel whenever I want. Only the destination has been chosen for me.

Panama City.

Hazel's plan has now become mine. She wants to be rid of me. But if she thinks I will disappear without finding out why Jesse is dead, she doesn't know me at all. Stuffing the money, ID, and ticket back into the bag, I head farther into the forest.

38

I TRAVEL THROUGH THE WOODS, swiftly. This is a popular trail for joggers and dog walkers on the weekends, but it's almost deserted today. A woman with a black Lab passes by me and we exchange obligatory greetings. She doesn't seem to notice that I am wet, wan, trembling. That I am carrying an expensive leather bag on my solo forest walk. I pray I don't encounter anyone with an eye for such details.

At a fork in the trail, I turn left. The path will take me away from the coastline, toward the subdivisions and strip malls, back to the I-5. I need to get to Jesse's apartment, but more importantly, I need to get away from Hazel's house. From the scene of the murder. Jesse's murder.

Eventually, I emerge from the forest into a recently developed subdivision. I walk briskly past cookie-cutter houses, minivans, and SUVs in their driveways. My pantlegs are nearly dry, and I smooth my hair, slow my gait. I am just a regular woman out for a walk: not a person with a bag full of cash and a fake ID who has just discovered her lover's corpse. No one will notice me or think my presence unusual. And I pray no one is looking for me.

As I near a commercial district, traffic increases and pedestrians clutter the sidewalk. I feel safer here, less conspicuous, but I know I need to get off the streets. Stopping near a bus shelter, I dig in the bag and find my phone. An older woman is seated on the bench, and I ask if she knows the number of a cab company. She tells me, and I punch it into the phone. I will have the taxi take me to Jesse's apartment. There is a chance that the police will be there already, but I doubt that. Someone—Hazel probably—will need to come home, discover Jesse's body, and call them. She might claim he was an intruder. The cops will have to ID his corpse.

The phone rings in my ear as my eyes rove the area for a landmark to give to the dispatcher. The Trader Joe's is across the street, the parking lot where Hazel was supposed to leave my Toyota. It won't be there, of course. She doesn't want me to drive off into the sunset now. She wants me to get on a plane and disappear. Without ever knowing who Jesse was, or why he is dead.

But then I see it. At the back of the lot, far from the store entrance. My car.

"What the fuck, Hazel?" I mutter. Is this a trap? I hang up the phone just as the taxi dispatcher answers. Cautiously, I scurry across the busy street and enter the parking lot. My eyes are peeled for cops, security guards, Benjamin Laval, but the car and I are abandoned. And ignored.

The keys are on the back tire, just like Hazel said they'd be. Hurriedly, I open my trunk. Everything is there. Or it seems to be. But wait…the Nirvana T-shirt where I'd kept the netsuke is wrinkled, tossed on top of the pile of clothing. Digging through my backpack, I can't find the smooth carved snake. Hazel must have taken it. But why? To help me? Or to set me up?

Slamming the trunk, I hop into the driver's seat and reach carefully under the seat for my knife. It's not there either. I lean over and search the passenger floor. Squeezing over the console, I feel around in the back seat. My weapon is gone. Hazel undoubtedly took it. Was Jesse stabbed with my knife? Am I going to be framed for his murder?

A shopping cart crashes into a post, and I jump, my heart hammering in my throat. I need to get out of here. Someone could be looking for me right now. Righting myself, I fumble with the keys in the ignition and pull carefully out of the lot.

As I drive toward Jesse's apartment, I make a deal with myself. If the cops are there, I will ditch my car somewhere and go to the airport. I'll pack a bag, turn my cash into Bitcoin, and start my life over. People do it all the time. I will become Kelly Wilcox. I will accept all the things I do not know, and I will let Jesse and Hazel go.

His slack face, the punctures in his chest, the metallic scent of his blood revisit me and I feel queasy. But I push the images from my mind and keep driving until the blocky apartment building appears in the distance. I cruise past it, eyes darting around for any signs of police. Or Benjamin Laval's security detail. Or anyone suspicious. But all seems quiet, normal. An Uber driver delivers a pizza to the building next door. A woman with a green helmet rides past on her bike. At the end of the block, a landlord in sweatpants waters a sad flower bed.

Parking on a side street, I face the next hurdle. Getting inside. Last night, I'd opened the small office window as Jesse searched for my keys. If he hadn't closed it, I will be able to climb through it. I slip down the side of the building, concealed by the heavy evergreens that border it. The office window is closed, but the kitchen window is open a few inches. I yank it fully open and hoist myself onto the ledge. Wriggling inside, I land on the kitchen counter, out of breath.

With my feet on the parquet floor, I freeze, listening. The apartment is silent. The blinds are tightly closed over the barred windows, a single lamp burns in the living room, though it is daylight. Tentatively, I move through the space, peeking into the bedroom and bathroom, ensuring I am alone. That I am safe. At least for now.

My throat clogs with nostalgia as I take in the familiar surroundings. The dark gray couch where we'd sat and kissed; chatted about his sister and his nieces; had coffee and muffins. The table where we'd eaten coq au vin and sipped red wine. The bedroom where he had held me and made love to me and made me feel like I was desirable. Like I was enough. And then the frantic, almost animal sex we'd had in the entryway, against the kitchen counter, on the parquet floor.

Hazel's warning runs through my mind.

Jesse is not who you think he is.

"Neither were you, Hazel," I mutter to myself. I know I can't trust her, but those words ring true.

Something in this apartment will tell me who Jesse really was. And why he was murdered. I will find it, but I have to hurry.

39

I START IN THE BEDROOM. I'm not sure what I'm looking for, but I rummage through the closet and the dresser, lift the mattress and search beneath it. There is nothing unusual or incriminating. Just clothes, coins, a few dumbbells... The guitar case. I open it and find it empty. Did Jesse even play? I'd wanted to believe he had the soul of a poet, the body of a Greek god. I'd never asked him to play for me. Had I been a fool?

In the bathroom, I dig under the sink but find only Band-Aids, a box of condoms, and sports tape. On the counter sits a hairbrush suited to a thick mane of hair, not Jesse's short cut. In the shower, I note the vanilla-scented shampoo. They're signs of a female presence that I had ignored, hadn't wanted to see. Was that presence Hazel? Opening the medicine cabinet, I sift through bottles of over-the-counter pain meds, toothpaste, and sunscreen. I find Jesse's expensive facial cleanser: a spa brand. Reading the sleek tube, I recognize the name of the spa where I had my treatments. Hazel's spa.

My stomach churns with the knowledge. Hazel and Jesse were together. Lovers. A couple. I imagine them talking about me, laughing at me: at my body, my neediness, my pathetic circumstances.

I press a fist to my lips, stifling a sob of self-pity, while my whole body burns with their betrayal. My only friend and my lover were in cahoots against me. But why? Jesse is dead. Stabbed with my knife, most likely. Was that the plan? Or the plan gone awry?

I've accepted that lust and infatuation clouded my vision when it came to Jesse, but Hazel...Her friendship had felt genuine. Her tears and admissions of horrible abuse couldn't have been faked. And how could she be so heartless toward me after I saved her life? Maybe Benjamin Laval is not the monster. Maybe his wife is.

Scuttling back to the kitchen, I rifle through Jesse's cupboards. They are virtually empty: two plates, three glasses, a few coffee cups. There is no food except for a jar of peanut butter, a package of rice, a few cans of chili. And the protein supplements. Was Jesse really a trainer? He had to be. I'd googled him. I open the plastic tubs, sniff at the contents: chocolate, vanilla, strawberry.

In the last tub, I notice it. Peeking out of the off-white powder is a square of plastic. Just a corner. With my fingertips, I pull it out. It's a social security card. The name on it reads:

Carter Douglas Sumner

Who the hell is he, and why does Jesse have his ID? I plunge my hand farther into the canister, searching for anything else that Jesse might be hiding, but I come up empty. I dump all the containers into the sink, creating a small mountain of sweet-scented silt, but there is nothing of interest.

I need to google Carter Sumner. Hurrying to the small desk, I sit down at Jesse's laptop. It's password protected, of course. As I speculate as to the combination of numbers and letters that will grant me access, I realize how little I know about the man I'd considered my boyfriend. When is his birthday? What's his middle name? Did he have a childhood pet? A favorite grandparent? A beloved sports team?

At least I know Jesse was from Spokane. It's too simple, too obvious, but I type it in in desperation. Rejected. Panic flutters in my belly. I will have a limited number of tries before I'm locked out permanently. His nieces! Surely, he hadn't invented their existence. He'd told such specific anecdotes about them. He'd have to be a compulsive liar, a complete sociopath, to make them up.

One of them is called Ella, the other, Olivia. No...Olive. That's right. How old are they? Six and nine? Or five and eight? And which one was older? I calculate their birth dates in my head, and try their names, followed by their year of birth. The computer warns me that I have one more attempt.

With trembling hands, I sift through Jesse's desk for some sort of clue. At the back of the second drawer, I find a moleskin notebook, a black pen clipped to the cover. Maybe Jesse wrote down his passwords? There has to be something useful inside. I'm about to open the journal when a heavy knock at the door shatters the silence.

My pulse pounding in my ears is louder than the knuckles on the wood. I freeze, waiting for the word "Police!" But there is silence. And then another knock. Insistent. Menacing. This is not just a friend, a landlord, a delivery person. It is someone looking for Jesse. Or looking for me.

With the notebook in hand, I scurry back to the kitchen. As quietly as I can, I climb onto the countertop, bruising my shins on the sharp Formica edge, and scramble out through the window.

40

THE INTERNET CAFÉ IS DIM, grimy, and familiar. It may not have been smart to return to a venue I'd previously visited, but it felt safer than driving around, searching. I'm almost sure I haven't been followed; no one seems to be on my tail. Not yet anyway. And I know this place. I know they accept cash. I know the customers keep to themselves, mind their own business. People use a public computer for a myriad of reasons, not all of them legitimate.

I sit at the same desk as I did the last time I was here. My fingers touch the smooth outline of the social security card in my pocket as the computer boots up. The PC is old, slow, and cheap. When it is finally ready, I check the Seattle police online blotter. There are a handful of crimes reported: a carjacking in Tukwila; a Renton domestic incident where a woman shot her partner in the leg; two men arrested with drugs and guns after a traffic stop. But there is no report of a man stabbed to death in a luxury home northwest of the city. Surely by now Hazel has come home, seen the body, called the police.

Unless...she didn't call them. Unless...she didn't want the police to know that her lover had been murdered in her own home. But why? Was I meant to find my boyfriend's body? Was I meant to go down for the crime? If so, why would she leave me the money and the plane ticket?

Shaking my head to dislodge the swirling suspicions, I type in the name:

Carter Douglas Sumner

The results load slowly, and I feel my pulse quicken. Who is this man, and why did Jesse have his identification? The only possibilities I can fathom are shady, illegal, even nefarious. But speculation is pointless. Soon I will know the truth.

The screen displays a handful of news articles, all variations on the same headline from 2016.

Brothers charged in violent home invasion

Home invasion gone wrong lands brothers in jail

Pillar of the community badly beaten in home invasion robbery

Is Carter Sumner the villain or the victim? Did Jesse hurt him and steal his ID? Or does Carter have something to do with Jesse's murder? And what does Hazel know about this man? I click on the first article and read.

Two brothers face numerous charges after a breaking and entering on Mercer Island turned violent. The stately home on Ferncroft Road was broken into around 10:40 p.m. on July 25. Two men entered the residence by breaking a basement window and proceeded to steal several thousand dollars' worth of jewelry and electronics.

Before the intruders could flee, the homeowners, Donald

> *Fryer, 64, and his wife, Sunny Fryer, 59, returned home from a social engagement. Mr. Fryer was attacked upon entering his home and sustained serious injuries. Mrs. Fryer was bound at the wrists and ankles and locked in a closet while her husband continued to be brutalized. Donald Fryer was admitted to the hospital and remains in a medically induced coma. Doctors say his injuries are life-altering.*
>
> *Several days later, after reviewing surveillance footage and interviewing Sunny Fryer, police arrested two brothers for the crime. Sean Reginald Sumner, 29, and Carter Douglas Sumner, 25, were found in Othello and taken into custody by Seattle police. The Sumner brothers have been charged with breaking and entering, false imprisonment, theft under $5,000, and assault causing bodily harm. Sean Sumner has known ties to gangs and the drug trade. Carter Sumner has no record but is known to police.*

I feel no surprise that Carter Sumner is a criminal. Was he a friend of Jesse's? Did Hazel know him too? Or was he a victim, just like I was? Another target of one of their plots? I try searching Carter Sumner and Jesse Thomas together, but Jesse's name does not appear with the other man's. I add Hazel Laval to the search, but nothing new shows up. Hazel's name is associated with a few charity events: a gala fundraiser for breast cancer and a fashion show for children's literacy. She is a society wife, just like she told me she was. So, I go back to the second article about the Sumner brothers and read through it. The information is virtually the same, but about halfway through the piece, there is a photograph.

It was taken from a distance. There are a number of squad cars in the foreground, and a suburban street forms the backdrop. Several heavily armed police officers escort the two brothers away from a stucco bungalow. Their hands are cuffed behind their backs; their expressions are stony. The Sumner brothers are big men, with broad, muscled shoulders and thick necks, but the similarities end there. The older brother, Sean, is closer to the camera. His dark hair is cut short, and even from a distance, I can see that his eyes are a steely blue against his swarthy complexion. Notably, his nose appears to have been broken, more than once. The younger brother is farther away, but his hair is lighter, his lips fuller, his nose aquiline. Though it is impossible to see in the photograph, I know his eyes are hazel with flecks of gold. Because Carter Sumner is Jesse.

Or, more correctly, Jesse is Carter Sumner.

The discovery doesn't shock me. In fact, I feel nothing as I stare at my lover's image: the cold look in his eyes, the hard set of his jaw, the slight sneer on his lips. Jesse was a thief. He broke into a couple's home and beat them brutally. My boyfriend was a violent criminal. His arrest is the final piece of the puzzle, clicking into place.

On some level, I knew…not the details, of course, but the fact that Jesse's past was shady. I'd never asked about his bare apartment, his stick and poke tattoos, the car he surely couldn't afford. I didn't question him about his history because I had secrets, too, parts of myself I wanted to hide. And so I gave him the benefit of the doubt. Hazel, too. And now I am paying for that blind trust.

I look at the photo again, these two handcuffed men being taken away. I know Carter Sumner is dead. But where is his brother, Sean? And what does he know? He is my only link to the man I thought I knew. The man I cared about.

Only Sean Sumner can give me the answers I seek.

41

I DRIVE SOUTH TOWARD A strip of cheap motels and all-night diners. The sun is low now and the tall signs are lit, advertising all-day breakfast, free Wi-Fi, and adult channels. With the bag full of money, I could afford to stay somewhere decent, even luxurious, but without a credit card for incidentals, my options are seriously limited. And I need to keep a low profile. I am on the Laval security camera walking into the scene of a crime. My footprints and fingerprints are there, stamped in blood. I look guilty...just like Hazel wanted.

The exit that would take me to Uncle Jack's diner looms ahead and elicits a pang of remorse. I was supposed to work today at four. What did my boss, Randy, think when I didn't show up? I'd been consistently reliable, but he wouldn't be surprised. I worked for cash under the table. He wouldn't expect a written letter of resignation or two weeks' notice. And he owes me money from my last paycheck. Maybe he's glad I up and vanished.

I think about the day that Jesse came into the diner, sat down at the bar. His presence had thrilled me. He had sought me out after our garage encounter, and I was flattered. But now I wonder...Did he have another motive for finding me? Was it all part of his and

Hazel's twisted plan? It comes to me then, a quick flash of memory: Randy and Jesse exchanging a few muttered words. At the time, I'd assumed it was a simple customer interaction, but I'd noted the tense familiarity between them. Did Randy know Jesse? Or, more correctly, Carter Sumner?

The night when Jesse and I made love up against my car—*fucked*—in the alley behind the restaurant...Vincent had suddenly appeared when we were done. Or had he been watching the whole time? Had Jesse told him what we were going to do? Was it some sort of sick game? I am paranoid, suspecting everyone. But why wouldn't I? Hazel was my only friend. I had believed Jesse and I had something promising and real. But all along, they were playing me.

Five minutes later, I pull off I-5 and into a largely vacant parking lot. The Horseshoe Motel is set back from the highway, nestled behind a pancake restaurant and a bowling alley. The list of amenities is displayed on the overhead sign: ice machine, free Wi-Fi, business center. Access to a computer could be helpful.

A fan whirs as I enter the small office, the cloying scent of an air freshener no match for the odor of cigarettes and fast food. A middle-aged woman sits behind the counter with a book of sudoku puzzles. She looks up when I enter, her expression mildly annoyed.

"I need a room, please."

"Reservation?"

The place appears deserted. The vacancy sign is on. "No."

She heaves a sigh like this is a major inconvenience and not her actual job. She sets the puzzle book down with a smack. I pay cash up front and leave an extra hundred dollars as a security deposit. I will collect it when I check out.

"How many nights?" she asks me.

"One for now," I say, because I know I should leave. I should get on a plane and get the hell out of here...but not before I talk to Sean Sumner. "I'll pay you in the morning if I decide to stay on."

This seems to irritate her further, but she slides the key across the scratched countertop and returns to her puzzle book.

The first thing I do when I enter the hotel room is shove the strawberry-scented air freshener into a dresser drawer. I press my index fingers into my eyebrows, hoping the chemical scent is responsible for my headache, but it is likely a combination of stress, fear, and grief. Not for the death of Carter Sumner, but for the demise of Jesse Thomas. A man who had never even existed.

My car is concealed by a dumpster behind the bowling alley. If the police—or someone else—are looking for me, I don't want them spotting it parked out front. I had lugged my backpack full of clothing and toiletries to the end unit, along with the canvas bag containing my most precious items: my new passport, the money, and Jesse's notebook. As I head to the shower, I bring it into the bathroom for safekeeping.

The tub has rust stains, but the water pressure is good. I let it pummel my skull, hoping to wash away the anxiety and confusion gripping my head like a vise. Tomorrow, I hope to get some clarity. Because tomorrow, I am going to speak to Sean Sumner, Department of Corrections inmate number 62124.

Before today, I had never searched for an inmate. I'd had no reason to. It was far easier than I'd anticipated. The Washington State Department of Corrections has a comprehensive site. I typed Sean Sumner into their search engine, and it provided all the details I needed. Clicking on the name of the jail or institution even provided an address and a map. Next to each inmate's name was a link: *Register to be notified of release.* It sent a chill through me.

Had Donald and Sunny Fryer received a warning when Jesse was released from prison? Had they hired security and lived in fear that he might come after them again? And now their other abuser is out in the community, too. Sean Sumner is on a work release program, housed in a twenty-bed halfway house in Bellingham. No bars. No locks. No guards.

Turning off the water, I dry myself with a threadbare towel and wrap another one around my hair. I have slept in my clothes for so long that donning a clean but wrinkled T-shirt and fresh underpants feels like a luxury. Tearing off the bedspread, I climb into worn sheets. It is a real bed, at least, but I won't sleep. Tomorrow is too pivotal. And I can't be sure that I am safe here. That someone isn't going to kick this door in at any moment. But I can't spend the night in my car. Not without my knife.

I dig Jesse's journal out of the canvas bag and remove the pen clipped to the cover. Since I took the notebook from his apartment, I have been eager to sift through it. To find some clue as to who he really was and why he is dead. Sitting cross-legged, I open the book in my lap.

The first page has a name at the top.

Steven

And then, a series of letters and numbers.

Tri
EX 3 x 6—8, 25
KB 3 x 8—10, 25
Bi
Curl 3 x 8—10, 25
Shoulders

They are workouts—sets, reps, weights—for his clients. There are pages of them. Nothing valuable or interesting. I turn to a page with an *H* at the top. Does it stand for Hazel? The workout makes sense. Light weights, lots of reps, the focus on butt and abs.

I am about to toss the notebook aside when I spot something. In the top corner of the page, in a tiny scrawl, is a number: 206. It's the area code for Seattle. I flip through the journal, searching for further digits. Several pages later, I find four more numbers in the same precise handwriting. And then, on the inside back cover, three.

It's a phone number. It has to be. Jesse had been afraid to keep the number stored in his phone, and he didn't want to write it down in sequence, in case someone found it. But the area code gives it away. If I dial it, who will answer? It's not Hazel's number. Who was Jesse calling?

I grab the hotel phone and punch in *67 to block the caller ID. My mouth is dry, my pulse pounding in my temple as I listen to it ring. Once. Twice. Three, and then four times...

"Hello?" It is a man's voice, cool and deep. It sends a shudder through me. Do I ask who is speaking? Pretend I got a wrong number? But before I can say another word, the man speaks again. His voice is cold and mechanical.

"Lee? Is that you?"

The phone slips in my hand as fear grips my throat. Who have I called? How does he know me?

The voice travels from the receiver now pressed to my chest. "Tell me where you are..."

I slam the handset into the cradle.

42

RAIN SPATTERS THE WINDSHIELD AND headlights bounce off the puddles on the pavement, straining my eyes. It is 5:06 a.m. Soon, the late spring sun will rise, but for now, it is dark, the highway lit by streetlights and a stream of early morning commuters. I checked out of the motel, sacrificing the hundred-dollar security deposit in my haste to get away. I need to find Sean Sumner. And then I need to get on a plane.

I am driving north, headed for Bellingham. The small city close to the Canadian border is an hour and a half's drive from Seattle. The halfway house is on the edge of town, in a stately old home. Inside are twenty men, struggling to rebuild lives destroyed by the crimes they have committed. They are offered support services, like drug and alcohol counseling, employment training, and anger management classes...but finding work, and eventually a place to live, is up to them.

When the sun has risen and the city traffic thins, I pull into a drive-through coffee shop. I'm nervous to get out of my car—still worried someone could be watching me—but I need caffeine and some real food. Last night I'd had chips from the vending machine for dinner and my stomach is growling. I order a large coffee and a breakfast sandwich and move around to the pickup window. As I wait, I think about the man who answered the phone. The man who knew my name, who asked where I was. I know that I'm in danger now. There's no doubt. So why am I risking my safety to talk to Jesse's brother? What am I hoping to find?

My thoughts are jumbled and fuzzy—from anxiety and lack of sleep—but I try to make sense of this trip. It might be natural curiosity pushing me north, the need to know more about the man I was involved with. The man who tricked me into believing he was someone honest and decent. Someone who really cared about me. The man who was very likely sleeping with my only friend, an affair that had gotten him killed.

Or maybe I need to hear that, despite everything, Carter Sumner had a good side. Maybe I want Sean to tell me that his younger brother was a sweet boy once, warm and caring and loving. That he made bad choices, that he got himself into trouble, but that the Jesse I knew had existed. That he'd wanted to start a new life. That what we had was real. And then I can grieve for him. And let him go.

It is not too late to turn back. To head directly to Sea-Tac airport and get on that plane. To forget about this messy chapter and start my life over. I'm jarred from my internal debate by a teenage boy who leans out the window and passes me my order. Setting the cup in the console and the sandwich in my lap, I leave the parking lot. As I approach the highway, I deliberate for less than a second, and then I take the highway ramp headed north.

The coffee and sandwich fortify me, and the rain has ceased by the time I reach the first exit for Bellingham. Under a heavy gray sky, I wend my way through residential streets toward the halfway house. The directions are written on a slip of paper torn from Jesse's notebook, and my eyes dart from them to the road as I move deeper into suburbia. Do the people inside these quiet homes know about the twenty ex-cons living in their midst? Are they tolerant and supportive, believing everyone deserves a second chance? Or do they sign petitions, write letters to the city council, vandalize the property? *Not in my backyard…*

I park directly across the street from the halfway house. It looks like a normal home, large but innocuous, the lack of personal touches its only defining feature. The neighbors have hanging baskets of flowers, a tricycle on the porch, a pink flamingo planted in a flower bed. Sean Sumner's residence has nothing like this. It's a place to pass through on the way to a new life. Or back to jail if you screw up.

The dashboard clock reads 6:47 a.m. as I turn off the car. There is movement inside, the residents getting ready for their jobs in factories and kitchens, on the docks or in grocery stores. I sip the remains of my coffee, eyes glued to the front door, waiting for him to emerge. Will I even recognize Sean Sumner based on that one distant photo? Will he resemble Jesse in movement or mannerisms? Somehow, I feel sure I will know him.

The first man to leave the house is African American. The second, shortly after, is white but too small and wiry to be Sean Sumner. The online photo had depicted a big man, with a broken nose and piercing blue eyes. The next man who emerges could be Jesse's brother, but it's hard to tell. It's not until his icy blue gaze drifts over my car that I know it is him. Before I lose my nerve, I scramble out of the vehicle.

"Sean…," I call, crossing the street toward him. He turns, those cold eyes landing on me, but he says nothing. "Can I talk to you for a second?"

"I have work." He continues down the street.

"It's about your brother," I call after him, hoping that he'll turn around, talk to me, but he just keeps going. It's heartless to blurt it out like this, but I'm going to lose him. "Carter is dead!"

Sean Sumner stops. I see his shoulders rise in a deep, heavy breath. Slowly, he turns around and moves back toward me. "He can't be dead," he says, stopping a few feet away from me. "I'd be notified."

"I saw his body with my own eyes," I say, and my voice wobbles a little. "Carter was murdered."

A muscle twitches in Sean's jaw, the only sign that he has registered what I am saying. But I seize on it. "I'll buy you a coffee," I offer. "And tell you everything I know."

He glances at his cheap watch, and his internal debate plays out on his face. He's torn between his sense of duty and his curiosity, the need for information about his dead brother.

"Okay," he mutters.

Curiosity wins. I knew it would.

43

"I DON'T HAVE LONG," HE says when we are seated in a booth at a fast-food restaurant, watery coffees in paper cups in front of us. "What happened to him?"

I'm not sure if he's asking the cause of death or how his brother ended up murdered. "He was stabbed," I say, in service to brevity. "I don't know why."

"He was always pissing off the wrong people." He takes a sip of coffee. "I tried to keep him out of trouble."

I can't help but scoff. "The two of you broke into a home and beat an elderly couple."

He shrugs. "Clearly I failed."

Sean seems almost indifferent to his brother's murder. Inquisitive, but not sad or emotional. He must have hated his younger sibling. But even so, his apathy is abnormal. Creepy. Sean Sumner must be a sociopath. Or else, Carter was monster. A slight chill runs through me, as I think about my proximity to him. But I press on.

"Tell me about him," I say. "What was Carter like?"

He smirks darkly. "Were you one of his girlfriends?"

My face burns at his condescending tone. "Yeah. We were seeing each other."

"The ladies always fell for him," Sean says. "Carter couldn't get enough. He always had two, three, even four women on the go at one time."

I feel defensive. "The Carter I knew was kind. And caring. He loved his nieces. *Your* nieces."

He sneers. "Our sister never let us see the girls. She said we were a bad influence."

So, Jesse had concocted it all…the recorder concert, "Hot Cross Buns."

"He seemed so sincere," I murmur, almost to myself. "He seemed so…loving."

"Ask that old man how *loving* Carter was." Sean's face is hard, closed up. "My brother beat the shit out of that guy for no good reason. He was old and frail. We could have gotten away. But Carter got off on it. The violence and the power."

"But *you* went to jail. Jesse—*Carter*—didn't."

"My brother turned on me." Sean toys with a sugar packet, his fingers pressed with tension. "He played innocent. Said I dragged him into it. Said *I* beat that guy. He concocted this whole bullshit story about how he was the naïve little brother forced into a life of crime by the big bad bully."

"But that wasn't true?"

"I made mistakes. I made bad choices. But I fell into the life. Carter *chose* it." His face is twisted and ugly as he continues. "We didn't have the easiest time of it when we were kids, but Carter was born rotten. Bad to the core. From day one."

I remember reading that sociopaths are made—shaped by their environment and circumstances—but psychopaths are *born*. Their manipulative nature, their lack of remorse, their delight in hurting others, is genetic, predetermined. Had I fallen for a man who didn't have the capacity to feel love or warmth or empathy? Who delighted in toying with me physically and emotionally? Had I really been so needy? So gullible?

Sean takes a sip of coffee and continues. "But the prosecutor believed Carter and let him cut a deal. He got two years in jail. I got twelve, reduced to seven on appeal." He leans back in his chair, meets my gaze. "My own baby brother hung me out to dry. And it didn't bother him a bit."

I think about Teresa. Her anger toward me that will never dissipate. "You must really hate him," I say.

"Carter was always weak. His lawyer manipulated him. Convinced him that turning on me was the only way to save himself. The person I really hate is Benjamin Laval."

My coffee sloshes in its paper cup. My mouth opens but the words won't come. The circuitry in my brain is overloaded by this information. Finally, I whisper: "*Benjamin Laval* was your brother's lawyer?"

"I know. He's a big shot. Still not sure how Carter could afford him. My brother had connections, though. Shady friends with a lot of money."

Sean Sumner thinks I'm impressed that Carter secured such a high-powered attorney. He keeps talking, though his words feel far away now, like I'm at the bottom of a deep well and he's on the edge of it.

"I never want to go back inside," Sean continues, oblivious to my distraction, "but if I ever get a clear shot at that bastard, I'll risk it." He takes a sip of his coffee. "Someone will take him out one day. Laval is crooked. He's screwed over way too many people. Bad people. He surrounds himself with security, but someone will get through."

I meet his cold blue eyes. "When I found your brother's body, it was in Benjamin Laval's house."

His face pales with genuine surprise, but he sits back, affects a casual pose. "Carter must have really pissed Laval off."

"Yeah. He must have."

"So, Laval killed him. Or had him killed, more likely." Another dark chuckle. "He'll get away with it, though. He's too smart. And too ruthless. He won't be taken down for getting rid of a low-level dirtbag like Carter."

We don't speak for a moment, both of us processing what we have learned, what it all means. Sean Sumner's blue eyes dart to his wrist again. He sits forward abruptly. "I have to go. I can't be late for work."

We get up and hurry outside. "Thanks for the coffee."

That's it. That's all he says as he walks off toward the center of town. I stand for a moment, watching him go. There is more I want to ask, more I need to know, but it's too late now.

I'd come to Bellingham to find answers. I am leaving with more questions.

44

IT DOESN'T TAKE A DETECTIVE to put the puzzle together. Jesse—*Carter*—hired Benjamin Laval to represent him after the breaking and entering. During that time, Jesse must have met Hazel. There had been a spark between them—two gorgeous but damaged people, a forbidden attraction. Benjamin convinced Jesse to turn against his brother in exchange for a shortened sentence. When Jesse got out, he and Hazel began their affair in earnest. But Benjamin Laval discovered it, and he—or one of his henchmen—stabbed Jesse to death.

Now I wonder if Benjamin was the horrible abusive husband Hazel had made him out to be. Or had she concocted the whole story so that I'd help her run away with her lover? Could Hazel have lied so convincingly? I had seen the damage: the bruises on her back, the black eye. It could have been faked, but it had felt so real. It still felt real.

My role in the scenario is murky. Why did Jesse find me and seduce me? What purpose did that serve? He had made love to me—sometimes gently, sometimes so passionately it bordered on rough. Why would he do that if he was in love with Hazel, planning a life with her? And if Hazel was on her way to the airport, why had Jesse gone into her house?

These are questions I will never have answered. Because I am going to get on a plane, *today*, and I am going to start my life over. I have wasted too much time, taken too many chances. I need to take the money and ID Hazel left for me, and get the hell out of Dodge. There is only one thing I must do first.

Traffic is already thickening, though I'm still ten miles from downtown Seattle. I will bypass the city, head straight to Sea-Tac. When I am close, I will ditch my car, collect what belongings I can, and take a cab to the airport. I'll get on the first flight to Dallas, transfer there for my South American leg. And no one will ever hear from me again.

There is a weigh station for transport trucks, and I pull into it, stopping my car some distance from the big rig occupying the scale. My hands tremble as I grab my phone, dial the only number I know from memory. The Sumner brothers—their crimes, trials, and betrayals—have put my relationship with my sister in perspective. What I did to her is not unforgivable. Not comparatively, anyway.

She answers on the third ring, her voice cool and suspicious. She doesn't recognize the number of this street phone, of course. She probably thinks it's a spam call, or a telemarketer. My voice is hoarse, barely recognizable, when I say her name. "Teresa..."

There is a long silence and I expect her to hang up, but she speaks. "Where are you?"

"I'm leaving the country," I tell her. "But I couldn't go without talking to you first."

Her response is frosty. "About what, Lee?"

"About what I did." The lump in my throat makes it hard to speak, but I press on. "I was going to tell you that I saw Clark with that woman. I really was. But I needed money. I was in danger. I was desperate...I'm so sorry."

"You've told me all this before."

"I know, but now…now you know how bad it was. Now you know that I had to disappear. That I wasn't safe!"

My sister sighs exasperatedly. "Clark and I are married now. I really don't think it's possible for you and me to have a relationship. Not after what you did to him."

She hasn't changed her stance, hasn't softened over time. "Okay…"

"Clark had an addiction. He has mental health issues. And you took advantage of that."

Clark couldn't keep it in his pants. Thankfully, she can't see me rolling my eyes. "Got it," I say, and it almost sounds sincere. "But I'm going to call you, okay? Once a year. Just to check in."

"If you want, but I'm not going to change my mind."

"Tell Mom and Dad that I love them. And that I'm fine."

And then I hang up. I have done what I can, and now I need to go. Dropping the phone into the console, I drive slowly toward the highway entrance. But before I even reach it, the phone rings again. Teresa clearly has more to say. Maybe she wants to give me a piece of her mind—*another* piece. Is it possible that she's already reconsidered my apology? Could she be prepared to accept it, to accept *me* back into her life? Would I stay? Risk my safety to try to rebuild my relationship with my sister? My family? I don't know.

I pull over and grab the phone. On the call display, I see the name…

Hazel.

My heart skitters in my chest. I don't know if I should answer. Hazel played me, used me, set me up. But she also saved me. With a fake passport, money, a plane ticket. What could she possibly have to say to me after all she has done? My curiosity gets the better of me, and I accept the call.

"Hello?"

"Hello, Lee." The voice is calm, male, familiar. It is the same voice that answered when I dialed the number I found in Jesse's journal. The deep masculine voice that called me by name, that asked me where I was.

"This is Benjamin Laval. We need to talk."

My throat is thick, coated with fear. "About what?"

"You need answers. And I have them."

He beat his wife; I feel sure of it now. And he killed Jesse. That is without a doubt. "We can talk now. On the phone."

"This isn't a secure line," he says. "And I have something to give you."

Still, I hesitate. Because I was ready to get on that plane with my remaining questions. I'd convinced myself I didn't need to know why I'd been manipulated and used. Why Jesse found me and seduced me. Why he'd gone into Hazel's house and gotten himself murdered.

"You're not in any danger from me." Laval intrudes on my thoughts. "We're both victims, Lee. Of Jesse. And of Hazel."

I believe him—in this regard, at least. So, I name a park on the south side of the city, a safe, public space. "Meet me there in half an hour."

"See you then," he says, and he hangs up.

With my hands sweaty on the steering wheel, I pull back onto the highway.

45

I LINGER IN THE PARKING lot for a few moments, observing him. Benjamin Laval is dressed down in dark jeans, a linen shirt, and a gray jacket, but his distinguished air is palpable despite his casual attire. He appears to be alone, though I suspect his security team is not far away. A black SUV at the back of the lot looks suspicious. The windows are tinted, so I can't see who is inside, but I assume it's a bodyguard. Perhaps more than one.

Climbing out of the car, I cross the grass toward him. He's standing behind a park bench, eyes focused on a distant stand of trees. I should be afraid of him—I know he is violent, cruel, and ruthless—but I'm surprisingly calm. If Benjamin Laval wanted me dead, I would be by now.

He turns as I approach, his eyes appraising me. "Thanks for coming."

"No problem."

"Shall we sit?"

We do, a couple of feet between us, our eyes facing forward. He starts the conversation off.

"I represented a young man named Carter Sumner. You know him as Jesse Thomas."

"Yeah, I know," I say, glancing over at him. He doesn't ask me how I know, and he doesn't meet my gaze. He just keeps talking.

"I got him the shortest possible sentence for a violent breaking and entering. Two years. He only served fourteen months."

He is the hero in his own story. It's evident in his confident, self-satisfied tone. Of course, he doesn't mention Sean Sumner, who spent seven years inside, locked away because Benjamin convinced his younger brother to turn against him. Laval's job was to represent his client's interests. Everyone else could go to hell.

"I felt for the kid," Benjamin continues, his voice taking a fatherly turn. "He was young and surrounded by bad influences. When he got out, I helped him start over. I got him a job as a trainer at a gym. I gave Carter a new name, a chance to build a legitimate life. And then he met my wife, Hazel."

"And they became lovers," I say, because I have figured this out. So far, Benjamin Laval has told me nothing new.

He shifts his body to face me. "My friend owns the gym where Jesse worked, and where Hazel exercised. He promised to keep an eye on them for me. Or an ear in this case. That's how I learned they were planning to kill me." He smiles, an eerily casual grin. "They couldn't stop whispering about their clever little plan. Jesse was going to stab me to death. They were going to frame you for the murder."

"Frame *me*?" I scoff. "Why would *I* want you dead? What possible motive could I have when we've never even met?"

He leans his arm against the back of the bench, calm and composed. "A homeless woman lived in the park near our house. Hazel took pity on her. Took her food. Gave her gifts. Even money. And then that woman became obsessed with her. I was in the way."

Realization dawns, hot and ugly. That's why Jesse sought me out, lured me in. So they could kill Benjamin and set me up. My lover pushed me to help Hazel with his sad story about his abused mother. He probably stole the knife from my car and had planned to use it as the murder weapon.

"They tricked you into letting yourself into the house. You were meant to discover *my* body, not Jesse's."

My throat is hoarse. "Who killed Jesse?"

"My security detail. It's their job to protect me."

"It's their *job* to stab him over and over again?"

"I'm sorry you had to see that," he says coolly. "They were supposed to have taken care of the body before you arrived."

"And where is it now?" I ask. "The body?"

"Gone. No one will ever find it. Jesse Thomas never existed."

"And the murder weapon?" Because it had to have been my knife. Why else was it missing from my car?

"Dealt with," he says without further explanation.

"What about Hazel?" I ask, out of some misplaced sense of loyalty. "What will happen to her?"

"Hazel will pay for what she did. What she *tried* to do." His smile is predatory. "She actually thought she could outsmart me. She's a stupid, delusional girl. She was way out of her depth."

Benjamin will destroy his wife. And I can't blame him. But something twists in my chest…Concern? Pity? Because despite all she has done, Hazel saved me. And I know that Jesse was charming, manipulative, and merciless. Had he used Hazel like he used me? She is so weak and damaged from her husband's obvious cruelty; it's no wonder she fell under Jesse's spell.

Start over. Rebuild your life. Jesse is not who you think he is.

Benjamin interrupts my internal musings. "I need to ensure that you won't talk to anyone about this."

That's why he's really here. To protect himself. To cover up a murder.

"It wouldn't look good for you," he continues. "You were in my home without permission. Your prints are everywhere. The obsessed stalker narrative could still play out."

It's a threat. "I won't say anything," I promise.

"It's best if you leave Seattle," he says, eyes boring into mine.

"You have no family or friends here. And you lost all your money when the Aviary went under."

Of course a man like Benjamin Laval would look into my past.

"I have a friend with a successful restaurant in Austin." He withdraws an envelope from a jacket pocket. "He'll take you on as a sous chef. It's a great opportunity."

So, he *doesn't* know everything. He doesn't know that Hazel already offered me an escape route.

"There's money here. A plane ticket. And my friend's contact details. Start your life over, Lee. And forget you ever knew Carter Sumner. Or my wife."

I take the envelope. Because if I don't, if I refuse to go quietly, he will dispose of me. Like he did Jesse.

"You'll never hear from me again," I say as I stand. "I promise you that."

I walk briskly back to my car, eyes forward, shoulders squared. It is only when I reach for the door handle that I realize I am shaking.

46

AFTER MONTHS ON THE STREET, feeling hopeless and afraid, I suddenly have options. I have money, two plane tickets, and a job waiting for me. I can rebuild my life as Lee Gulliver. Or I can start a new one as Kelly Wilcox. It is a heady feeling, both exciting and terrifying. My escape is so close, but I am not free—or *safe*—yet. And I am not sure who to trust…Hazel or her husband.

I park my car at a meter and slide my finger under the flap of Benjamin Laval's envelope. Inside, I find a flight itinerary—a direct flight to Austin, leaving tonight. It's just a four-hour journey, nonstop to a new life. There is a stack of money there, too, hundred-dollar bills. Glancing around to ensure no one is watching me, I thumb through them. Twenty-five grand. With the money from Hazel, I have seventy-five thousand dollars. It's a lot. Enough to rebuild. Almost enough to repay my debt to Damon. *If* he found me.

Shoving the envelope into the canvas bag, I get out of the car and slip into the familiar café. I pay at the counter, then head directly to *my* computer. This place feels comfortable now, but it will be the last time I visit. Because, while my destination may be unknown, I know I can't stay in Seattle. My freedom, even my life, is in jeopardy here. I have promised to disappear, and I plan to. My first online search is the restaurant in Austin. It is indeed successful, well-known, and probably a good opportunity for me. I could regain some semblance of my old life. Reestablish a relationship with my family. Teresa wants nothing to do with me, but one day, Clark will betray her again. He'll have another affair. And then she will need me.

But if I go to Texas, Benjamin Laval will keep tabs on me. He'll make sure I keep my mouth shut. And if he ever needs to, he will send me down for Jesse's murder. If the body ever resurfaces, or Sean Sumner reports his brother's murder, Benjamin will come for me. As long as that man knows where I am, I will never stop looking over my shoulder.

My next search is Panama. I know little about the country except for its famous shipping canal and what Hazel told me: that it's the perfect place to hide from the past, to use cash to start your life over. I learn that the Central American country is located on an isthmus, the bridge of land that connects North and South America. It is bordered by Costa Rica to the west and Colombia to the southeast. The Caribbean Sea touches the north coast, and to the south, the Pacific Ocean. It is beautiful and prosperous and culturally vibrant.

Obviously, I can't fly into a foreign country with a bag full of cash. But I've noticed Bitcoin ATMs scattered around the city and setting up an online crypto wallet only takes me a few minutes. If I choose this plan, I can deposit my cash at an ATM here and claim it when I get to Panama. And then I can start my life over. Get a job at a restaurant in Panama City or open my own place. Maybe build a little fish shack on the Caribbean. Thanks to Hazel and Benjamin, I have enough money now. But Hazel will know where I am, know that I am living as Kelly Wilcox. And Hazel Laval can't be trusted. She is capable of having her husband murdered and setting me up for it.

So, who do I fear the most? Which life is the safest? Or do I start over on my own terms? Take this money and build a brand-new life somewhere else? A seaside village in Scotland. A stylish arrondissement in Paris. A funky neighborhood in Berlin…

Jesse's journal and pen are still in my canvas bag. I dig them out and open the notebook full of exercise programs. And then I bring up my flight options. If I choose Panama, when can I leave? It is a long flight—over eleven hours, but the distance makes me feel safer. I write down the first flight, leaving tonight, with a three-hour stop in Houston. It departs just after the Austin flight. My next option is not until tomorrow. If I spend one more night at the motel, will I be safe?

As I peruse another travel site, Jesse's pen rolls off the table and lands with a heavy clunk. Reaching down to retrieve it, I realize it has broken, the top half completely severed from the bottom. Picking up the two pieces, I notice that one half of the pen contains a USB stick.

I have never seen this before—a working pen with a concealed thumb drive—but it's probably not that unusual. Out of curiosity, I plug the storage device into the computer. I'm expecting more exercise routines, maybe a nutrition schedule, but two audio files pop up. They are labeled simply: *Tape 1* and *Tape 2.*

My brow furrows as I inspect the pen further. It's an actual pen, but I notice a small microphone embedded in it, and the clip is an on/off switch. I have heard of these covert recording devices, these "spy gadgets." They are sometimes marketed to students to record class lectures, but they're perfect for surreptitious taping. So, what—and who—had Jesse recorded?

I need to listen to these files, but not here, not in public. I need headphones. There were a pair in my trunk at one point, but I haven't seen them since my iPhone was stolen. And would they be compatible with this computer? Scanning the room, I see a guy seated near the door wearing earbuds plugged into the desktop. With the canvas bag in hand, I approach him.

"Excuse me?" I tap the desk to get his attention. His eyes dart up to me and he quickly closes his onscreen window. Whatever he was perusing—porn probably—he doesn't want me to see it.

"Yeah?" He's instantly wary of me…and for good reason. My clothes are worn and rumpled. Despite the night at the hotel, I am exhausted, wearing my stress and fear on my face.

"Can I borrow your earbuds? I'll give you fifty bucks."

He snorts. "You serious?"

"I only need them for a few minutes. Half an hour, at the most."

"I'm using them," he says, clocking my desperation. "Make it a hundred."

"Fine." I fish in the canvas bag and remove two fifties.

"I should've asked for more," he mutters as he unplugs the cord and hands them over.

He could have asked for two, three, even five hundred dollars. I am that curious. I am that desperate.

Back at the computer, my hands fumble to plug the headphone jack into the socket. Wiping the earbuds vigorously on my shirt, I insert them into my ears. And then I hit play on the first audio recording.

Within seconds, I wish I hadn't. Because what I am hearing makes my blood run cold and my stomach churn. I am listening to a crime being committed. And in the thick of it, Jesse's voice is clear, concise, and inhuman. I realize…this is not Jesse at all. This is Carter Sumner. The criminal who beat an elderly man for no reason. The defendant who sent his brother to jail for his own actions. Carter is—*was*—a sociopath. A monster. A master manipulator. Jesse never existed. Hazel didn't know him any better than I did.

With a trembling hand, I click on the second audio file. It is just as heartless, just as gruesome. I keep listening as a sharp pain stabs my temple, the circuitry of my brain overloading with the cold-blooded violence I am exposed to. Why did Carter record this? It incriminates him. But not only him, and I realize this was insurance. Because Carter's voice is not the only one captured here. Now I know that I am in greater danger than I ever realized. Even with Carter gone, I am not safe. Because the other voice is that of a murderer too. And if that person finds out I have heard these recordings, I will be killed.

Removing the earbuds, I try to steady my breathing, to calm my fluttering heart. But my body feels beyond my control: nerves tingling, pulse racing, limbs paralyzed by the shock of what I have just witnessed. Everything I thought I knew is wrong. Everyone I know has lied to me. And I have brushed up against pure evil. But if I leave now—*right* now—I can save myself. There is no time for strategy or analysis. Forcing myself to move, I drop the thumb drive into my bag; then I return the earbuds and hurry out of the café.

In my car, I lock all the doors and pull onto the street, my tires chirping on the pavement. My eyes dart to the rearview mirror, afraid that I am being followed, terrified that someone will realize what I have just heard. The thumb drive in my bag feels like a bomb, a beacon, a grenade. I must get rid of it, fast, get it out of my possession. But what I do with it will affect so many people, change their lives forever. And it will change mine. Because there is one thing I have gained clarity on.

There is no one I can trust.

PART FOUR

HAZEL

47

WHEN I WALKED INTO THE house that day and saw my husband seated at his desk, my first feeling was relief. I had successfully thwarted Jesse's plan to kill Benjamin. My lover had arrived at the back door, found it locked, and turned away. If he *had* forced his way inside, the fact that I hadn't planted Lee's knife was the final clue. Our plan could not go ahead. Jesse had left. Benjamin was alive. And I had protected Lee.

But when my husband swivels in his chair and his eyes meet mine, I see it: barely contained rage. Hatred. Disgust. "Hello, Missy." His tone is oily. "Where have you been?"

I swallow the fear coating my mouth. "At the gym. Where else?"

His face is implacable. "What are you wearing?"

Lee's clothes are shabby, ill-fitting. My husband knows I would never go out like this. "Vintage," I say, giving him a weak smile.

"Your friend was here."

"Oh, Lee?" My voice comes out high-pitched and strangled, but I press on...a faint sense of hope. "Yeah, I was going to lend her some dressy clothes. For a job interview. She borrowed my car. I walked back."

"Not her," he says, his lips curling into a malicious smile. "Your *other* friend."

I cock my head, feign innocence. But he knows. I was an idiot to think I could fool him.

"*Jesse*, I think his name was?"

I'm not sure how to play this. Do I pretend Jesse is a stranger to me? A simple intruder? Maybe a stalker? If I deny our relationship, Benjamin will know I'm lying and will punish me. If I admit we were lovers, I am as good as dead. But I have to ask…

"Where is he?"

"Oh, he's gone, Hazel." The smile is still in place. "You'll never see him again."

He doesn't tell me if Jesse is dead or alive, only that he got rid of him. Benjamin paid him off probably. I know now that Jesse loved money more than he loved me.

"I know all about your little plot, my darling." Benjamin stands, towering over me. "Did you really think you could kill me and get away with it?"

"No…" The word comes out a whisper. I take a step back.

"Clearly you did. You and your so-called *boyfriend*." He smirks. "You're so stupid, thinking you could trust him. But he never cared about you, Hazel. He was only after your money."

He's right. But how did Benjamin know? Had he beaten and interrogated the truth from Jesse? Or paid him for it?

"You never even knew his real name." Benjamin smiles when he sees me blanch. "Your lover's real name was Carter Sumner. He was a criminal. A dirtbag. A real piece of shit."

He paces around his office, like he is in court. Habit, I guess. "I was his lawyer in a violent breaking and entering case. One of his criminal associates hired me to represent him. That's how he found you, Hazel. He targeted you."

My head feels thick and foggy, and the information isn't sinking in. I knew Jesse had a shady past. The signs were there in his home, in his tattoos, and the ease with which he suggested my husband's murder. But to think that he was an entirely different person, someone Benjamin knew and I didn't, makes me wobbly. I reach behind me, hand scrabbling for the bookshelf to steady myself.

Benjamin clocks my obvious distress and smiles. "He used you to get to me, Hazel. To take what I've built through my skill and talent because he had none. He was a loser. And a user. And you fell for him."

I open my mouth to deny or apologize or beg forgiveness, but no words will come. There is nothing I can say as my husband continues. He is in litigator mode, making his closing arguments.

"Carter Sumner would have moved in with you, married you even, and then…he would have taken it all. You were nothing but a means to an end, Hazel. Disposable. Like garbage."

Do I lie? Beg forgiveness? And then it strikes me. I don't need to cringe and cower. Because it doesn't matter what Benjamin does to me now. Soon I will escape. Or I'll be dead, either by his hand or my own. At least I will be free. I have nothing left to fear.

And so I smile.

"Well, it was worth a try."

He slaps me across the face—unusual for him—but I can safely assume that he won't allow me out in public for the next few days. And he is shocked by my insolence. It is entirely brand-new. He's had me under his control for so long.

His voice is a growl. "You devious bitch."

"I used Jesse, too," I say, a wicked smile on my lips. "To get rid of you. And for sex. Which was incredible, by the way." I am taunting him, goading him. And it feels so fucking good! His face is red with rage; a vein bulges in his temple. He's on the verge of losing control. If he murders me—right here, right now—it will all be over. And he will go to jail for it. Even Benjamin Laval can't get away with killing his wife, in his own home, with his bare hands.

"Go to the room." He shoves me forward and I stumble, but I don't fall. I glance over my shoulder, another smile.

"Whatever turns you on, Chief."

Casually, I head down the stairs.

As I lie on the floor, the thin blanket over me, I think about what my husband told me about Jesse—Carter Sumner. He knew who I was when he approached me that day at the gym. Knew I had money, a beautiful house, and that I was under the thumb of a powerful man. Could he sense my desperation? That I would be easy to use and manipulate? And our plan to escape to Panama…Was it all just a ruse? My husband is right about one thing: I am stupid. Gullible. Pathetic.

My mind drifts to Lee and I pray that she got away safely, that she didn't go with Jesse. I pray that she took her new identity, and her plane ticket, and started over. Lee can live the life I had wanted. As a new person in a new country. The life Jesse had talked me out of because he wanted more. He wanted everything: the cash, the mansion, the prestige. And now he is gone, and I am trapped here.

I think about my own escape plan, how difficult it will be to execute now. I'll need Benjamin to let me out of his self-styled dungeon. I'll need to earn back his trust so he'll give me the space I need to get away, to fake my death. Drowning again? It probably makes the most sense. But my thoughts are muddled by stress and fatigue. I feel exhausted. I feel defeated. Only one thought gives me comfort. One way or another, I will soon be free. I close my eyes and fall into an exhausted sleep.

48

THE WEEKEND PASSES IN A blur. I only know the day by my husband's presence. He hasn't returned to the office, so it must be Saturday or Sunday. Eventually, I realize that he's not going back. He's working in his study because I can't be left alone. Even with Jesse out of the picture, Benjamin no longer trusts me…for obvious reasons. I had plotted his murder, to take everything he's built for my own. Is he slightly afraid of me now? It's an uplifting, even giddy, feeling.

But I play the penitent, ask my husband for forgiveness. I tell him I was manipulated by Jesse, bullied into his scheme—which is not entirely false. Eventually, Benjamin buys it. Of course he does. He thinks I am weak and stupid, incapable of power or agency. He doesn't suspect that my remorse is just a ploy to get out of the basement room. Because I can't enact my plan if I am shut away as a prisoner. And so, when my husband lets me out, I revert to my former role. I cook his meals, clean his house, take his punishments, all with a knowing glint in my eye. As the days pass, his unease is still palpable. He has not returned to his downtown office and remains locked away in his study for hours on end. He has stationed Nate inside, the big man standing near the front door, eyes subtly following me around the house. I am a lab rat trapped in a cage: studied, monitored, ultimately disposable.

One morning, after I set Benjamin's eggs in front of him, I tender a request. "May I go see my mother today?"

"No."

It's the answer I expected, so I don't respond, don't press. I had hoped to say goodbye to her, but in a way, I already did, long ago. She won't know I am gone, so she won't miss me. I have made my peace with it. But as I'm cleaning the kitchen, I notice Nate chatting to my husband, their heads bent in serious conversation. Moments later, Benjamin approaches me.

"If you want to spend your time with a zombie, go ahead," he says. "But Nate will drive you."

"Thank you." My smile appears grateful.

From the back seat of Nate's SUV, I watch the city fly past. This will be my last sojourn into Seattle, a place I have always considered my home. Now it feels like a foreign country. My world has dwindled to such a tiny radius—gym, grocery store, state park—that venturing outside of my orbit is strange and new.

"Thanks," I say to Nate, who has yet to speak.

His eyes meet mine in the mirror. They are questioning.

"For convincing Benjamin to let me visit my mom."

"You can't keep a person from their mother," he says, flicking on his indicator. "That's just wrong."

But everything about my relationship with Benjamin is wrong. And Nate knows that better than anyone.

The care home is calm, serene even, with a soft color palette and natural light flooding in through large windows. The manager, Greta Williams, a birdlike woman drowning in a chunky cardigan, leads me to a back garden where my mother is seated in a cushioned chair. She is facing a wild rosebush, the fragrance wafting toward me as I approach. Fat bumblebees flit between the pink blossoms, and my mom watches them, rapt. When I look at her face, I see a small, contented smile.

This is why I stayed with Benjamin, why I signed his contract and followed his rules. My mother is at peace here, maybe even happy. Despite all she has lost—her memories, her identity, her daughter—she is comfortable and cared for. I pull up a chair and sit next to her. Was she always this tiny? She was petite but strong; I felt it when she held me in her arms, comforted me, and supported me. Now she is softer, her body fragile and brittle, wasting away.

"Hi, Mama," I whisper, and she turns her face toward me. It is there for only a second…a flicker of recognition. She knows me, I am sure of it. And then her eyes go blank again and she turns back to the view.

I take her hand, soft and papery, and talk softly to her about our memories, the good ones only. The hard times, the mistakes, our financial struggles are all forgotten and forgiven. All I remember are the laughs, the cuddles, the unconditional love a parent has for a child. The only pure love I have ever felt. I gloss over my marriage and my affair and tell her that she raised a strong and vital woman. That I have taken control of my own destiny. That I am not a victim anymore. She doesn't notice the faint remnant of bruising under my eye, mostly camouflaged by makeup now, or the swelling on the right side of my lip from Benjamin's slap. I kiss her on the cheek.

And then I say goodbye.

49

WHEN I GET HOME, BENJAMIN is ensconced in his study. He doesn't emerge, doesn't ask after my mother's welfare, doesn't check to see if I am upset. It would be out of character—frankly, disconcerting—if he did. I can just hear his voice, serious and professional, through the closed door. I know better than to interrupt. And I feel no need to say goodbye to him.

I turn to Nate. "I'm going to take a bath."

He nods, gives me a small smile of compassion. Nate has a mother. He understands what I'm going through. He is human…unlike Benjamin. I climb the stairs slowly, my body weary. Resigned. But my spirit feels light. Because I am ready. Ready to let go. And ready to make my husband pay.

Inside the luxurious bathroom, I lock the door behind me and turn on the bathtub taps full blast. The hot water gives the air a steamy, jungle feel, and the sound of the rushing water will camouflage my voice. I won't leave a suicide note: Benjamin will feel nothing when he reads it…except maybe relief. No guilt or shame or regret. And he will destroy it instantly. Tell his friends and colleagues that I was depressed, unhinged, ill. Public humiliation is the only way I can hurt him.

Propping my iPhone on the quartz countertop, I hit record. Leaning close to the camera, I begin to speak. "My name is Hazel Laval," I say, my voice just above a whisper, shaky with nerves and emotion, "and I'm about to kill myself."

Over the past few days, I had come to accept that suicide was my only option. With my husband home and security on high alert, there was no other way to set myself free and protect my mother. But before I died, I would destroy Benjamin. I still had the power of my voice. A recorded suicide note, indicting my husband for his abuse and shared online, would ruin him. He'd be fired from his job, shunned from his social circle, maybe even held criminally responsible for my death.

"My husband, Benjamin Laval, is cruel and abusive," I continue. "He's treated me like a slave for years. He made me sign a Total Power Exchange contract giving him complete control over my life. He locked me in a room when I disobeyed him and he mentally, physically, and emotionally tortured me. I can't…no, I *won't*…take it anymore. But there is no other way out. By the time you see this message, I'll be dead. Benjamin Laval killed me. I hope he will pay for it. Somehow."

When I am done recording, I open a scheduling app. In one week, my video will post to all my social media channels. I had never been very active online, but I'd curated a sparse but perfect feed: photos of meals I'd cooked, ocean views, a selfie in a gorgeous outfit. But this video will blow away the façade. And, God willing, it will blow up my husband's life.

After I turn off the taps, I reach under the sink and remove a bottle of lemon-scented cleaning solution. A few days ago, I'd emptied it, washed it, and filled it with vodka. If Benjamin found a bottle of liquor concealed in the bathroom, he'd have been suspicious. And I would have been sent to the basement room. At the back of the drawer in my vanity rests a bottle of sleeping pills. My husband never allowed me to have more than twelve pills at a time, but I've been stockpiling them. I've got twenty-eight tablets now. More than enough, combined with the vodka. I will fall asleep, slip under the water, and I won't come up. By the time Benjamin or Nate becomes concerned and picks the lock or breaks down the door, it will be too late. I'll be dead.

My hands fumble with buttons and zippers as I slowly, methodically, remove my clothes. I already know what it feels like to drown: the intense pressure in the lungs, the moment of panic as the body instinctively fights to breathe, followed by a deep, heavy rest. The cold softened the experience for me the last time. This time, the substances will do it. And Lee won't be there to wrench me from the water.

Shaking the pills into my hand, I notice that I am trembling. I am ready, this is the best—the *only*—way, but now I'm frightened. I am a young woman, and I am about to die. Despite my circumstances, there is a flicker of life force inside me that doesn't want to be extinguished. I take a large drink of vodka. Liquid courage.

It is in that moment that I hear the front doorbell ring.

I should not be diverted from my plan—who knows when I will have another opportunity. I should swallow these pills, wash them down with more vodka, and climb into the tub. But Nate's muffled voice travels through the floorboards, followed by the voice of a woman. My curiosity is piqued. Unannounced guests are rare at our house, female ones even more so. Could it be Lee? Come to confront me for double-crossing her? Or to thank me for saving her? Dumping the medication back into its bottle, I grab a floral silk robe off the hook on the back of the door and slip into it. Tentatively, I move into the hallway.

The voices are clearer now. I hear the woman again and perhaps an unknown man. Benjamin has joined them, too. His anger and belligerence travel up the staircase. "This is a fucking outrage," he bellows, and the female voice responds, inaudibly. If it's Lee at the door, I must protect her. She is no match for an angry Benjamin.

Wrapping my thin robe tighter around me, I hurry down the stairs in bare feet.

As I scurry toward the entryway, it becomes clear that the female interloper is not Lee. Her voice is calm, authoritarian, and her words are just audible. She is reading the Miranda rights. But to whom?

I burst into the foyer. "What the hell is going on?" But it is obvious. My husband is being arrested. A muscular uniformed officer is cuffing Benjamin's hands behind his back. Like he is a common criminal. Like he is a threat to society. My chest flutters with a combination of shock, elation, and hope.

The woman, a detective I assume, given her no-nonsense blazer and slacks ensemble, approaches me. "Are you Hazel Laval?"

"Yes."

"My name is Detective French. We're arresting your husband for conspiracy to commit murder."

"Murder?" I feel chilled and exposed in my thin silk robe, my teeth chattering through my words. "Whose murder?"

Her face is grave, her lips pressed into a thin line. "Yours," she says.

50

I STAGGER BACK AS IF shoved. French reaches out, cups my elbow for support, but I don't collapse. Somehow I remain upright, though my mind is reeling with the news. *And* the logistics of it. Had Benjamin and I been simultaneously plotting each other's deaths? Or had he found out about Jesse's and my plan to get rid of him and decided I needed to die? I almost saved him the trouble. If the police had arrived an hour later, I'd have been dead.

The detective's hand is steady on my arm. "Would you like to sit down?"

I nod, let her lead me to the living room, where I sink into the sofa. Behind me, I hear Benjamin instructing Nate.

"Call David Vega. Get him to meet me at the station." And then he addresses the cops. "We'll have this dismissed at arraignment, and you'll have egg on your face."

I turn in my seat to watch the uniformed officer escorting my husband out the door. The whole scenario feels unbelievable, dreamlike. Moments ago, I had only one way out of my abusive marriage, and now my husband is being taken to jail. Something bubbles up inside me: optimism. Because if Benjamin is behind bars, he can no longer hurt me. I'll be safe. And I'll be free.

As if he can read my mind, Benjamin calls back to me. "Don't worry, Missy. I'll be home soon." Despite his pleasant tone, it is a warning. A threat. A visible shiver runs through me. French clocks it.

"Don't worry. He won't be."

"Are you sure?" My voice is husky. "Is he going to jail?"

"He'll be processed and sent to holding," she says. "He'll likely be arraigned tomorrow. Given the seriousness of these charges, and his extensive resources, I'll be surprised if he gets bail."

"You don't know him," I tell her. "He's powerful. And connected. He's a criminal defense lawyer!" My panic is building. Benjamin was planning to kill me. If he gets out, he will finish the job. I feel light-headed. Weak. Sick.

The detective attempts to calm me. "You'll be assigned a victim's advocate to guide you through the legal process," she says. "You'll be kept informed of his release, *if* it happens."

If. It's not good enough.

"You might want to consider getting your own lawyer," French says, her voice low and confidential. "This could get messy."

There's no doubt about that. And I have no one else to lean on. No friends. No family. Benjamin has made sure of it. I can hardly reach out to my circle of acquaintances, the spouses of my husband's colleagues. *You may have heard Benjamin has been arrested for planning to murder me. Would you like to try that new wine bar on Pike?*

"Most people can't afford it," the cop adds, glancing around at our luxurious surroundings, "but it can make things a lot easier."

She thinks I am rich, for obvious reasons. But despite my fine home filled with expensive art and furnishings, I don't have my own money. Benjamin gave me credit cards that I was allowed to use for clothes, groceries, and beauty treatments. I asked him for cash when I needed it, but he wouldn't necessarily oblige me. And the safe in his study is practically emptied of money. I had found the code, written on a slip of paper tucked behind a picture frame. The money was now with Lee, who was hopefully in Panama.

"I'll do it," I tell her, because I have to protect myself. "Can you recommend someone?"

"I'll see that you get a list of lawyers who handle these kinds of cases."

"Thanks."

She stands, suddenly cool and perfunctory. "We have a warrant to seize the computers and smartphones as evidence. Can you show me where they are?"

"O-of course." I get up and lead her toward the study, but Nate blocks our path.

"Can I see the warrant?" he says. He is loyal to Benjamin. He is still on the payroll. Despite our affinity, Nate is not my ally. For all I know, he could have been tasked with my murder. But he'd had ample opportunity to do it, and he hadn't. So how had my husband planned to get rid of me?

The officer hands Nate a document and he looks it over. Apparently, it's all in order because he steps aside. Detective French summons two uniformed officers with a wave of her hand, and I lead them into Benjamin's sanctuary.

The laptop is there on the desk, hooked up to a massive monitor. The police must have confiscated my husband's phone when they arrested him because I don't see it. "Did he have any other devices?" French asks me. "An iPad? An extra phone?"

"No. Not that I know of."

"We'll need your phone, too."

"But why? I'm the victim here."

"There might be texts or emails between you and your husband that we can use as evidence in our case against him."

My husband's correspondence with me was only ever instructions: what he wanted for dinner, what clothes I should wear, where I was to meet him for an event. I'm almost sure there is nothing to incriminate me on my phone. I never texted Jesse; we were careful about that. The police will only find trivial chitchat with my superficial friends. And Lee. Our conversations were so much deeper. But over text, they were logistical only. I remember the flurry of calls the day she went to the spa, but they are easily explained. A friend with car trouble. A friend who has moved on.

And then I remember the suicide video.

"My phone is upstairs," I say as panic flips my stomach over. "I…I was about to take a bath."

"Officer Deane will take you upstairs," French says, waving over a strapping young man in uniform. "I promise we'll get your phone back to you as soon as possible."

Why do I need an escort? Again, I feel like she suspects me of something, like she knows there is more to this story. But perhaps she just thinks I am too weak to make it up the stairs. I give the young officer a complacent smile and allow him to trail me to the upper level.

As we approach the bathroom, I turn to officer Deane. "I…I'm going to be sick," I tell him, and I know it's convincing. I am pale and clammy; I clutch my stomach for effect. "Can I have a moment?" He nods. To him, I am a woman who has just learned that her husband wants her dead. Nothing more. I hurry into the bathroom and lock the door.

Inside, I turn on the sink to camouflage my movements. My phone is on the edge of the tub, and I grab it, quickly canceling the scheduled video. Then I delete the recording and the app. I have already ensured my files don't sync to the cloud. The police don't need to know that I ever thought about killing myself. No one does. Because now I want to live! If Benjamin goes to jail, I will be a free woman. I can be happy! I can have my life back!

Putting the vodka-filled bottle of cleaner back under the sink, I shove the sleeping pills into the drawer and turn off the taps. I look at myself in the mirror, wan and shaky, but safe. For the moment at least. I must remain calm. I must protect my secrets. With my phone in hand, I exit the bathroom.

Officer Deane is leaning casually against the opposite wall when I emerge, but he rights himself quickly. "Here it is," I say, handing the phone to him. I notice the plastic gloves he is wearing, the plastic bag he drops it into. It's all so official, and I feel vulnerable again.

"You can get dressed," he says, "and we'll take you down to the station."

"Why do I need to go to the station?"

"Your perspective is important. It's standard procedure."

"But I have nothing to say. I had no idea my husband was planning to kill me!" The words sound like a foreign language in my ears.

"It's our job to build a case for the prosecutor. If we don't do it thoroughly, your husband could get off."

Fear sends a tremor through me, rattles my bones. If Benjamin gets released after this, he will be lethal. The officer sees my angst and presses on.

"As the intended victim, you might know something useful."

The *intended victim.* But I have so much to hide. "Of course," I say. "But can't we just talk here? I'm really not feeling well."

"Detective French would like you to come to the station."

I could crack under a harsh interrogation, spill all my secrets, my own deadly plans. But if I refuse to go, it will look bad. I will look guilty. And so, I give him an obliging nod.

"Give me a few minutes."

51

THE POLICE STATION IS LOUD, frenetic, rank with testosterone. I keep my eyes forward, alert only for Benjamin. He is somewhere in this building, and I am still terrified, even here. Detective French leads me to an interrogation room that is much smaller—and beiger—than the ones I've seen on TV. After ushering me to a wooden chair, she offers me water, soda, or a sandwich. She is being kind to me; she has clearly been trained on how to handle victims of a crime. But she is not my friend. I must not forget that.

She slides a couple of sheets of paper across the table toward me. "Here's some information on crime victim programs that you can access. And a list of victims' rights attorneys."

"Thanks."

"If you need a break at any time, just let me know."

The police are under increased scrutiny of late, their actions and attitudes judged and analyzed. Detective French is being gentle, professional, playing by the rules. The force is concerned about lawsuits, about bad press. I know this is protocol. Still, my guard is slipping in the face of her manufactured kindness. I mustn't let it. I glance at the pane of one-way glass and picture the men behind it. The same ones who took my husband away, who wandered through my house looking for evidence and taking photographs. Some of them are still in my home right now. The ones who aren't watching me.

"I need to know if I'm in danger," I say. "What does conspiracy to commit murder mean? That Benjamin was planning to kill me? How? And who ratted him out?"

"We'll make sure that you're safe," French says. It is meant to sound reassuring, but it comes across dismissive. She ignores the rest of my questions. "Tell me about your marriage."

"We didn't have a marriage." At least I can be honest about this. "I mean, we did, legally, but it wasn't a relationship. I was Benjamin's property."

"How so?"

"We had a contract. A *Total Power Exchange* contract. I did what he told me to do, or I'd be punished. If I refused him, he'd end our marriage. He'd kick me out of the house with nothing. And he'd throw my mother out of her nursing home and onto the street."

Empathy flits across her features, but her voice remains professional. "We're going to need to see this contract. Where is it?"

"It will be in his safe," I say. When I'd grabbed the money for Lee, my gloved hands shaking with nerves, I'd noted the stack of documents, but I'd been too afraid to sift through them. Too worried that Benjamin or Nate would catch me in the act. I'd quickly grabbed the money buried under the pile of papers and shut the door. "It's in his study."

"Do you have the combination?"

"No," I lie, thinking about that slip of paper hidden behind the picture frame. I can't admit that I know about it. Or that I know what's inside. "I was never allowed access."

She nods, writes something down, though I am being recorded. "You said that Benjamin *punished* you. Physically?"

"Sometimes."

"I'm sure this is difficult, but can you tell me how?"

"He would whip me with a cat-o'-nine-tails. And I had to spend hours alone in a basement room." My throat feels thick. "But the emotional abuse was worse."

"What did that look like?"

"He insulted me. He made me feel stupid and worthless." A tear slips from my eye. "He didn't let me see my own mother."

"And yet, you stayed with him?"

I bristle. This detective has drifted into interrogation mode. "Why *do* abused women stay?" I retort. "Fear. Shame. Lack of options... All of the above."

She realizes her mistake, opens her mouth to correct it, but I cut her off.

"You don't understand the kind of power Benjamin has over me. I don't have my own money or bank accounts. I'm not allowed to choose my own friends. Or order my own meals in restaurants." A shudder rips through my chest. "He controlled my body. He made me get breast implants."

"I'm sorry, Hazel." French's voice is conciliatory. "That's awful."

"My mother is a hostage." I'm crying now, fat tears falling onto the table. "If I don't do what he wants, she's as good as dead."

French reaches behind her for a box of tissues. She waits as I dry my tears, blow my nose. And then she continues.

"Did your husband have other lovers?"

"I don't know." And it is true. "He worked a lot. And he traveled. It's possible."

"And you?" she prods. "Did you find comfort in anyone else?" Her expression is soft, nonjudgmental. But I won't fall for it.

"No." My face is hot and I hope she thinks it's outrage. "I wasn't allowed to go anywhere without his permission. Even if I'd wanted to, I couldn't have had an affair."

"You must have left the house on occasion?"

Does she know something? Is she trying to catch me out? "I

was allowed to go to the grocery store," I say, my voice steady. "Sometimes for lunch with friends of Benjamin's choosing."

"Can you tell me the names of those friends?"

"Sure." I recite their names as the detective writes them down: Vanessa Vega, Laurie Gamble, a handful of other high-brow women I saw on occasion. If the police contact them, they'll be appalled. They'll gossip and speculate about the situation over wine and canapes. But that's the least of my worries now.

"Did your friends know about the abuse in your marriage?"

"No. They weren't real friends. I couldn't be honest with them. If I opened up, they'd tell their husbands, and it would get back to Benjamin."

"So, no one knew what your husband was doing to you?"

"No."

"You must have had *someone* to talk to?"

Lee. She knew it all. She had listened and supported me. Our friendship may have been a con, but there had been genuine moments.

"No," I say. "I had no one."

"Do you work out?" she asks casually, eyes on the papers before her. "Pilates? Exercise classes?"

My stomach plunges with dread. This line of questioning could lead straight to Jesse. But I maintain my composure. "I jogged mostly. In the park near my house. But I was allowed to go to yoga classes and to the gym."

"And the name of your gym and yoga studio?"

I tell her, as breezily as possible. Obviously, Jesse can't still be working there. Benjamin would have paid him off, beat him up, sent him packing. But what if one of the other trainers had noticed our chemistry? Our disappearing acts? Or what if one of Jesse's colleagues knows where he is? If the cops find him and ask him about me, what will Jesse say? He can't reveal our plot without incriminating himself, but my chest feels tight with dread.

"Any hobbies?" she asks.

"I like to bake," I tell her.

"Nothing outside the home?"

I shake my head.

"That should do it for now," French says, flipping her notebook closed. "Is there someone I can call for you? Someone who can come get you and be with you?"

The only person I can imagine comforting me right now is Lee, but she is gone. And if she isn't, she certainly won't support me. She will hate me for my betrayal.

"There's no one," I tell her. "I'm completely alone. That's how Benjamin wanted it."

She taps the sheet of paper on the tabletop. "Get yourself a lawyer, Hazel."

And with those words, my interrogation is over.

52

I SLOUCH ON THE BATTERED leather sofa, a mug of herbal tea warming my hands. The waiting area has brick walls, potted plants, and a middle-aged receptionist who glances over at me sporadically, her eyes gentle and compassionate. I had called several lawyers from Detective French's office; Rachelle Graham was the only one who could see me today. In fact, she was one of a small handful who agreed to see me at all. My husband is well-known in the legal community and has a reputation as a ruthless brawler who does not like to lose. This makes me an unappealing client. But Ms. Graham is righteous and brave. She is up for the challenge.

An Uber brought me to this office in trendy Belltown, a downtown neighborhood close to the waterfront. Our appointment isn't until six, but I have been sitting on this sofa for an hour and a half. I have nowhere else to go. I'm afraid to go home. And I feel too vulnerable to browse through shops or cafés while I wait. Too exposed. My husband was plotting my murder. I could still be in danger.

Finally, the office door opens, and a man emerges: ill-fitting gray suit, receding hairline, scuffed dress shoes. His face is pink, eyes watery, and I wonder if he has been crying. The woman who escorts him to the exit is tall with cropped hair, dark skin, and an aura of steely competence. They exchange a few words in the hallway—his voice emotional, hers reassuring. When she returns, she addresses me.

"Hazel Laval." I obediently jump to my feet. "Rachelle Graham," she says, taking my hand in her strong, warm grip. "Come on in."

In contrast to the bohemian serenity of the waiting room, her office is cluttered, chaotic…a mess, basically. But she doesn't apologize or make excuses. She ushers me toward a chair, still warm from the man in the gray suit. Rachelle sits behind a desk rendered invisible by files, papers, devices, law books.

"Let me tell you a bit about myself," she begins. "I was a prosecutor for seventeen years. You might think that their interests and yours are the same, but that's not necessarily the case. There are politics at play. Personal agendas."

I nod because my throat feels too tight to speak.

"You need a strong advocate who works for *you.* Someone who knows your rights. And who knows the system backwards and forwards. I can guide you through the criminal court process and explore avenues in civil court. My only objective is to see that you get compensation and justice."

She doesn't need to sell me. I am in. We discuss her fee and I assure her I can pay. I have access to my credit cards—for now, at least. And there are valuable items in my home that I can sell. Rachelle instructs her assistant to prepare a contract, and then she opens a laptop perched atop a pile of documents.

"So…your husband has been arrested for conspiring to murder you."

It almost sounds comical in her breezy tone. "Yep."

"Tell me…"

And I do. Against the soundtrack of her fingers on the keyboard, I tell her about our Total Power Exchange contract, about Benjamin's cruelty and control.

"I need to see that contract."

"The police will have it by now," I say. And then I tell her that my mother's well-being kept me captive, that she would die on the street if I ever left my husband. "I had no life of my own," I finish. "I was no more than a pet. A possession."

"Did you have a prenup?"

"Of course. Benjamin made sure that I'd get practically nothing in the divorce. And my mother's care would be terminated."

Her fingers stop moving. "So, why kill you?"

My eyebrows shoot up in response to her question.

"I mean, he had you under his thumb. You did everything you were told. If he divorced you, he'd have to pay you a pittance. So, why does your husband want you dead, Hazel?"

I know about attorney-client privilege. I know I could tell Rachelle Graham the truth: that I was having an affair. That my lover and I were planning to murder my husband. And she would be legally bound to keep my secrets. But when I begin to speak, more lies come out.

"I have no idea. He must hate me."

"Why? Were you cheating on him?"

"No!" The word flies from my lips so easily.

"Then why would he hate you? What did you do?"

"I…I've been more assertive lately," I say, which is only true of the day he confronted me about Jesse. "I've been less obedient. Just…not doing as I'm told. Talking back. It infuriated him."

She exhales through her nose. "I'll be a stronger advocate if I know the truth, Hazel. As your lawyer—"

But I cut her off. "That is the truth."

My words sound firm, convincing in my own ears, but her brown eyes meet mine with suspicion. For a moment, I fear she'll dismiss me, tell me she can't work with a dishonest client, but eventually she breaks her gaze and changes course.

"You have a right to know the case the prosecution is building," she says, setting her laptop aside. "I'll find out what evidence they have and who they're calling as witnesses. You'll likely have to testify."

My chest clutches at the thought of facing Benjamin in a courtroom. Of the questions his legal team will ask me and the lies I will be forced to tell. "I can't."

"In Washington State, they can subpoena you. If you refuse, you could be charged with contempt."

And if I testify, I could be charged with perjury. "But I didn't know Benjamin wanted me dead," I try. "There's no point! I have nothing to say!"

"I might be able to arrange video testimony so you don't have to see your husband," she offers. "But I'm not going to lie to you. A trial will be ugly. Benjamin Laval is known to be a barracuda. His team will come at you. They'll disparage your character, bring your credibility into question. And they will be vicious."

My heart palpitates as I imagine the assault. I am no match for David Vega and the other attorneys at my husband's firm. They will interrogate me, badger me, and I will crumble. Fall apart. Incriminate myself. I will be caught out as a liar. A slut. And an attempted murderer myself. This whole situation feels like a runaway train, and every time I open my mouth, I stoke its engine.

"There's a chance this won't even get to trial," she says. "Your husband's team will be working every legal angle to make this go away."

"Go away?" I struggle to take a breath. "If he gets out..." I trail off, press my fingers into my eye sockets, feel the dampness of the tears welling there.

Rachelle's voice is calm, soothing. "For now, he's behind bars."

"But I could still be in danger. Who was he conspiring with? I need to know."

"I'll see what I can find out," she says, brow furrowed. "Have the police arranged an officer to guard your home?"

"They said they'll have a car out front."

"Change your alarm code," she instructs. "Do you have a gun in the house?"

"No. I don't know." Tears spill over at the thought of my inability to defend myself. I'm like a sitting duck, in a glass mansion. "Maybe Benjamin does. But I don't know where it is."

Rachelle gets up and moves around the desk. She gently pulls me to my feet, holds me at the elbows. "I'm on your side, Hazel," she says, eyes penetrating mine. "I'm going to keep you safe. And I'm going to get you through this."

Now I know why the man in the gray suit was crying. Rachelle Graham's fierce protectiveness in the face of so much hostility undoes me. Not since my friendship with Lee have I felt this sort of compassion, this type of support. Tears stream down my face. "Thank you," I mumble, sniffling pathetically.

Abruptly, Rachelle steps back, resuming her professional manner. "Let's take care of the paperwork," she says. "And then I'll get to work."

53

AND SO, I GO HOME because there is nowhere else. I have no friends—and even if I did, I wouldn't jeopardize their safety with my presence. A hotel is an option, but with my financial limitations, I don't want to spend the money. I need to pay Rachelle Graham. I will need to hire a divorce lawyer eventually. And I will have to start my life over—if I make it through this. If I don't end up in jail. Or dead.

The cop car stationed at the end of the driveway gives me no peace of mind as I wander through the cavernous house. I know better than anyone the many ways in and out of this place. One conspicuous squad car is not going to deter a person who is determined to get to me. There must be ways to circumvent the alarm system. Nate is gone, of course. He is on Team Benjamin. For all I know, he could be the one I am meant to fear. Surely he had knowledge of Benjamin's plan at the very least.

I am too anxious to eat, but I move to the kitchen and turn on the kettle. There are several calming tea blends and I select one, drop a fragrant tea bag into a mug. When the water boils, the whistle is like a scream, and I hurriedly remove it from the heat with a trembling hand. As the tea steeps, I grab a large knife from the block and tentatively finger the blade. Lee slept with a knife for protection every night. She was willing to plunge it into flesh, insert it deep into a man's belly to protect herself. Jesse—*Carter*—was going to stab my husband to death for a life with me. Would I be able to do the same?

I'm fooling myself. I am weak, a coward. But I add a shot of Benjamin's bourbon to my tea for fortitude. And then I carry the knife and the mug to the sofa.

Despite my exhaustion, sleep will be impossible. My brain throbs with the effort of sorting through the day's events. There is too much to process. A sleeping pill would put me out, but I need to be on my guard. Because my husband may be behind bars, but he wants me dead. And Benjamin always gets what he wants.

When my cell phone rings, the sun is up, the early morning rays filtering through cedar trees and into my vast living room. I prop myself up on the sofa, where I must have drifted off. Clearly, the sedative effects of the bourbon were powerful on someone not used to drinking. My fingers feel fat and clumsy as I fumble for the phone.

The caller is my lawyer, Rachelle Graham. I clear my froggy throat, try to sound alert and awake. "Hello?"

"Your husband is being arraigned this afternoon," she tells me without preamble. "It's a serious charge but given who he is, he could get bail."

"Detective French said he wouldn't! She said I didn't have to worry!"

"*If* he does, I'll talk to the prosecutor about conditions. A no contact order and a restraining order."

"C-can I stay here?" I ask. "This is *his* house."

"You've lived there for almost a decade, Hazel. It's your home, even if your name isn't on the deed."

"But the prenup?"

"Given the circumstances, you should be able to challenge it. You'll have to get a divorce lawyer to review it, but I'm sure she'll find grounds to change or even nullify it."

"Can you do that?" I ask hopefully. "I don't know if I can afford another lawyer."

"That's not my area of law. But a divorce attorney can petition the court to have Benjamin pay your legal fees."

"Okay," I say, but my voice wobbles. This is all too much. I am overwhelmed, getting confused, coming undone.

"We'll worry about that later," Rachelle says, picking up on my angst. "But for now, stay put. Let's see how his arraignment goes."

"Is there any chance the case could get dismissed?" My husband's threat to the arresting officers replays in my mind.

"That almost never happens at arraignment." I hear her deep intake of breath as she recognizes Benjamin's power. "But pack a bag. Get your affairs in order. Just in case he comes home."

I shower quickly, knowing how vulnerable I am in this glass enclosure, hot water obscuring the sound of an intruder's approach. With my hair wet, I pack quickly and efficiently: clothes, toiletries, medications, and jewelry. I stuff as much into the suitcase as I can; if Benjamin is released, I'm not sure when I'll be able to return. Hopefully, at some point, I will be allowed to safely collect the rest of my belongings, but I don't know when.

As for getting my affairs in order…I don't even know what Rachelle means. I have spent most of my adult life sheltered, living under my husband's thumb. In many ways, I'm like a child. The simplest financial tasks are beyond my comprehension. I don't have my own bank accounts. I don't know how to pay bills. I don't know if I own anything of value or if it all belongs to my husband.

I am shoving a handful of socks into the suitcase when the doorbell rings. My heart lurches in my chest. Good news does not show up at my door.

Stumbling down the stairs, I realize that I am holding my breath.

I inhale slowly, an attempt to calm myself as I move to the front door. Through the glass panel of the entryway, I see the police officer tasked with guarding me. I clock his calm, almost jovial expression. My shoulders relax when I see Vanessa Vega standing next to him. She is wearing jeans, a cropped jacket, and stylish flats. She is holding a casserole dish. Relief bubbles up in me, makes me temporarily buoyant. Vanessa may not qualify as a friend, but she is certainly *friendly*. I pull open the door.

"She's fine," I tell the officer before he can speak. I usher Vanessa inside.

"Eggplant parm," she says, referencing the dish. "Heat it in the oven at three-fifty for an hour."

"Thank you." It is a kind gesture, and my throat thickens. "That's really sweet of you."

"It was an excuse," she says, voice lowered. "We need to talk."

"Okay. Would you like tea?"

"I don't have time. David didn't want me to come but I told him that you're my friend. It would be rude not to bring you a casserole at least."

My *friend*. Though our relationship had been nothing but shiny surfaces.

Vanessa leads the way to the kitchen. "Benjamin's going to get off," she says, putting the casserole in the fridge. "You know that, right?"

"My lawyer said—" But she isn't finished.

"David and the other partners are consumed with the case. They're meticulous and brilliant. And they're *ruthless*. They *will* get the case dismissed, Hazel. It's only a matter of when. You need to be ready."

Feeling unsteady on my feet, I slide onto a barstool. Vanessa takes a seat next to me.

"You need your own lawyer."

"I have a lawyer. A victim's rights attorney."

"Good. You'll need a divorce lawyer, too." She cocks an eyebrow at me. "Obviously you want to divorce him."

"O-obviously," I stammer, though my thoughts have been on more pressing matters. Like the threat on my life.

"And your prenup won't hold up now. Not after he planned to kill you." I'm impressed by Vanessa's knowledge. Was she a lawyer once? A paralegal? Or has she gone through a divorce herself? I have never asked who she was before David Vega.

"Do you still have your credit cards?"

"Yes."

"Go to the bank and get cash advances. Benjamin will cancel your cards as soon as he gets a chance." Her eyes drift around the open room. "There are a lot of valuable items in this house. The art. The sculptures. You should hire an asset advisor. I'll send you a name."

"Thanks."

She turns to face me. "What about your LLC?"

"My what?"

"Benjamin makes a lot of money. I'm sure he filters some of it through a limited liability corporation in your name. Did you sign anything?"

"I signed a lot of things. I signed whatever he asked me to."

"You need access to that account, Hazel." She digs in a designer purse, extracts a matching wallet. From it, she presents a business card. "George Scofield is a forensic accountant. Call him."

I stare blankly at the card. "I…I don't know what that is."

"George will find out what Benjamin earned during your marriage. I'm sure it's hidden…in businesses, offshore accounts, creative investments. But George is great at finding out where the bodies are buried." She realizes her mistake, pats my hand. "Not literally."

There is a weight on my chest, and I struggle to take a breath. I don't know how to do this. To hire lawyers and accountants and to fight for what is rightfully mine. My vision blurs as tears well in my eyes.

Vanessa rubs my back. "I know this is a lot to take in. But I couldn't stand by and let Benjamin destroy you. Not like he did his first wife."

My head snaps up. "His *first* wife?"

"He didn't tell you about Karolina?" But it is obvious he didn't. "Christ," she mutters, shaking her head. "We were told not to mention her. That it was awkward and uncomfortable for Benjamin. And David said the marriage was a *blip*. A mistake. That Benjamin shouldn't be haunted by a bad choice he made years ago."

Since I became Mrs. Laval, Vanessa has been the closest thing I've had to a real friend. But she'd still adhered to Benjamin's wishes. She'd still kept his secrets. My voice is breathy, incredulous. "Tell me now."

"They were only together for a couple of years. She was from Poland. When she left him, he said she was homesick. He blamed cultural differences." She rolls her eyes. "But he was horrible to her. Condescending. Controlling. Like he was with you."

I am speechless. Benjamin had another wife. Another life that I knew nothing about. When we met, he made it seem like he was a workaholic, a playboy, unable to settle down...until he met me. I'd believed I was special, the only one. But, of course, it was a ruse. And he wanted to keep his first wife a secret. Because he had tried to destroy her, too.

"She went back to Poland. Benjamin was determined that she'd get nothing in their divorce. She fought back, though. David told me she filed against him from her home country."

Who was this woman who had been brave enough to walk away from Benjamin? Strong enough to fight for what she deserved? How had she not allowed him to crush her spirit, like he had mine? Unlike Karolina Laval, I am weak and small. Easily controlled by my husband. Easily manipulated by a con man like Carter Sumner.

"I wasn't close to Karolina. None of us were. So, when she left, we just...forgot about her. No one ever heard from her again."

Vanessa suddenly glances at the watch on her wrist. "I have to go. My daughter has a dentist appointment." I follow her to the front door, where she turns to face me.

"Call George. And a divorce lawyer. I'll email you the name of an asset advisor."

I nod, though none of this is sinking in through the storm of information.

"Take care of yourself, okay?" She hugs me and it is warm and comforting but over so quickly.

"Thank you," I call as her shoes *tip-tap* down the paved driveway. She acknowledges me with a wave of lacquered fingernails.

I close the door. Alone again.

54

BENJAMIN'S COMPUTERS HAVE BEEN confiscated, but they were all password protected, anyway. Thankfully, my iPhone has been returned to me. I find it on the kitchen counter and take it to the sofa. Tucking my feet underneath me, I tap in my passcode: Benjamin's birth year, per his request. It is possible—even likely—that Karolina Laval has reverted to her maiden name. If so, I won't be able to find her. But I pray that she hasn't. Because I need to connect with her. Even talk to her. I need her to tell me how I can defeat my husband.

Facebook seems the most logical place to start. I tap the app, wait as it updates and then opens. I'm not sure how to spell her first name, but I try it with a *K*, the more common European spelling. Facebook offers me three profiles. One has a different spelling of Laval. One lives in Chile. And one is right here, in Seattle, Washington.

I click on the local account. It is dormant, the last post—a GoFundMe link for a child with cancer—was shared eight years ago. Karolina must have dropped social media when she dropped her husband. The account's privacy settings are tight, and I sense my husband's hand in that. Benjamin keeps his wives sheltered, protected. He would have had all of Karolina's passwords, would have subjected her to random social media checks. I peer at the small profile picture: a pretty blond woman cuddling a French bulldog. Is this Karolina, my predecessor? The woman who got away.

The message icon is prominently displayed, and I tap on it. A window opens, a portal to this woman who fled, returned to her life in another country, on another continent, but with whom I feel so connected. Of course, if she has abandoned her account, she may never receive my message. But if there's even a chance that my plea might find its way to her, I have to try.

My finger hovers over the tiny keyboard as I attempt to summon the right words.

> Hi Karolina,
>
> I believe that you were once married to Benjamin Laval of Seattle, Washington. I am his current wife. I recently discovered that my husband was planning to kill me.

I stop, backspace over that. It sounds too crazy to be true. It *is* too crazy to be true, and yet, it is. *Was.* Shaking my head, I dislodge the thought, focus on this missive. I type again.

> I am divorcing my husband. I would really like to talk to you about your experience with him. If you are open to a conversation, please send me your phone number. Or call me at 206-555-2722.

And then I add:

> Please, Karolina. I need your help.

After I press send, I feel bolstered. The thought that there is a woman out there who has survived Benjamin Laval gives me hope. I imagine Karolina living in her own apartment on a colorful square in Warsaw. Or in Kraków with its chapels gilded with gold. She freed herself. She created a wonderful new life. She got what she deserved after years of suffering Benjamin's brutality and control. Maybe—just maybe—I can do it, too.

Seizing on my moment of strength, I slip on a cardigan, grab my purse, and hurry outside to the police officer. When he sees me approaching, he gets out of the car.

"Good morning," I say, offering him a grateful smile. "Do you need anything? Coffee or tea?"

"I'm fine. Thanks, though." The young man is lighthearted, even cheerful. This could mean I have nothing to worry about. Or it could mean that he's not taking his job very seriously.

"I need to go to the bank," I tell him. "Can I drive myself?"

"I'll take you," he insists. "Which bank?"

God, I don't even know. I'm embarrassed to admit it to him. But I fish out my credit card and direct him to the closest branch.

Pulling up to a bank in a police car feels odd and conspicuous. At least the officer doesn't insist on accompanying me inside. I hustle into the building and join the small line. This is not the first time I have visited a teller, but it has been years. I affect the same calm, bored stance as the other patrons, reading posters about term deposits and mortgage rates. When it is my turn, I approach a young woman with smooth skin, smooth hair, a hip but professional outfit. She looks straight out of college, a girl with her whole future ahead of her.

"I'd like to make a cash advance on this card please." I slide my credit card across the counter.

"You're aware of the interest rate on cash withdrawals?"

I'm not. "Yes."

"How much would you like?"

"The maximum amount, please."

She nods, her eyes on the screen. She clicks her mouse a few times, taps at the keyboard before she speaks. "I can give you seven thousand dollars on this card."

"That's it?" I blurt, and then lower my voice. "But the credit limit is eighty thousand dollars."

"Yes, but there's an outstanding balance of twenty-two thousand. And you've made several cash withdrawals at various ATMs over the past few months."

"But I haven't." Benjamin explicitly forbade it. And he checked all my credit card bills for complete compliance.

She shrugs. "Someone using your card did."

My brow furrows. Could Jesse have taken my card without me knowing? Or Lee? But they don't know my PIN code. My husband does. He knows every password, every security code. But why would he take cash out on my card when he was expecting me to be dead?

"If you're sure that you didn't make the withdrawals, you can file a report." She doubts me, I can tell. She thinks I'm a spoiled, scatterbrained housewife who's forgotten about her trips to the ATM.

"How much was taken out in cash?" I ask.

She clicks her mouse again, eyes roving over the screen. "Fifty thousand dollars."

Fifty grand. It's so much money. And such a precise figure. I wonder if this was Benjamin's backup plan. If his plot to kill me failed, if somehow I survived, he knew I would do this. I would try to access money on this card. And Benjamin wants me to have nothing. He wants me to suffer.

"Anything else?" She sounds slightly irritated by my questions and confusion. Fishing in my wallet, I slide her another card. A black one this time.

"How much can I get on this?"

"This isn't a credit card, it's a charge card," she says. "The borrowing fees can be as high as five percent. You can take out as much as you like but you'll have to pay it back in full on your next bill."

Not my problem.

I smile at her. "I'd like a hundred grand, please."

As the officer drives me home, I check my phone. I'm not sure of the time difference between Seattle and Poland, but I pray that Karolina saw the message, that she responded, that she is willing to talk to me. There is no response, and my mood sinks. But it is still early. There is still a chance.

When I enter my silent house, I go straight to the kitchen. I don't feel hungry, but I know I should eat. I need to stay strong for what's ahead of me. Whatever it is, it will not be easy. I heat up some of Vanessa's eggplant parm in the microwave. It is fragrant with garlic and basil, and my stomach growls. I haven't had a proper meal in so long. I take my plate to the breakfast bar and check the phone again. This time, there is a notification: one new message.

You can call me, it says. And there is a number.

My food is forgotten as I punch in the international digits, my pulse audible in my ears. Karolina Laval is my inspiration, my hope. She survived her marriage to Benjamin and her divorce. If she can do it, I can too. Of course, Karolina may not have planned to kill him. Benjamin may not have hated her as much as he hates me.

A man answers the phone, in Polish.

"Hello," I say, enunciating each word. "Do you speak English?"

"Yes."

"I'd like to speak to Karolina, please."

"My name is Peter Brus." His English is accented but perfect. "I am Karolina's brother."

"My name is Hazel Laval. I sent Karolina a message on Facebook."

"Yes, I know," he says. "You're married to Benjamin Laval."

"I am," I admit. "For now..."

"I'm sorry for you." I hear the hate in his voice. "That man is a *potwór*."

I don't know the meaning of the Polish word, but it's clearly not anything good. "That's why I'm calling," I say. "I need to talk to Karolina about getting out of my marriage. I want to know how your sister did it. How she divorced Benjamin and got away from him. How she was able to start over."

"You can't talk to her," Peter states.

"I understand that this is hard." Desperation makes my voice shrill. "I'm sure it's upsetting for her to revisit those years. But I know what she's been through. And I promise I'll be sensitive to her feelings. I just..." My voice cracks a little. "I need her help."

"You can't talk to her," Peter says, and his voice is adamant, even angry, "because my sister died four years ago."

55

"HOW?" I BLURT, BEFORE REALIZING that this is a highly insensitive question. "I... I mean, I'm sorry."

"Car accident," he says. "That's what the police called it. But there were no skid marks. She didn't slow down or try to swerve."

"You think she crashed her car *on purpose*?"

"Karolina drove straight into a concrete barrier at full speed." His voice remains steady. "She wasn't wearing her seat belt."

My mouth falls open, but I can't say the word. And I don't need to... because Peter continues.

"Suicide," he says. "But Benjamin Laval drove her to it. He murdered her."

I close my eyes, afraid to ask. "What did he do to her?"

"When they were married, he treated her like a dog," he growls. "She wasn't allowed to see us. Or even talk to us. My father got sick, and Benjamin wouldn't let her come home. My father died calling out for her."

My chest hurts. My head throbs. This is so much worse than I expected.

"When Karolina finally left him, he made sure she got nothing.

Not even our mother's jewelry that she brought with her to America."

"I could look for it," I suggest. "I could send it."

But Peter ignores the offer. "Benjamin had videos of my sister doing degrading things," he continues. "He sent them to her employer. To her friends. To our church."

It is classic Benjamin. So cruel and vindictive. His enormous ego couldn't take a woman leaving him.

"Your husband murdered my sister," Peter says. "He deserves to rot in hell."

"H-he does," I stammer. "And I'll do everything in my power to make sure he pays for it."

The laugh that travels down the line is bitter. "Benjamin Laval will never pay. Not in this life." There is a slight pause, an intake of breath. "And he will never let you go."

With those ominous words, Peter hangs up.

The eggplant and cheese have congealed on the plate, the once-enticing scent now turning my stomach. I feel lost and hopeless, sick at the thought of what Benjamin did to Karolina. What he drove her to. My husband's plan to murder me may have been intercepted, but he will find a way to destroy me. Just like he did his first wife. Unless I can destroy him first.

I find the card Detective French gave me and call her. She answers almost instantly.

"I found something out," I tell her. "Benjamin was married before."

"And he never told you that?"

"No. He told our friends to keep it from me. And now his first wife is dead." I relay the story Karolina's brother told me, how there were no skid marks, how she wasn't wearing a seat belt. "Peter Brus thinks it was suicide. That Benjamin tortured her and harassed her until she couldn't take it anymore."

"We'll look into it," French promises, taking down the details. "I'll talk to the police in Warsaw. And interview Karolina's family."

"Thank you." I hang up, feeling slightly more positive. Benjamin may have destroyed the first Mrs. Laval but he won't destroy this one. I am going to fight back. I will take him down for what he did—to Karolina and to me. At least, I will try. My appetite has finally returned, and I go to the kitchen, reheat the casserole. I am eating it when my phone rings again.

"Good news," Rachelle says when I answer. "Your husband pleaded not guilty as expected. But the judge denied him bail. He'll be remanded until the next hearing."

Relief runs down my back and shoulders like warm honey. "Thank god."

"With your husband's wealth and connections, the judge considered him a flight risk. It's a big win, Hazel. It means the courts are taking the case seriously."

"Why wouldn't they?" I ask. "Benjamin wanted to kill me."

"I know." Rachelle sighs. "But it can be complicated with someone as high profile as your husband."

I know what she means. Benjamin could have had the judge in his pocket. Could have paid him off or been owed a favor. This is how it works in the world of powerful men like my husband.

"I called Detective French," I tell her. "Benjamin's first wife died under mysterious circumstances."

"That's tragic," she says after I've relayed the full story. "And it's definitely disturbing that he didn't want you to know. But I'm not sure it's relevant to your case."

"A dead wife isn't relevant? Another woman Benjamin tortured and harassed?"

"Karolina died in Poland four years ago, long after she left Benjamin. It's been ruled an accident by police."

"But her brother doesn't believe it. He thinks Benjamin drove her to kill herself!"

"If there is evidence of Benjamin's harassment, the prosecution could use that," Rachelle says hopefully. "What about those degrading videos? Does her brother have copies?"

"I don't know," I murmur. I think about having those horrible videos dragged out into the light again. Of hurting her family and sullying her memory.

"I'll talk to French," my lawyer says. "And I'm arranging a meeting with the prosecutor to go over their case. I'll find out what they've got, and then we can meet to discuss it."

"Okay."

"In the meantime, you're safe. Benjamin is behind bars. Try not to worry."

But of course, I will worry. Rachelle Graham doesn't know my husband like I do.

I hang up the phone and move to the window. The police car is still there. Surely if Benjamin is my only threat, they will call it off. Resources are limited, police stretched too thin. It is a never-ending story in the news. But the car doesn't move. I watch it, arms folded around myself, for seconds, then minutes. I leave, make more tea, return to the window. The car is still there. So why are the cops leaving the officer outside my home when Benjamin is being held in jail?

Because they don't think I'm safe either.

56

I WAKE EARLY, MY BODY yearning to go for a run. My life with my husband revolved around exercise. The endorphins kept me sane, kept me alive. Would it be safe for me to jog along the trails? Or would I be vulnerable in the thick forest? The gym is no longer an option. Not if Jesse could still be there. Not if there could be questions about our relationship.

In the kitchen, I bake raspberry oatmeal muffins, the process of measuring, sifting, and mixing soothing, meditative. My thoughts have been consumed by my husband's arrest, the revelation that he wanted me dead, but now they drift to my ex-lover. Slowly but surely, I had realized I couldn't trust Jesse. It became apparent when his relationship with Lee turned sexual. That's when I knew that Jesse would take whatever he wanted, fulfill his own desires with no regard for my feelings. I'd felt gullible and naïve then, but now I feel downright stupid. Because now I know that Jesse—Carter Sumner—targeted me. That he knew I was sad. Lonely. Pathetic. I was the perfect dupe.

Pouring the batter into the greased tins, I imagine the scene when Jesse entered my home and found Benjamin—his former lawyer—waiting for him. Nate would have been there, too, large, imposing, protective of his boss. My husband would have threatened Jesse at the very least. Likely, he'd have had Nate rough him up. Or worse. As the muffins bake and I clean up the mess, I wonder if Jesse is still alive. If he is, has he gone back to Spokane? Was he even from there? Everything he told me could have been a lie.

I wonder, not for the first time, if Lee is with him. The note of warning I'd written her may have gone completely unheeded. *Jesse is not who you think he is.* Would she believe me? She was so enamored, just like I had been. Lee might think I was jealous, trying to sabotage her relationship because I was so miserable in my own. She may have tossed the plane ticket, taken the money, and started a new life with Jesse. But one day, she will learn the truth about him. I just hope it won't be too late.

The timer on my phone trills and I remove the muffins from the oven. The fragrance is enticing, and I eat one while it is still too hot, the cake falling apart in my hands, the fruit burning my mouth. When they have cooled slightly, I set the most perfect muffin on a napkin and walk down the driveway toward the police car.

The cheerful officer from yesterday has been replaced; sometime in the night there was a shift change. The woman who gets out of the car is tall, strong, attractive in a stern way.

"I brought you a freshly baked muffin." I smile at her.

"No thanks."

"It's raspberry oatmeal. Still warm."

"I'm good."

What kind of robot turns down a warm muffin? "Okay..." I feel awkward. "I need to get some exercise. Would it be okay if I go for a run?"

"Not a good idea," she says, leaning an arm on the roof of her car. "You're safest in the house."

"Maybe you could take me to a yoga class? Wait in the lobby?"

"My orders are to protect you here. Inside your home."

"But the other officer drove me to the bank," I tattle. "It's just a yoga class."

"I can't speak to what Officer Campbell did. I'm just telling you *my* instructions."

An unpleasant, panicky feeling wells up in me. I'm a prisoner. Just like I was before.

"Do a yoga video," the officer says, and I catch a hint of condescension in her tone. "You've got enough space. I'm sure you'll survive."

Chastened, I turn on my heel and head back to the house, my face hot. I feel belittled by the robust officer's comment. I imagine her punching heavy bags, breaking boards with a single kick, flipping full-grown men over her shoulder. She thinks I am weak and frou-frou, a useless trophy wife, a kept woman. And she is probably right. When I enter, I go straight to the kitchen and toss the muffin into the trash.

When my anger has cooled, I take the cop's advice and search YouTube for a yoga video. I need something calming and centering that will help me cope with this sense of powerlessness. The options are multitude and specific:

Yoga for beginners
Yoga for kids
Yoga for perimenopausal women
Yoga for women who've just found out their husband wanted to kill them

Selecting a forty-five-minute Yoga for Stress workout, I prop my phone on the coffee table. I'm about to hit play when the device rings out in the silent house. It's my lawyer.

"Detective French called me this morning," Rachelle says. "She spoke to the Polish police. About Karolina Laval."

"And?" My heart leaps into my throat. Her tone is unreadable, but I pray this will be good news. That the cops have discovered something the prosecution can use against Benjamin.

"The Polish force did a thorough investigation into her death and concluded it was a car accident. Excessive speed and wet road conditions were contributing factors."

"They made it look that way," I cry. "But it was suicide! And Benjamin drove her to it!"

"*Who* made it look that way?"

"I…I don't know," I stammer. "The cops?"

"That's a serious accusation," Rachelle says, her voice measured. "I don't think you want to go down that road, Hazel."

"They need to talk to Peter Brus," I say, feeling scolded. "He told me that Benjamin tortured his sister. That Karolina drove into that concrete barrier on purpose."

"French spoke to Karolina's mother," my attorney says. "They had to get a Polish translator, but Mrs. Brus was very forthcoming."

"What did she say?"

"She spoke very fondly of her former son-in-law," Rachelle says with a sigh. "She said that Benjamin and Karolina were happy together for many years, but eventually Karolina wanted to come home. Even after the divorce, Benjamin was good to the family."

My stomach twists. I already know where this is going.

"When Karolina had her accident, Benjamin covered her medical expenses. When she passed away, he paid for the funeral. Mrs. Brus told the police that he set up a memorial trust for the family, in Karolina's name."

"Will French talk to Karolina's brother?" My voice is shrill, desperate. "Please?"

"Peter Brus sounds like a very sick man."

"What do you mean *sick*?"

"Apparently, he has substance abuse issues. And paranoid delusions. His own mother doesn't speak to him."

This is how my husband operates. He paid off Karolina's family. Anyone who refused to be bought was destroyed, painted as delusional, a drug addict. It would have been so much easier with me. Because I have no one.

"The Seattle police are still working on the case," Rachelle continues. "They haven't given up. But the first Mrs. Laval isn't relevant."

But she is. I know it. Peter knows it.

"Try not to worry," my lawyer says gently. "You're safe. Benjamin can't hurt you anymore."

As soon as I hang up the phone, I let out a guttural scream. Rage and frustration burn my throat, my face, my belly. My husband is a Machiavellian mastermind, and Karolina's family was no match for him. The police are no match for him. Snatching up the books and magazines artfully arranged on the coffee table, I hurl them about the room. There is a heavy designer bowl on a side table, and I raise it above my head, smash it on the floor. The tempered glass shatters, remnants skittering across the hardwood. Our black and white wedding photo, in its pride of place, hits the far wall. The glass breaks with a satisfying crack.

Surrounded by the mess, I stop, suddenly sheepish. The cameras... Who is watching me now? Where does the footage go? I must look wild, feral, unhinged. Or perhaps I seem like a spoiled princess having a tantrum. Neither is a good image for me. I get the broom and sweep up shards. Tidy the magazines. I am picking up the wedding photo when my phone rings again. It's the Arbutus Care Home. I am breathless as I answer it.

"Is this Hazel Laval?"

"It is."

"This is Greta Williams." Her tone is somber. "From your mother's care facility."

My heart twists with panic. "Is my mom okay?"

"I'm so sorry to tell you this..." Her words are tremulous. "Your mother has gone missing."

"Missing? What do you mean *missing*?"

The tiny woman inhales. "It seems she wandered away from the facility."

"How could that happen?" I cry. "The place is supposed to be secure!"

"We're flummoxed," Greta says, and I hear the tears in her voice. "We take great pains to ensure our patients are safe and protected. I…I honestly don't know how she could have disappeared."

But I do. Benjamin is behind this. His people have taken my mother. To hurt me. Or to warn me. But surely he wouldn't harm her. He is shallow, cruel, a heartless narcissist, but only a true psychopath would injure an innocent old lady.

Greta continues. "We have a nurse and two security personnel combing the area. The police have been called. We'll be speaking with them soon."

"I'm coming down there." The uptight cop outside will have to make an exception for a missing mother.

"There's no need," Greta says, and I can tell she's nervous, afraid I will be angry and combative. That I will kick up a fuss at them for losing my mom. But I can't blame Greta or the staff of the Arbutus Care Home. Because my husband is behind this.

"Sometimes dementia patients will return to their old homes," Greta says. "Can you give us her last address? Or a place she lived when she was particularly happy?"

"Sure." I rattle off the address of our cramped apartment from memory. Was my mom happy there, despite the financial strain? My childhood home, a small bungalow in Ballard, was full of arguments and tension. But there must have been good times, too. I give Greta that address as well.

"We'll find her, Hazel," she says. "I promise we will."

But it's a promise she can't keep. Because my mother is not lost. Someone from Benjamin's network of shady contacts has her. I hang up the phone and let the tears of fear, rage, and frustration come. Rachelle Graham had tried to assure me that I was safe, that Benjamin couldn't hurt me anymore. But she has grossly underestimated him.

57

WHEN MY PHONE RINGS A couple of hours later, I snatch it up hopefully. I want it to be Greta Williams with good news about my mom. But the name on the display is my lawyer's.

"You need to come to the King County prosecutor's office," she tells me. "We can go over the case against your husband together."

"Okay...But something terrible has happened. My mother has gone missing from her care home."

"Shit. I'm sorry," she says. "Have the police been called?"

"Yes. But I think Benjamin is behind it."

There is a slight pause, and I wonder if Rachelle thinks I'm hysterical, full of tales of dead first wives and kidnapped mothers.

"Sometimes old people wander off," she says. "Let the police do their job. You need to get down here."

The King County prosecuting attorney's office is located in a heritage building close to Pioneer Square. Two buildings—one housing the courthouse and administrative offices, the other the King County jail—are connected by an internal skybridge. The surly, carb-denying officer escorts me into the mosaiced lobby where Rachelle Graham is waiting. Her expression is tense, her greeting perfunctory as she takes my elbow and leads me to the bank of elevators.

We ride up with a man and woman, both in suits, who get off several floors before us. When we are alone, my attorney speaks.

"Any news about your mom?"

"Not yet."

"I know it's bad timing, but you need to focus. This is critical."

"I'll be fine." But my voice quavers, belying my nerves.

"Take a deep breath, Hazel. Pull yourself together." Rachelle's voice is firm, commanding, almost cold.

The elevator shrugs to a stop then. Inhaling through the tightness in my chest, I step off and move forward.

Inside the office, we are met by a young woman in a pencil skirt who escorts us to a meeting room. Rachelle ushers me inside and closes the door behind us. I take a seat in one of six chairs set up around a round, midsize table. On it, there is a laptop.

"I'm going to play you a recording that is going to be very hard to listen to," Rachelle says. "It's audio of your husband hiring a man to kill you."

So that's how they caught him. Benjamin must have propositioned an undercover officer to get rid of me. It will be chilling to hear my husband plot my demise, but somehow satisfying that he was outsmarted. I, at least, had plotted with a known accomplice, someone I thought I could trust, not some random hit man.

Rachelle's fingers alight on the laptop's trackpad, and she clicks on the audio file. My husband's voice—distant but clear—emerges from the speakers.

"Thank you for coming," he says.

The undercover officer's voice is closer to the concealed microphone. Clearly, he was wearing a recording device. "It's not like I had a choice."

"You're only free because of me," Benjamin says. "I'd say that you owe me. Wouldn't you?"

My brow furrows, but I know these stings can be elaborate. I focus on the continuing conversation.

"You were paid, weren't you?" the would-be hit man grumbles.

"A reduced rate." There is a soft chuckle. "Even your boss can't afford me." Benjamin's arrogance is gross, distasteful, and completely expected. He continues. "You knew this was the deal all along."

The cop lets out a heavy sigh. "Yeah...I guess I did."

My breath catches in my chest. Something in that sigh is familiar. There is a prickle at the back of my neck as the assassin asks, "What do you want me to do?"

And with those few words, I know. This man is not an undercover cop. He is Jesse Thomas. But not my lover, not my hope. He is the man who punched me so easily. Who came up with the plan to murder my husband and blame Lee. He is Carter Sumner: the criminal, the liar, the murderer for hire.

Benjamin continues, his voice smooth. "My wife's name is Hazel Laval. I want her gone."

"Dead?"

"Permanently gone, yes."

They are both so calm, so casual, as if they are talking about sports or the weather, not snuffing out my life. I don't realize that I am vibrating until Rachelle's hand lands on top of mine. She pauses the playback. "Do you want to stop?"

My husband hired my boyfriend to kill me. Of course I want to stop. I want to run from this room, straight into traffic. I want to sprint to the ocean and dive in, go under. It is all too much. Too sick. Too humiliating.

"Keep going," I say, my voice hoarse, barely audible.

"It's going to get worse," Rachelle warns.

But I nod my acquiescence. With my hand held in her tight grip, it continues.

"I'm not killing a woman for nothing," Carter Sumner says. "I'm not going to risk going back inside."

"Twenty-five grand now. Twenty-five when she's dead."

Fifty thousand dollars. My husband is wealthy beyond belief, but that is all my life is worth to him.

"Okay." Carter is clearly pleased with the figure. "How do you want me to do it?"

"It needs to look like an accident."

"That's gonna take time," my former lover advises. "I could shoot her tomorrow. A break-in gone wrong."

"Far too suspicious, I'm afraid." Benjamin is cool, composed. There is nothing but a faint rustling for a moment, and then I hear a low whistle.

"She's hot," Carter says, and I realize my husband has shown him my picture.

"She's a beautiful woman on the outside. But inside…she's dead. Empty. Totally vacuous."

Carter smirks. "Dumb girls are not a problem for me."

Fuck you both.

"Good." There is a smile in my husband's voice. "Because I want you to seduce her."

"For real?"

"It's the best way to get close to her. She's lonely. Weak and needy," my husband explains. "You'll have her under your thumb in no time."

"So, what, do I just walk up to her and ask her out?" Carter queries. "I mean, where would I even meet a woman like Hazel?"

"I'll get you a job at her gym," Benjamin offers. "I know the owner. And clearly you know a thing or two about working out."

"Thanks." Carter takes it as a compliment. "Not much else to do inside."

"Hazel will fall for you," my husband assures him. "You're strong, good-looking, and you'll pay attention to her. That's all she wants. And if you're dating her, it'll be easier to get her out on the water."

"You want me to drown her?" Carter sounds oddly pleased with the suggestion.

"I'll provide a boat. And these..." I hear the crinkling of a plastic bag. "I took a couple of her prescription pills. You can crush them up in her drink."

"Two Xanax and two sleeping pills?" The sound of the plastic is louder in Carter's hand. "Is that enough?"

"I don't want this to look like an intentional overdose. And this is more than enough to make her weak and groggy," Benjamin assures him. "When she's starting to nod off, toss her in. The water's cold." I hear the smile in his voice. "Hazel will never wake up."

I reach for the wastepaper basket and vomit into it. Lee saved my life that day. I thought she'd disrupted my plan, destroyed my future, but if I had gotten into that boat with Jesse, I'd be dead. I am only alive because of her.

Rachelle Graham gets up, retrieves a tissue box from a credenza. "There's more," she says. "But maybe that's enough for today."

"No." I wipe my mouth with a tissue. "Keep going."

Her lips are pressed together in a grim line as she clicks the trackpad.

"Sounds easy enough," Carter says brightly. "And if you want me to bang your hot wife, that's a bonus."

There is some more banter about logistics: the boat, the timing, Benjamin's schedule. I hear the exchange of money happen—the twenty-five thousand in cash. And then the recording stops.

"There's another file," Rachelle says, but there is a coolness in her tone. When I meet her eyes, they have hardened against me. What has she concluded about my relationship with Carter Sumner? I feel nauseous and jittery, terrified of what I'm about to hear next, but there is no point in delaying it.

"Play it," I say.

This time, Carter's voice emerges from the speakers first.

"You were right..." There is a chuckle in his voice. "She's totally fallen for me. I think she's *in love*."

"I'm not surprised," my husband says, his words dripping disdain.

"She thinks we're running away together," Carter says. "That we're going to have a *future*."

I feel the weight of my lawyer's eyes on me, but I don't meet them. She knows I'm a liar now. A cheater. My gaze is locked onto the shiny surface of the table, tracing the whorls in the wood.

"How sweet," my husband sneers. "Where to?"

"South America," Carter says, showing his lack of geographical knowledge. "She thinks we're going to take the boat up to Bellingham and get on a plane to *start our new life together*." He is imitating me, mocking me. Hate and anger churn my guts.

But Benjamin is pleased. "Nice work."

"She wants you to think she committed suicide," Carter continues, like a schoolboy trying to impress his teacher. "She's going to leave a note."

"I'll destroy it," Benjamin says calmly. "A suicide would reflect badly on me. This needs to look like an accident. Hazel jogs along the cliffside trails. She tripped. Fell in. The current swept her away."

"She's going to swim out to my boat," my former lover explains. "That way, she'll be wet and cold and probably close to hypothermia. I'll give her tea with the pills in it. We'll motor north for a bit. And when no one's around, I'll toss her in."

Like a bag of garbage.

"Good," Benjamin says. "But do it quickly. Don't travel too far north. When I get home, I'll call her acquaintances to ask if they've heard from her. And I'll alert the cops in the morning. Eventually, her body will wash up onshore somewhere. They'll find her own drugs in her system...if her corpse is still intact."

"And when do I get my money?" Carter asks, because of course that's what he cares about. "I don't want to wait for her body to show up."

"When she's been gone thirty-six hours, I'll release your next payment. It won't be safe for us to meet then, but I'll arrange for a drop-off."

They discuss a locale—a bar off I-90 near Judkins Park. Nate will deliver the final twenty-five thousand.

And then my husband says, "Well done, Carter. Or, I guess I should call you Jesse." And the conversation ends.

Rachelle says nothing but she is watching me, judging me. I don't look up, not yet. My face is burning with shame, humiliation, and fear. I have been caught out. Trapped in a massive lie. Finally, I raise my head and meet her steely gaze.

"You need to start being honest with me," she says.

58

THE WHEELS IN MY HEAD turn frantically. Rachelle had asked me point blank if I had a lover and I'd denied it. But now she knows I was sleeping with Jesse—with Carter. That I thought we were going to run away together. That somehow our plan went awry. But she doesn't know about our plot to kill Benjamin. Or about Lee. And I must keep it that way.

"We were lovers," I admit. "I didn't tell you because I felt ashamed. I *feel* ashamed. I was such a fool."

"Talk to me, Hazel. And no more lies."

A large part of me wants to come clean, to confess what my lover and I were planning to do. To let the calm, capable attorney pick up the pieces of my shattered life. Surely, if I admit that I couldn't go through with the assassination of my husband, that I double-crossed my lover to save my friend, my punishment will be lenient. But I can't risk it now, not while my mother is missing. I can't go to jail while she is still out there, in Benjamin's clutches. So, I will play dumb, play innocent.

"He told me his name was Jesse Thomas. He was a trainer at my gym."

"And when did you find out his real identity?"

"Just now," I lie. Because I can't admit that my husband told me my lover's real name. That he caught us conspiring against him. "I heard Benjamin call him Carter."

"Carter Sumner," Rachelle says. "A former client of your husband's. He was charged in a violent breaking and entering. Any idea where we can find him?"

"I…I don't know. I haven't heard from him since…" I trail off.

"Since when?"

"I tried to swim out to his boat," I tell her. "But it was too cold. I was too weak. I had to turn back. I saw him a few more times after that. At the gym. But he was angry with me. He felt betrayed. Like I chose my husband over him."

"Okay," she says, but I hear the skepticism in her voice.

And then it dawns on me, and my stomach drops. "But he handed in these recordings, right? He must be cooperating with the police." Would Carter reveal our plot to save himself? Send me down for *his* plan? Of course he would.

Fool me once…

"The thumb drive was submitted anonymously. Dropped off at a precinct in South Seattle. The duty officer didn't even see who left it there."

"But it had to be him. Who else would have a copy of these recordings?"

"Your boyfriend made these tapes to cover his own ass. If he got caught, he'd implicate your husband. A murder for hire is a much lighter sentence than first-degree murder."

The thought of the two men who had used and abused me going down for their plot to kill me elicits a tiny flicker of joy in my chest. But I know it will not be that simple.

"Carter either dropped the thumb drive off and disappeared," Rachelle continues, "or he gave it to a friend. Had them deliver it if Carter got into trouble."

"Is it enough?" I indicate the laptop with its audio files. "To convict my husband?"

"Audio recordings are hard to prove. The police can do spectrographic analysis on the voices, but it's not always conclusive."

I press a hand to my mouth as my heart plummets. We need more evidence. Or Benjamin and Carter are going to get away with it.

"The first wife's death was accidental," she says dismissively, "but the police have found another ex-client of Mr. Laval's who says Benjamin solicited him to kill you last year. For twenty grand."

Christ. Was my husband shopping for a deal?

"But the guy is a convicted drug dealer and a car thief. He has a serious credibility problem."

"What else do they have?" My throat is tight, my voice high-pitched.

"Investigators are still poring over video footage from your home. But it seems only you were recorded. Benjamin doesn't show up at all."

"He controlled the cameras." My voice is bitter. "He didn't want a record of the way he treated me." Or his encounter with Carter Sumner. Benjamin knew that his hit man had turned on him, that Carter was planning to attack. He'd turned the cameras off that day, and he had lain in wait. But what about Lee? She had entered my home the same day. "Was there anyone else on the cameras?" I ask.

"Like who?"

"I don't know." I won't bring my friend into this, not if I don't have to. "Just…anyone?"

"No one except Nate Mattias, the security guard."

It is like Lee was never there. The cameras were off. Her fingerprints were in the house but not on record anywhere. And the police don't know that I'd never had a friend of my own in my home. To them, Lee never existed. She is safe.

"They're looking into his bank records," Rachelle continues. "They're hoping to find the cash withdrawals from his cards or accounts. There's no transaction if there's no exchange of funds."

"But we heard it on the recording!"

"The defense will poke holes in that." Her sigh is defeated. "We really need to find Carter Sumner. The prosecutor might be able to upgrade your husband's charges from conspiracy to solicitation of murder for hire, but that'll be hard if we can't find the hit man."

The *hit man.* God, I was a fool.

Unless…there had been something authentic between Carter and me. I know that my boyfriend had agreed to murder me for fifty thousand dollars, but maybe, when he met me, he couldn't do it. Even though he lied to me, cheated on me, manipulated me, I still want to believe that his feelings for me were real. That he handed that thumb drive over to the police to save me. But deep down I know this is wishful thinking. I know he was just trying to save himself.

Rachelle closes the laptop. "The pretrial hearing is in a few days. We'll get a better idea of what the defense is planning. I'm sure they'll file motions to dismiss."

"*Dismiss?*" I feel dizzy, nauseous. "We have him on tape planning to kill me!"

"The prosecutor will do everything she can to keep him behind bars for a long, long time. But there are legal issues to consider here. Evidentiary chain of custody. Two-party consent laws."

I don't know what any of that means, but I can tell she is concerned.

"Like I said, audio testimony is a tough sell. But we still have a few days to dig up more evidence." She gives me a small smile, but something has shifted in her. Rachelle doubts me now. She thinks that I am lying. Hiding things. And she is right.

"All we can do now is cross our fingers and wait," she adds.

My life is on the line, and she is suggesting I rely on crossed fingers? But Rachelle knows. I am powerless over my fate.

I always was.

59

FOR THE NEXT TWO NIGHTS, I don't sleep. My body feels coiled and restless, like my skin is too small, like my insides are being slowly, invisibly crushed. My mother has still not been found. She has been gone for three nights and the thought of her trapped, alone, and afraid makes me cry for hours. I worry and fret and stew over my lack of agency and freedom. I am prohibited from helping with the search, from even leaving the property. Easygoing Officer Campbell must have been reprimanded for his leniency because he now insists that I stay inside with the doors locked. I must trust that others are trying to find my mother, that they care as much as I do.

I send a list of addresses to the care home: the dental practice my mom used to work for, her best friend's house, the pool where she used to swim laps when I was a kid. I give them the details of Benjamin's vacation home on Orcas Island, and his condo adjacent to the golf course in Semiahmoo. (I tell them that my mom spent time there, not that I suspect she could be held captive.) Greta Williams promises her security guards will visit the local spots on a rotating basis. She assures me that she'll give all the addresses to the police, who will check into them when they can. But it's not enough. I should be out there, scouring the city, looking for my mom. But I am stuck here. Trapped and powerless.

A missing bulletin is placed with the local media.

"A senior citizen has wandered away from her care facility in Northeast Seattle," the news anchor says, voice tinged with professional concern. "Melanie Sinclair is sixty-seven years old and suffers from dementia." A recent photograph of my mom, looking frail and vacant, appears in the top right corner of the screen. There is a birthday cake in front of her, aglow with candles. I wasn't in attendance. I wasn't allowed to go. "If you see Melanie," the polished announcer continues, "please stay with her and call the Arbutus Care Home or Seattle Police."

If Benjamin—or Nate, or another one of my husband's lackeys—abducted my mother he has not told me how to get her back. What does he want in exchange for my mom's release? I can't stop the prosecutor from coming after him; they have already built their case. Our prenup ensures I'll get basically nothing in the divorce—although I might be able to challenge it given recent events. Is that why Benjamin took my mom? Or was it just to hurt me? To punish me. To show me that he can still get to me.

I spend my captivity tearing through the house searching for clues to my mother's whereabouts. I dig deep into closets, explore the basement crawl space, pull boxes out of the garage, and meticulously sift through them. Deep in a dusty crate, I find an unfamiliar ring of keys. There are three keys of varied shapes, but none of them are labeled. Is my mother behind a locked door somewhere? Secreted away in a storage locker? Held captive in a seedy back room? The thought makes me feel sick.

When the police came with the search warrant, they went through my husband's study, including the safe. They riffled through all the cupboards and drawers, but they were unable to find the Total Power Exchange contract. But it has to be here somewhere. If I can find it, it will at least validate our toxic arrangement. Benjamin's preliminary hearing is impending. If the investigators can't find the money trail, more credible witnesses, or further recorded conversations, Benjamin could be set free. Of course, Carter Sumner is the smoking gun. But if they find him, if he tells the police everything, all three of us will end up behind bars.

When the day of the hearing arrives, the contract has still not surfaced. Neither has my mother. It's been days now, and the thought makes me sick to my stomach. I sit at the breakfast bar, nibbling a piece of dry toast and watching the clock. My attorney has advised me that the "prelim" could take a couple of hours. The prosecutor will present her case: the evidence and the witnesses, from which I have been excluded. I'd begged not to be put on the stand, terrified that my husband's lawyers would eviscerate me, but now I am having doubts. Would my testimony make a difference? I pray that the judge will believe there is probable cause that Benjamin Laval committed this crime, without my attendance.

After an hour has passed, I abandon my cold toast and pour two fingers of bourbon into a glass. I wince as the strong liquor hits my palette and burns my esophagus, but it has the desired numbing effect. There is nothing I can do now but wait. And hope. *Cross my fingers*, as my lawyer so helpfully advised. The alcohol makes that slightly less torturous.

As if to punctuate the sentiment, my cell phone rings. Rachelle Graham's heavy breath prefaces her words. "The case against your husband has been dismissed, Hazel. I'm sorry."

The glass slips from my hand, hits the counter, but it doesn't break. My knees crumple beneath me and I clutch the edge of the sink for support. I feel like I'm drowning, like the air has been sucked from the room. But my attorney continues, as if I am attentive, listening.

"The judge said there was insufficient evidence to prove that a crime was committed by the defendant."

"But the recordings?" I manage, though my words are a gasp.

"Hearsay," she explains. "The defense team argued they didn't have the opportunity to cross-examine Carter Sumner. And without a voice sample from him, there's no way to prove his identity or the authenticity of the recordings."

My mouth gapes wordlessly, the only sound an ugly croak.

"Your husband's lawyers said that the audio could have been tampered with. Even faked."

"Faked?" I find my voice. "By who?"

"By anyone with a grudge against Benjamin Laval," she says. "In his line of work, he has no shortage of enemies." There is a slight pause. "Or it could have been someone from his personal life."

My jaw clenches. "What about the money he paid to Carter Sumner?"

"There were no cash withdrawals taken from any of Benjamin Laval's accounts," she states, her voice resigned. "There were, however, several cash advances taken on *your* personal credit card. In the amount of fifty thousand dollars."

"I didn't take any money out!" I cry. "I wasn't allowed to!" *That's why I had to steal the fifty grand for Lee from Benjamin's safe,* I don't add.

"Your credit card statements were submitted to the court." I hear the suspicion in her voice, and I know...*Benjamin did this. He set me up.*

"And there was nothing incriminating on the video cameras?" I ask rhetorically. Because I know there was not.

"Most of the footage was of you, Hazel."

I think about my recent meltdown, all caught on film. The psycho throwing magazines and photographs, smashing the pricey glass bowl. And then I snap to. "When is he being released?"

"It'll be a matter of hours. You should get out of the house."

"Where should I go?" I am asking myself as much as I am her.

"There are local women's shelters that will take you in. I can send the addresses. But if you feel your husband is a threat to you..."

"*If*? He killed his first wife! He kidnapped my mother!"

In Rachelle Graham's pause, I hear my own words. I sound hysterical. Deluded. This is what my husband wanted all along.

"You might want to find a shelter in a different town," she continues. "You're going to lose your police protection. As far as the law is concerned, you're no longer in any danger."

But I am. I'm in much more danger now.

"Or…," she says, her voice tender, maternal. "You could consider checking yourself into a facility. Somewhere safe and secure, where you can get some rest. Maybe some counseling?"

She thinks I'm insane. Breaking down. She thinks I should be locked up.

"I'll be fine," I snap. "I can take care of myself."

"Okay," she says with a sigh. "Good luck, Hazel."

But it means goodbye.

60

MY BAG IS ALREADY PACKED, but I grab another suitcase, throw everything I can into it: art, figurines, designer clothing...anything that might be valuable. If I am going to survive, start over, I will need money. Perhaps the hundred thousand dollars I withdrew on the charge card will be enough, but I know nothing about budgets or the cost of living. And I have not worked since I was a girl. This is the only way I know to support myself.

Leaving town is tempting, but I must find my mom first. There are parts of the city I can stay, places where Benjamin would never venture. The seedy parts, where people do whatever they have to in order to survive. I will need a disguise, though. If I cut my hair, bleach it blond, Hazel Laval will disappear. Blend into the scenery. Another faceless, nameless person hiding from her past.

The car is a problem. The Mercedes belongs to Benjamin. He could report it stolen and have the police deliver me directly to him. But I have enough cash to buy a cheap used vehicle, a bland sedan that no one will notice. Lugging my suitcases outside, I look for the cop car at the end of the driveway. I'd hoped the officer who'd been protecting me might offer me a ride, but he is already gone. Called off. I am completely alone and vulnerable. My heart thudding with fear, I call a taxi.

The driver takes me to a used car lot where I purchase a 2009 Hyundai Elantra—a nondescript gray four-door—for three thousand dollars cash. The salesman had wanted to negotiate, to offer me bells and whistles and test drives, but I am on my way in less than an hour, the car insured for a six-month term.

My next stop is a hair salon in a run-down strip mall southeast of my home. "Cut it off," I tell the stylist, who is a heavyset woman whose hands smell of cigarettes. She is the antithesis of my former hairdresser, Karl. "And I want to go blond."

It's a drastic change and it won't suit me. Getting the pigment out of my dark hair will require bleach and damaging chemicals, but she sets to work without comment. Two and a half hours later, she is done. I am transformed.

"What do you think?" she asks as we both take in my reflection.

The cut is rudimentary and too old for me. The color washes out my complexion. I don't look good, but I look different—and that is all that matters. I traded on my looks for a long time, but they're nothing but a hindrance to me now. For this next chapter, I must rely on my wits and courage to survive.

"It's perfect," I tell her. "What do I owe you?"

Back in the Hyundai, I take I-90 east, heading toward the sprawling suburbs of Bellevue, Kirkland, and Redmond. These cities are home to tech giants such as Microsoft, Amazon, Google, and Nintendo, their hotels catering to the wealthy sector. I press on past them, looking for a cheap roadside motel that will accept my money with no questions asked. There would be more options south of the city, but I don't want to be too far from my mother's care facility.

I think about Lee living in her car. If I was as brave and hardy as she was, I would pull into one of these uniform subdivisions and go to sleep. I'd leave the keys in the ignition, be ready to take off at the first sign of trouble. But I remember the pain she was in when she woke in the mornings. Her embarrassment when she had to pee in the bushes. I am already so exhausted, so on edge, so close to breaking down. And unlike Lee, I have money. And that means I have options.

Finally, I hit a stretch of fast-food restaurants, truck stops, and gas stations. I pull into a run-down inn with its sign partially burnt out: OTEL. I feel confident they will take my cash. And I am right.

Inside the room with its cheap, dated décor, I lock the door and check my phone. No one has contacted me: not the Arbutus Care Home, not my husband, not the police. This device is my last remaining vulnerability. Benjamin could have his firm's investigators track it. But surely that will take some time. Tomorrow I will replace the phone and give the nursing home my new number. For now I put it into airplane mode.

I climb into the thin sheets smelling strongly of artificial spring flowers and I try to sleep.

61

MORNING LIGHT SEEPS IN AROUND the edges of the floral curtains, and I wake, momentarily discombobulated. It takes a second for my surroundings to become familiar: the industrial carpet, the laminate furniture, the chemical odor of fabric softener...My fingers find their way to my short haircut as my eyes drift to the suitcases pressed up against the door. It comes back to me in a rush: I am in hiding. I am in danger.

I shower and dress quickly, ears alert for any sounds of trouble. I hear nothing but the roar of the highway, the occasional slamming of a car door. I repack my suitcases and haul them both out to the car. I won't come back here tonight. It is imperative that I keep going, that I stay one step ahead. A moving target is harder to hit.

When I am on the road, I take my phone off airplane mode, check for messages. Nothing. I had hoped that Greta Williams would call to tell me that my mother had miraculously reappeared. Now that Benjamin is free, he has no reason to keep her. Except that he does. My mother's disappearance keeps me here, in Seattle, looking for her. And Benjamin thinks he can find me first. A chill skitters down my neck, rattles my shoulders. I shake it off. And focus.

As the highway stretches out before me, my fear dissipates, replaced by an unfamiliar sensation. It is freedom. For the first time in years, I can do what I want—without permission, demands, or limitations. Reveling in the moment, I vow that I will never live as a prisoner or a captive again. The exhilarating feeling is short-lived, though, tainted by the fact that I am running for my life. My wants and needs have changed. I'm in survival mode now—food, shelter, and a new phone—the modern necessities of life. I pull into a shopping center that is sure to have an electronics store.

Inside, I buy a cheap phone with a six-month plan, paying cash and using Benjamin's address on the contract. Hurrying into a public restroom, I toss my old phone into the garbage. As I walk back to my car, I call the Arbutus Care Home and give them my new phone number. After that, I contact Rachelle Graham's receptionist and give her the same information. And then I drive.

Since my mom vanished, I've been desperate to participate in her search. If she is truly lost—not abducted—she will make her way to a familiar place. A place with good memories and positive energy. Somewhere she will feel safe and comfortable. I drive to my childhood home in Ballard and cruise through the neighborhood until I spot our old house. Despite significant updates, I recognize it. But would my mother? And would she come here? While there were some happy times, this is where her marriage to my dad fell apart. It might not be the place or the time she wants to revisit.

I drive toward the university and the Intramural Activities pool where she did her twice-weekly swims. There are a handful of students and retirees milling about out front, but none of them are Melanie Sinclair. And there's no point going inside. She wouldn't be admitted without a membership card, and she hasn't had one for years. I drive on, toward her apartment building, the tower where we lived post-divorce. Though I circle the block several times, she is nowhere to be seen.

Tears of frustration are blurring my vision, and I pull the car to the side of the road. My mom is not in any of these familiar locations because Benjamin has her. He took her to hurt me, to keep me in Seattle, searching for her, so that he could get to me. Digging in my purse, I extract the ring of keys I found in that box. They are useless. My mother is locked away behind some unknown door, and I can't find her.

After blowing my nose and dabbing at my eyes, I pull back onto the street. I haven't eaten today, and while I have no appetite, I know that I must. If I'm going to find my mom, outsmart my husband, I need to stay strong. Sharp. Healthy. I drive to a fast-food restaurant and order a wilted chicken salad.

I'm seated at a corner table, when the unfamiliar ring of my new cell phone startles me. Only two people have this number. Ignoring the glowers of a woman at a nearby table, I grab it and answer.

"It's Greta Williams calling from the—"

I cut her off. "Did you find my mother, Greta? Is she okay?"

"We found her," she says, and I hear the catch in her voice. "I'm so sorry, Hazel. Your mother was found dead."

The world goes dark, silent, like I have fallen down a deep well of pain and loss. I want to scream and thrash and rail against this news, but I am paralyzed. My face is wet with tears, though I don't realize I'm crying. A wounded moan seeps out of me, my fist pressed to my lips.

"Hazel?" Greta asks. "Are you okay?"

But I don't respond. I can't. Because another emotion is bleeding through my grief. A dark, burning hatred toward Benjamin Laval. He murdered my mother to hurt me. Took an innocent old lady, lost and confused, and snuffed out her life. It is depraved. Psychotic. Beyond the pale. I stand, make my way to the exit on shaky legs.

"Wh-what happened?" I manage to ask when I am outside.

"There are no signs of foul play," Greta continues. "Or any visible injuries. The coroner will investigate, of course, but it appears that she just wandered off and slipped away. Peacefully and quietly."

My husband is clever. He'd have made her death look natural. Like my drowning would have. Like Karolina's car accident had. "I need to see her."

"I don't think you want to." Greta's voice is shaky. "She passed several days ago. There is already a degree of decomposition."

The words make me feel faint, dizzy, and nauseated. I lean against the stucco façade of the restaurant for support. "Where did you find her?" I murmur.

"A dogwalker found her in Bedford Park," she tells me. "It's not far from here."

"I know it."

"There's a wooded area, with a small creek. It's a beautiful spot, Hazel."

I want to believe that my mom died gently, surrounded by nature. That her last moments were serene and peaceful. But a sob shudders through me because I know...My husband did this. My mom died frightened and confused. I double over with pain.

"As you know, her funeral arrangements have been preplanned and paid for. But we will need you to come in and sign a few documents."

"I...I can't." My throat clogs with emotion. "Not right now."

"When you're ready," she says gently. "Take your time. And, Hazel...I'm so sorry for your loss."

I nod, try to thank her, but I can't form words. I hang up the phone.

Bedford Park is not far from the apartment my mother and I shared. It has a children's playground, a grass field currently taken over by angry Canada geese, and, in the northeast corner, an expanse of forest. That's where I am headed now, moving briskly past kids playing Frisbee, a family with a chubby toddler on the swing set, a couple of teens vaping on a bench. The path that leads into the brush is narrow; tall grasses lick at my arms, angry brambles just beyond them. The evergreens are tall and lush, and they block out the light of the high spring sun.

In the distance, I hear the gentle babble of the creek and I move toward the sound. Eventually, I come across an offshoot from the path, overgrown and barely noticeable, and I cut deeper into the undergrowth. Blackberry bushes grab at my clothes, try to scratch my skin, but I push through until I emerge into a small clearing. The creek is little more than a trickle now, not the rushing brook of my childhood. But I remember this place.

My mom and I had picnicked here a handful of times. It was never fancy—ham and American cheese sandwiches, a bag of chips, and a couple of sodas—but it had been special for us. A treat. When we were here, we didn't worry about bills or money or keeping up with our friends and neighbors. We'd talked and we'd laughed, and we'd enjoyed each other's company.

A sob of grief—and of relief—erupts from my chest. My mom escaped from the nursing home and came here of her own volition. Somehow, I know it. She had grasped that wisp of a memory, and she chose this spot to lie down and let go. Benjamin didn't take her. He didn't kill her. My mother had a peaceful death, surrounded by nature, beauty, and happy memories, no matter how diluted.

My cheeks are wet, and I realize I am crying. It is loss and joy and release. Because I know my mom's life was short and difficult, but it was not without moments, like the ones we shared here, of beauty.

Finally, I say goodbye.

62

I AM DREAMING. MY MOTHER is there, young and pretty, her dark hair blowing in the wind, dangly earrings kissing her cheeks. We are at the beach, and we have a dog, though we never had a dog. It is medium-sized, black and white, smiling with its tongue lolling. My mom calls to it: *Pepper! Come here, boy!* It lumbers happily toward her, and she ruffles his fur.

Hazel! The wind whips her voice, but she is calling me now. *Come see Pepper!*

Happily, I move toward them. Though my mom is a younger version of herself, I am not. We are roughly the same age, but this doesn't bump for me. It feels normal. Mother and daughter together. Natural and right. And then Pepper turns on me, his teeth bared.

He is no longer a friendly family pet. He is a snarling, snapping beast, all fangs and claws, blood and saliva. He lunges for me, and I shrink back, cry out, but no sound comes from my throat. I am weak and defenseless as this angry creature attacks, tearing into my skin and tissues, cracking my bones. The only sound I can make is a whimper, a moan. I am utterly defenseless as the creature clamps down on my neck. And then I wake up.

I'm in a pool of sweat, in another motel room, this one even seedier than the last. It is quiet outside the plastic blinds, a soft gray light slipping through them. According to my phone, it is predawn. But I know I must leave, right now. The dream felt ominous and terrifying. It unnerved me. Hurriedly, I slip into my clothes, zip my suitcases, and head out into the silence.

The motel rooms are dark, their occupants asleep, as I wheel the two suitcases across the dimly lit parking lot toward my sedan. My car is at the side of the building, invisible from the main road. Even the highway is quiet at this hour. But soon it will fill with big trucks and commuters, and I will feel less alone.

I lift the heavy bags into the trunk and close the lid gently, conscious of my slumbering neighbors. Opening the locks with a beep, I move to the driver's side. My hand is on the door handle when a calm voice slithers over my shoulder.

"Hello, Missy."

He has found me. Like I knew he would. I never had a chance.

I turn to see my husband—handsome in a casual outfit, still perfectly pressed—smiling at me. The menace in his grin is evident as he moves toward me. I should run. I should attack. But all I do is cower away, press myself up against the car. When he stops, he is so close I can feel his breath.

"I like your hair," he says, reaching out to touch it, but I jerk my head away. There is derision in his voice, and in his cold gray eyes. He is toying with me. Enjoying my fear. The false compliment is all part of the game. "It's a bit light for your complexion, but I'm sure you look better with makeup on."

I grit my teeth to keep from lashing out. I will not be goaded. I will not play.

"You made a valiant effort to escape," he says, taking a step back, allowing me to breathe. "But did you really think you could just walk away from me, Hazel? That I would just *let you go* after you planned to kill me?"

"You planned to kill *me*," I snap.

Benjamin laughs darkly. "It's comical, isn't it?"

"Hilarious," I growl. And I have to ask, "How did you find me?"

"You gave your new phone number to the nursing home. The nursing home *I* pay for. It was easy to get access to your mother's updated records."

"She's dead," I tell him, my voice trembling only slightly. And though I have convinced myself my mother's death was peaceful, natural, and on her own terms, I must be sure. "Did you take her, Benjamin? Did you hurt her?"

"For God's sake, Hazel." He rolls his eyes. "Do you think I'm a monster?"

"I do, actually."

"I had nothing to do with the crazy old lady's demise," he says flatly. "But it played into my hands nicely."

"How so?"

"Your accusations were the rantings of a delusional woman. I've paid for your mother's care for our entire marriage. Why on earth would I hurt her?"

Behind him, a light flicks on in one of the motel rooms. The chunky blinds block out all but the slimmest shards, but I know someone is awake in there. They have heard us. They will intervene if things get violent. I just need to keep my husband talking.

"You'd hurt my mom to hurt me." I raise my voice slightly. It can't be obvious.

"I suppose I could have, but I didn't." He smiles cruelly. "You have my condolences, though. You really are alone now, aren't you?"

"I always was," I retort. "You saw to that."

"But now you have no family. No husband." He presses his lip out in a fake pout. "And no lover."

"I ended it with Carter," I tell him, cheeks burning with indignation. "I'm not as stupid as you think I am. I figured out that he couldn't be trusted before you did."

"He played us both," Benjamin admits. "But especially you. Did you really think that you and *Jesse* could build a life together? Where were you going to run off to? Brazil? Colombia? Uruguay?"

He begins to pace in a tight circle, like he did that day in his study. Like he has done so many times in a courtroom. It is habit. He can't help himself. "How were you going to live?" Benjamin orates, oblivious to the lighted room. Or just indifferent, unafraid. "Carter Sumner had never worked an honest day in his life. And neither have you."

"I worked before I met you," I snap. "I would have gotten a job. And built a new life."

"Maybe..." His smile is condescending. "But your boyfriend convinced you to kill me so that you could have it all. The house. The cars. My money..." He smirks again. "All Carter took from me was twenty-five grand. He took your heart. Your hope. And your dignity."

My face is burning, my body tense with hate and indignation. He still has the power to make me feel small and stupid. My fingers grip the car key concealed in my hand, and I want to stab it into his eye, his neck, his ear. If I am quick enough, I can do it, jump into the car, and get away before he kills me. My eyes dart to the lightened room. If I scream, will someone come before Benjamin can hurt me?

But I won't let my husband see my fear, my defeat. I lift my chin higher and meet his gaze. "Why do you want me dead, Benjamin? Why not just divorce me? The prenup you made me sign already stipulates that I'll get nothing."

"It's not about money, Hazel," he says. "It was never about money."

"Then why?"

The light in that room snaps out, and with it my hope. Whoever is behind those blinds has decided this is a lovers' quarrel, a simple domestic spat. They've chosen to mind their own business, to leave me to my demise. Benjamin will triumph, like he always does.

"My relationships with women are...unique," my husband continues.

He means *sick. Twisted. Toxic.*

"When I'm grooming a woman to become my slave, it is imperative that she goes in blind. I can't have her finding my previous wives and asking a lot of questions that might dissuade her from signing my contract."

"I'll sign an NDA," I offer quickly. "I won't say a word. I promise."

But I am lying. Because if a woman came to me, asked me what it was like to be married to Benjamin Laval, I would tell her. I'd have to. I couldn't send an unsuspecting girl into his lair, subjecting her to a lifetime of abuse and pain.

"I tried that with Karolina," he says. "But my first wife slandered me. She told everyone who'd listen that I was cruel. That I was a pervert."

"And so you killed her," I say, raising my voice again.

"*I* didn't kill her," he says with mock offense. "The roads were slick. She was driving too fast. It was an accident."

"Her brother knows the truth. He knows you drove her to commit suicide."

"He's a paranoid drug addict. Mentally ill. His own mother has disowned him."

"Well played," I say. If I can keep him talking long enough, maybe someone else will wake up. Maybe someone will come. Someone will help me. "But you almost got caught getting rid of me. Carter Sumner double-crossed you."

"Those recordings were a surprise, I'll admit, but I knew they'd be inadmissible." He chuckles. "We had the entire courtroom suspecting that you tampered with them to set me up. Even your own lawyer believed it."

I had heard the doubt in Rachelle Graham's voice when she

called me. Did she think I was crazy? A con artist? All of the above?

"And there was no other evidence," Benjamin continues. "I got cash advances on *your* credit card to pay Carter Sumner. You paid for your own murder, my darling." He is gleeful, so pleased with himself. "It's genius, I know."

"What now, Benjamin?" I ask. Because I am done listening to him gloat.

"You need help, sweetheart. I'm going to see that you get it."

"What do you mean, *help*?"

"You're a danger to yourself, Hazel. We all saw the video footage of you tearing the house apart like a maniac. And you were stockpiling sleeping pills. Hiding vodka under the bathroom counter. And you made that heartbreaking suicide video."

I canceled the scheduled video. I know I did. I'd deleted it, too. Benjamin had hacked into my phone somehow. He'd found the file.

"I'm concerned about your sanity. So, I'm going to have you committed." His smile is self-satisfied. "I've already put the plan in motion."

"If you release my suicide video, you'll be humiliated," I retort. "Everyone will know you treated me like a slave. That you're sick and toxic and perverted. That you made me sign a Total Power Exchange contract."

"A *what* contract?" And I see the glimmer in his eye. "There was never any contract. I don't even know what you're talking about."

He destroyed it. When? Recently? Or years ago?

"Here's what's going to happen, Hazel," he says, and he begins to pace again. "I'm going to take you in for a psychiatric assessment. Do you remember Dr. Veillard?"

Of course I remember Benjamin's friend, the shrink. The psychiatrist had never cared about my problems, had only prescribed drugs to mask my pain.

"He's agreed to evaluate you for involuntary care. Dr. Veillard knows your psychological history. He knows about your crazy accusations against me. He's very concerned for your mental health and well-being."

Fury makes my body tremble all over. I want to fly at him and attack him, claw his face with my fingernails until he is raw and bloody. But that will only play into his narrative. He is too smart for me. I am overcome by hopelessness and defeat. To my mortification, tears spring to my eyes.

"Don't cry, my darling." More fake pity. "Karolina had to die for what she did to me. You're getting off easy."

"Where is Carter?" I ask, and my voice wobbles.

"Don't tell me you still care about him?" Anger makes his voice louder. "He used you. He targeted you."

It is a trigger. My husband's calm demeanor is slipping. "Tell me where he is," I demand. "I want to see him. To talk to him."

"Wow," he growls. "You really are crazy."

A voice in the darkness then, a female, concerned: "What's going on out here?"

I glance around my husband to see a diminutive woman standing next to the laundry room door. She is a housekeeper or a maintenance worker, judging by the heavy ring of keys attached to her belt. This woman is small, but she is brave. In her hand is a cell phone, poised to dial.

"Just a little argument with my wife," Benjamin says, turning on the charm. "We'll keep the noise down."

"Are you okay?" She is addressing me.

"She has mental health issues," my husband explains. "She needs—"

But I don't hear his words because my arm is wheeling at him, the ignition key pressing through my clenched fingers like a shiv. My target is his eye or his neck, but I miss, grazing his cheek. Still, I feel the drag of his skin, see the slash of blood, and hear his guttural scream of pain, rage, and shock. He flinches, steps back, just for a second, but it is enough. I yank open the car door and heave myself inside, slamming it closed behind me. I press the lock button and fumble to get the key into the ignition. Benjamin punches the window—once, twice—and I scream, terrified the glass will break. His face fills the frame, red and seething, a portrait of rage.

"Open the fucking door!" he hollers.

I shriek, honk the horn, draw more attention as I struggle with the key. The woman is running the other way, but she is on her phone, calling for help. The police will come but it will be too late by then. If Benjamin gets his hands on me, I am dead. The key slips into the ignition and I turn it, bang the car into gear, stomp on the gas. I fly toward the exit, but Benjamin is running alongside me, hands scrambling for purchase on my car. He thinks he is that strong, that invincible, that he can stop my escape with his bare hands. He grips a windshield wiper, but I accelerate, and it tears off in his hand. I hit the main road, merge onto the highway, and I drive.

In my rearview mirror, I see my husband's silhouette, standing alone beneath the neon sign. I watch his shoulders rise and fall with each heavy breath, his hand moving to the gash on his check. He is watching me drive away, but he is not letting me go.

He never will.

63

I FLY ALONG THE HIGHWAY for at least ten, even fifteen minutes before I consider where I'm going. My escape had been pure instinct, complete adrenaline, but now I must strategize to ensure my continued freedom. Because my husband will be strategizing my capture. If the police were called, I know how Benjamin would paint my getaway. He'd say his wife is delusional, suicidal, refusing the help she so desperately needs. She attacked him like a wild animal that was cornered, sick and deranged. I am dangerous—to myself, and to others. They will all come looking for me.

Now that my mom has passed, there is nothing tethering me to this city. But where should I go? If I drive north, I will be at the Canadian border in a few hours. I'd be safer in a different country, but Benjamin has my passport; I won't be allowed in. I could continue driving south, all the way to California, disappear in a big city like San Francisco or L.A. Or I could go east through Idaho and into Montana. It is the less expected route. I have never lived in a rural environment. Benjamin won't think I can hack it.

I take the next exit, crawl through a quiet shopping complex until I find the freeway headed east. The sun is up now. Morning commuters drive toward the city to work, parents take their kids to school, big trucks make their deliveries. No one else on the road is fleeing for their life, for their freedom. I am alone in this tenuous situation, but I can do this. If I keep my wits about me, if I strategize carefully, I can outsmart my husband.

Benjamin knows the make and model of my vehicle. He would certainly have noted the license plate number and given it to his security team and maybe the police. I will need to trade this car in for a new one, but I will wait until I get to Montana. An out-of-state plate will draw too much attention, garner too many questions.

My appearance is another issue to deal with. Everyone will be looking for a woman with short blond hair. I'll buy a box of red hair dye, color my hair at the next motel. In the meantime, I should pick up a hat at a gas station. And then there is my phone…Shit! They could be tracing me right now, tracking my movements! I fish deep in my purse with one hand, ready to throw it out the window.

But the highway is swimming before my eyes and there is a heavy pressure on my chest. Sweat prickles my hairline and my fingers and toes have gone numb. I'm going to pass out, right here on the freeway. Struggling for air, I take the nearest exit and manage to pull into a gas station, lurching to a stop just as my body shuts down. I am crying and shaking and gasping for breath. It's a panic attack; not my first one, but the first one while driving. The first one that snuck up on me at such an alarming rate. My body is telling me what my brain refuses to accept. I cannot do this. I am not equipped to live my life on the run. And I am no match for Benjamin Laval.

I was stupid and naïve to even try.

Defeat settles on me like a heavy blanket. My husband has won. He beat me…Not physically this time, but emotionally, spiritually, financially. He got to Karolina in Poland. How could I think that I'd be safe in Montana? It might take days, weeks, even months, but Benjamin will find me and lock me away. And when—*if*—I got out, I'd have nothing. Literally nothing. Not even a car to live in like Lee had.

After only a few days of running, I am already so tired, already so worn down. I am not cut out for this. A life of fear, of constantly looking over my shoulder, will break me. I give up. I surrender. But I won't be Benjamin's prisoner again. There is another way to end this: a victory in its own right.

Wiping the tears from my face with my sleeve, I breathe through my nose, slowly, steadily until my heartbeat returns to normal. A sense of calm settles over me. Acceptance. This, I know I can do. I have come close before. When I am composed, I get back on the road. This time, I head west, toward the coast.

The factories and warehouses give way to tech campuses and then to high-end shopping centers as I get closer to my former home. As I draw near, the surroundings become familiar and yet uncomfortable, filled with a dark kind of nostalgia. I pass the grocery store where I shopped for Benjamin's dinner, where I had left Lee's car hoping she'd find it. There is the café where I met Vanessa Vega on occasion, playing the role of dutiful happy housewife. I fly past the gym where I tried to change my body to please my husband. Where I was seduced by my trainer. Where I was targeted for murder.

Taking a sharp right, I pull into the parking lot of a quaint church, its clapboard siding freshly painted white. There is a charity shop around the back of the building, its proceeds going to support refugees establishing a new life. Lugging the suitcase of valuables into the store, I am greeted by a middle-aged woman with a warm face.

"Oh my," she says, rushing to help me with the heavy load. "What have we here?"

"There's some art and some sculptures. Some designer clothes. It's valuable stuff," I say. "I recommend you get it appraised."

She presses a hand to her chest, touched. "This is so generous of you."

I don't tell her that it's not. That I have no use for these items, not where I'm going. "I just want the money used to help people," I say. And then I hurry back to my car.

Eventually the road leads me away from the commercial district, winding its way through tall cedars, past the stately but forbidding houses perched above the slate-blue ocean. I am approaching the glass house where Benjamin controlled me for so many years. Will the security guard stationed outside notice my vehicle as I race past? It is a chance I must take. Because my destination is the beach where I nearly drowned. Where Lee used to sleep. Where she saved my life.

But she won't be there this time.

I continue to the end of the road and park the Hyundai in Lee's old spot. The bushes are thick with leaves and unripe whiskery berries. The car will be well concealed...if anyone thinks to look for me so close to home. Benjamin will expect me to run. To at least *try* to hide. He won't suspect that I will surrender so easily. That I will return to the scene of the crime.

Pushing through the brambles, I make my way down the slim trail that leads to the beach. The sky is a flat gray, the ocean almost colorless, the air full of briny sea mist. The scent is salty and pungent, but the air kisses my skin. My feet slip on the smooth rocks, make a percussive accompaniment as I head toward that beached log. The spot where Lee and I sat together, drank coffee from a thermos, ate fruit or pastries or scones, and talked about a different life. As I approach it, I feel an insistent vibration, hear a faint buzz.

It's my cell phone in my jacket pocket—no wonder I couldn't find it in my purse. I expect this call will be from the Arbutus Care Home, about my mother's paperwork. I won't be able to sign it now, but it won't matter. She is gone. At rest. Her remains are to be cremated. It's all been paid for. And I have already said goodbye.

But when I retrieve the phone, it says *Seattle Police Department* on the call display. I'm not sure if I should answer. Is this just a ploy to trace the call? To track my location and take me in? But curiosity gets the better of me.

"Hello?"

"This is Detective French calling," she says, all business. "We need to talk to you."

I don't ask how she got my number. She is a detective after all. "About what?"

"A jawbone washed up on a beach near Port Townsend," she states. "The dental records match Carter Sumner's."

This is not what I expected, but I am not surprised. Not that Carter is dead, anyway. It makes sense that Benjamin killed him. To cover his tracks. And because he hated him.

"Nate Mattias has been arrested for the murder," the detective continues. "And he's talking."

Is it a warning? A threat? I feel cold all over, oddly numb. "What is Nate saying?"

"At first, Nate said that Carter Sumner broke into your house to attack your husband. He said he killed him in self-defense. To protect his employer. But that explanation didn't exactly stand up."

"Why not?"

"Mr. Sumner was stabbed sixteen times. And his body was dismembered." A sour taste rises in my throat as she continues. "If it was simple self-defense, it wouldn't have been so violent. Or so gruesome."

"And he wouldn't have had to hide Carter's body," I add.

"Exactly." French takes a heavy breath. "Nate Mattias has implicated your husband in Carter Sumner's murder. He says Benjamin instructed him to kill Carter. That Benjamin stood by and watched as he did it. Benjamin discovered that you and Carter were having an affair."

So, Benjamin is going to pay after all. A lightness fills me up, a sense of vindication, of justice. I allow myself to smile, even though I know what this means.

"The police will be bringing your husband in soon. And he's going to tell his side of the story." The detective articulates my concerns. "If there was more to your relationship with Carter Sumner, if there is anything you and he were hiding, Benjamin is going to use it. He's fighting for his life, Hazel."

I close my eyes. I won't fight Benjamin, not anymore.

"We can help you," French continues. "I *want* to help you. But you have to talk to us first. If your husband killed Carter Sumner, we can make him pay."

But I will pay, too. I swallow thickly, the words stuck in my throat.

French takes my silence for compliance. "Where are you? I'll send a car."

"No thanks," I say softly.

"It's time to stop running, Hazel." And she is right about that. "Tell me where you are."

"Good luck," I say, but it means goodbye. I hang up the phone.

For just a moment, I sit on that silvery log and stare out at the ocean. I am done fighting. I am opting out. This is where Hazel Laval will disappear. Cease to exist. For real this time. I drop to my knees on the beach, close my eyes, connect, in some strange way, to my mother. And then I start to dig.

The sand is damp and cold and my hands cramp with the effort. But I keep digging, deeper and deeper. Finally, my fingers alight on a corner of plastic, and I tug at it. It was buried farther down than I remember, but I manage to pull it out and shake off the sand. Inside the plastic sleeve is a passport. Jesse—Carter—had promised to get me a new one. He'd told me it was easy on the dark web. And it was.

I got one for Lee. And I got one for myself.

Picking up my phone, I call and order a taxi. Then I throw the device and my jacket into the water. The jacket will drift away; at least I hope it does. The phone will be easier to find. I turn and pick my way back up the trail. At my car, I pull the remaining suitcase out of the trunk and toss my car keys into the bushes. When the cab pulls up, I hop in.

"To the airport, please." The driver nods, and we drive off, past the stunning home where Hazel Laval lived in such misery. But Hazel is dead now, gone. Soon she will be reinvented, reincarnated, risen like a phoenix. Because there is more than one way to play the game.

And there is more than one way to win it.

EPILOGUE

"KELLY!" MY SERVER CALLS, AND after a second, I turn. It still takes me a moment to respond sometimes, even though I've been Kelly Wilcox for nearly three months now. "There's a woman here to see you."

"Thanks, Alvaro." Setting down the heavy knife, I wipe papaya juices off my hands with a damp towel; then I move from the outside kitchen into the restaurant. It is tiny—a hut, even a shack—but it is mine. There are only twelve seats inside, but more tables are set up on the sandy beach, offering superb views of the crystal-clear ocean. We serve freshly caught fish with tropical fruit salsas and icy cold beers. The food is light, fresh, and simple. I have grown to love it.

Occasionally, I will make a dish from the Aviary's menu, but supplies are limited on Isla Carenero. Twice a month I must take a short ferry ride to Bocas Town to stock up on staples. Despite this inconvenience, I have taken to island living: the jade waters of the Caribbean Sea, the salt-fine beaches, and the diverse group of travelers who find their way to this remote destination.

When I'd first arrived in Panama City, I had taken a job at a bustling high-end restaurant. But without a résumé, I'd had to start at the bottom. I could have worked my way up, showcased my skills, but I felt uneasy in the cosmopolitan city, conspicuous. I was still growing into my new identity then; I wanted to do that somewhere less accessible. And I wanted to run my own restaurant again. This small island in the Bocas del Toro Archipelago gave me that.

A blond woman sits alone at a beachside table, sipping a tiny cup of café con leche. I assume she's here for a job. I am actively looking for help. My restaurant, the Nest, is located near a hostel, and we are busy servicing backpackers from all over the world. These travelers are young, adventurous, and self-involved. They don't ask questions. They are remarkably incurious.

As I approach, the woman turns, her chin-length bob swaying, and my stomach drops. "Hi, Kelly," she says, standing up.

My mouth opens, my eyebrows rise, but no words come.

She introduces herself tentatively. "My name is Nora Harmsworth."

But it's not. Her name is Hazel Laval. And I wondered if I would ever see her again.

Over these past few months, I have processed what Hazel did to me. And what she did *for* me. I have analyzed our friendship and what it meant to each of us. I chose to come to Panama knowing she could find me. Because I still have questions. But I'm still not sure I can trust her.

"Can we talk?" she asks, and I see that she is nervous.

"Give me a second." I move back through the restaurant to the small fridge outside the back door. I grab two frosty bottles of beer. We're going to need them.

"Let's talk on the beach," I suggest, handing her a chilled bottle. She follows me toward the water, where we lower ourselves onto the powdery sand. We sit side by side, facing the ocean like we did in Seattle. But the warm, transparent sea is so different from the dark, unknowable Pacific. We are different now, too.

"Why did you come?" I ask, taking a sip of the cold, bitter beer.

"I had to know that you were okay. That you were safe. And happy."

"I am."

"Good." She smiles at me. "Your restaurant is really great."

"Thanks." The small talk is wearing thin. Hazel senses it.

"Jesse's real name was Carter Sumner," she blurts. "He was a criminal. A monster."

"I know."

She doesn't ask how I found that out. She just takes a long drink of beer. "He's dead."

"I know that, too." My eyes remain on the water. "I found his body."

"Oh my god, Lee." She glances around nervously. "I mean *Kelly*. Where did you find him?"

"In your husband's study."

"Jesus." She presses two fingers to her eyebrows as if she's in pain. "I tried to stop Jesse from going into my house. I locked the door. And I threw your knife into the ocean."

"So, *you* stole the knife from my car."

"Jesse told me to plant it in the house." She lowers her voice. "He was going to stab Benjamin with it. He wanted to frame you for the murder. But I couldn't do it. I'm not a killer." She turns to face me. "And I cared too much about you."

"What about the netsuke?" I ask. "Did you take that, too?"

She nods. "I wiped off your prints and put it back in Benjamin's study. It would have been evidence against you."

If she is expecting my thanks, I am not there yet.

"I'm so sorry you had to find his body," Hazel says softly. "That must have been awful."

"There was a lot of blood."

"Benjamin's security guard stabbed Jesse to death," she explains. "He must have taken the body somewhere and dismembered it. It was meant to disappear. But just before I left, his jawbone washed up onshore."

"God..." The beer in my stomach churns at the description. "That's gross."

"My husband has been charged with Carter Sumner's murder," Hazel says, seemingly unbothered by the gore. "He's in Seattle fighting for his life. And I'm here." She glances over and I see a glint in her eye. "Drinking beer on the beach with you."

"You beat him," I say.

"Finally."

"And we both beat Jesse... *Carter*."

"We sure did."

We sip our beers in silence for a while, eyes forward, each processing what we've learned and what we've been through. Finally, she breaks the silence.

"I was really damaged. But it doesn't excuse what I did to you. You must hate me."

"I did at first," I admit. "But I know how manipulative Jesse was. I fell for him, too."

"We were both weak then."

"And neither of us knew what he was capable of," I add. "I knew he was shady, but when I heard those audio recordings... and what he planned to do to you..."

"So, *you* turned them over to the police?"

"I dropped the thumb drive off on my way to the airport." I offer her a small smile. "Thanks for the plane ticket. And the passport and the money."

"It was the least I could do. After... everything."

"Yeah."

"It was real to me," Hazel says, swiveling toward me. "Our friendship. When we talked, I was honest with you. I know what I did was unforgivable, but our relationship meant a lot to me."

My throat tightens. I swallow some beer, try to wash the emotion away.

"I'm glad that you've built a new life," she says. "The Nest is fantastic. I... I'd love to eat here sometime."

When I don't respond, Hazel shifts awkwardly. "Maybe one day..." Slowly, reluctantly, she gets to her knees, begins to stand.

"It's a great place but it's a lot," I say, halting her movements. "I need some help, actually."

"Yeah?" She sinks back into the sand.

"How's your Spanish?"

"I'm on level eight of Duolingo."

I chuckle, but she continues. "I'm smart, Kelly. I learn fast and I work hard. And I can bake!"

"It's too hot to bake," I say with a genuine laugh. "But there's plenty to do."

"I'm in. Let me help you. Put me to work."

I look at her, at the brightness in her eyes, the lightness of her being. Hazel is a different person now. She is Nora Harmsworth. Strong. Independent. Happy... I still don't know if I can trust her, but I am willing to try.

We get to our feet and walk back toward my restaurant.

Acknowledgments

First, I want to thank you, the reader. *The Drowning Woman* is my twelfth published novel, and it is such a privilege to be able to bring my words to an audience. I am forever grateful to all the librarians, bloggers, Bookstagrammers, BookTokers, and bookstore employees who help bring books and readers together.

To my editor, Karen Kosztolnyik. What a pleasure to work with you again! Thank you for your calm wisdom and insight. I am so glad you connected with this story. Thank you to Rachael Kelly for being so supportive, organized, and responsive. Thank you to Sara Wood for this gorgeous cover design. Thanks to my production editor, Carolyn Kurek; my publicists, Staci Burt and Alli Rosenthal; and marketer, Theresa DeLucci. My gratitude to the entire team at Grand Central/Hachette in New York and to Donna Nopper and everyone at Hachette Canada.

To my agent, Joe Veltre. Thank you for standing by me while I meandered off into screenwriting, quit writing to open an ice cream shop, and switched genres several times (sometimes successfully, sometimes not). You have been such a wise and steady support through all the ups and downs (and now I am wondering why I didn't dedicate a book to you earlier). Thanks also to the amazing Olivia Johnson and the rest of the team at Gersh.

Thank you to my friend Noel MacDonald for sharing his years of experience as an outreach worker with the homeless population on Vancouver's Downtown Eastside. Noel gave me so much insight into the struggle of living on the streets: the daily traumas and indignities; the physical and psychological toll; and the cycle of poverty that is so difficult to break.

To my friend Tanya Shklanka: Thank you for our many conversations about the good, the bad, and the ugly of having your own restaurant. (Zocalo was the best!)

Thank you to my brother Joel Gook and my brother-in-law Charlie Chin for sharing your Panama travels with me.

Thanks to Nora Harmsworth, for having such a great name for a character, and for supporting Christianne's Lyceum of Literature and Art and their scholarship program.

Thank you to the incredible author community. I feel like I have so many supportive writer friends, far and wide. A special thanks to my blurbers: Ashley Audrain, Mary Kubica, Chevy Stevens, Marissa Stapley, Samantha M. Bailey, Ashley Winstead, Liz Nugent, and Laurie Elizabeth Flynn. I am such huge a fan of your work and your endorsement means the world. And shout-out to my writer crew here in BC: Eileen Cook (for providing her genius insights on an early draft, and for meeting regularly to talk writing over Brussel sprouts); Roz Nay for the brainstorming, and for making me laugh daily via voice memos; Chevy Stevens for always being available for support, advice, and an animal video; and Daniel Kalla for the twist-sharing and brunches.

And to John, who is surprisingly creative despite his analytical career. You are always my first brainstorming partner and my first reader. Love and thanks.

About the Author

Robyn Harding is the bestselling author of *The Perfect Family*, *The Arrangement*, *Her Pretty Face*, and *The Party*, which was a finalist for the Arthur Ellis Award for best crime novel. Her book, *The Swap*, debuted at #1 on the *Globe and Mail* and *Toronto Star* Canadian Bestsellers lists. She is the screenwriter and executive producer of the independent film *The Steps*. She lives in Vancouver, British Columbia, with her family and two cute but deadly rescue chihuahuas.